A Knight's Destiny

For the Love of a Shaw
Book Three

By:

Debbie Hyde

Debbie Hyde Books
Cover images by: The Killion Group Images &
Jon Tyson @ Unsplash

Cover Design by: Debbie Hyde & Nevaeh Roberson
ISBN: 9798692569288

This book is dedicated to the loving memory of Miss Haily Page Englin. Haily instantly captured the heart of every person she ever met. Haily's smile and love made the world in which we live a better place. She loved her family, friends, and her horse Spirit unconditionally. Our lives were remarkably changed from knowing Haily, whether it was for a few minutes or if it were for years.

We are all so grateful for the time that we had with Haily, even though we all feel that our time with her was too short. Thank you, dear sweet one, for being a part of our lives. We all know that Heaven is a happier, brighter place because it is now your home.

Chapter One

Just before noon, Elizabeth Dawson walked into the parlor on the main floor of her family's London home at Greyham Court. She found her older sister, Anne, laughing and carrying on with Evelyn Cramer.

It was a disgusting sight for Elizabeth, every time she saw these two together. They were always plotting something outrageous. One would think that Anne and Evelyn would give up on their ludicrous schemes by now, for none of them ever worked out like they had hoped they would.

Today, these two estranged master minds were plotting what they called '*a new adventure*' for Ms. Rhodes' End of the Summer Party. No matter how much these two bizarre friends schemed together, their wicked little tricks had not landed either of them a husband.

"Will Evelyn be joining us for lunch today?" Elizabeth did not even pretend to be polite on the matter. She really hoped that her sister's hateful friend would leave instead.

"Evelyn and I will be having our lunch here, in the parlor." Anne carelessly waved her hand at Elizabeth. "We do not care what you do for lunch, dear sister."

Evelyn giggled at Anne's response to her sister. Elizabeth tried to smile sweetly, but what she really wanted to do, was to grab Evelyn Cramer by her dark hair and drag her out onto the front steps. Since a lady could not do such a thing, Elizabeth turned to go.

"Your sister is so sad and boring." Evelyn giggled and swatted her fan at Anne.

Elizabeth rolled her eyes and continued walking away. She was halted by her sister as she reached the door.

"Oh, dear sister, be so kind as to tell the cook that we are expecting a couple more of our friends to join us, here in the parlor, for lunch today." Anne faked a pleasant smile at Elizabeth before turning back to Evelyn.

As Elizabeth turned around to, once again, leave the parlor, she was brushed aside by two men as they entered the room. The men hurried over to Anne and Evelyn. Elizabeth had to grab ahold of the door frame to steady herself.

Elizabeth's eyes widened in horror when she realized that these men were Roger Holden, the Earl of Statham, and the dirty looking Edmond Prescott. She knew right away that this duo was a bad combination.

"What is the meaning of this?" Elizabeth boldly asked.

"It has nothing to do with you, little sister. Now, run along and do as you were told." Anne rudely dismissed Elizabeth again.

"You would think that the little runt would know her place." Roger narrowed his eyes at Elizabeth as he sat down next to Evelyn.

"My place is here, in this home," Elizabeth stated proudly. "Yours is not." She looked between Roger and Edmond.

"Bold little twit, is she not?" Roger walked over and roughly grabbed Elizabeth by her wrist.

"The Duke would not want you and your friend in our home." Elizabeth stood tall and glared into Roger Holden's eyes.

"Enough, Elizabeth!" Anne snapped. She was growing tired of her sister's presence. "They are here as my guests. Besides, our dear precious little brother is, once again, nowhere to be found."

"I have not had a woman to challenge me like this in a while." Roger's grin was pure evil. Edmond was now at his side. "Whatever shall we do with you, little runt?"

"As long as I end up in the arms of Nicholas Shaw by the end of Ms. Rhodes' party, I do not care what you do with her." Anne carelessly waved her hand in Elizabeth's direction.

Shocked at her sister's words, Elizabeth's eyes widened as her mouth dropped open. So, this was her sister's plan? She was now

2

going to try and sink her evil claws into Nicholas Shaw. Anger, or hate, which she was not sure, now burned within Elizabeth.

"You are lucky that our brother has not already banished you for the things that you have done!" Elizabeth shouted at her sister.

"Mother would never allow that to happen." Anne was confident on the matter.

"If you try to ruin a good man like Nicholas Shaw, our brother will punish you, regardless of what Mother wants." With tears in her eyes, Elizabeth looked away from her sister.

"Oh, my dear little sister." Anne walked over to Elizabeth and patted her cheek. "Do not fret. I will not hurt your little Shaw friend too badly." Anne's voice now deepened, "Besides, you would not know what to do with him if you had him."

"You are so evil." Elizabeth's words caused Anne to slap her.

Evelyn, Roger, and Edmond laughed at Anne's actions. Elizabeth dropped her head and closed her eyes, so that she did not have to look at the evil group of people in the parlor.

"Evelyn, dear, you should try again for that little Earl of Hartford at the party. Maxwell Spencer needs to spend time with a lady and not dirty little port tramps." The four of them laughed even harder at Anne's outrageous suggestion.

"I cannot wait until Samuel gets home and deals with you." Elizabeth narrowed her eyes at her sister.

"I, for one, have had just about enough of you, little runt." Roger jerked Elizabeth's arm up in the air, pulling her to him. "And, since your sister does not care what happens to you, I have some wonderful plans for you."

With his free hand, Roger punched Elizabeth hard in the stomach. Elizabeth doubled over and gasped for air. Roger jerked her up again and slapped her across the face. Elizabeth cried out in pain just before a cloth sack went over her head. Moments later, her head was slammed into the door frame of the parlor.

Elizabeth was thrown over someone's shoulder, as she slipped into unconsciousness. The last thing she heard was her sister, Anne, and Evelyn Cramer's laughter as she was being carried away.

***

Nicholas Shaw leaned forward on his horse as he gave chase to the lone rider ahead of him. While surveying his family's land, Nick had seen the man coming out of the Eastern Forest, between his family's estate home and his uncle's home, Ellis Manor.

When the cloaked rider saw Nick, he took off at a full run. The man's actions told Nick that whoever he was, he did not belong on Shaw land, so Nick immediately started after him.

As Nick went to cross the road, he noticed his father approaching with a couple of the guards from Ellis Manor riding by his side. Since the mysterious rider had such a great lead on him, Nick gave up his pursuit. He reigned his horse in and waited for his father and the guards.

"Who was that?" Sir Phillip asked his oldest son.

"I do not know, Father. I just caught him coming out of the forest." Nick was more concerned with why the guards from Ellis Manor were here.

"Leave him be," Sir Phillip told his son. "Ride with me to Ellis Manor."

"Father, what is the matter?" Nick could already see the worry on his father's face.

"My brother was training a new horse and has been injured." Sir Phillip tried to maintain a straight face.

The guards from Ellis Manor could not give him enough of a report for him to determine how serious his brother's wounds were just yet. Sir Phillip was greatly worried about his older brother.

When Nick and his father reached Ellis Manor, they were greeted by his cousin Gavin. Gavin was his Uncle Matthew's oldest son and next in line for the family title.

"How is he?" Sir Phillip asked his nephew.

"His right leg is broken in about three places. He is resting in his room." Gavin was relieved but still quite emotional over his father's injury. "Father is expecting you. He has asked to see you the moment you arrived."

4

Sir Phillip nodded his head and followed Rosa up the stairs to his older brother's room. He was deeply concerned about his brother. Matthew had never had an accident with a horse before.

In many noble families, when there were two sons in line for the family title, the brothers fought as hateful rivals. This was not true for the Shaw family. Sir Phillip and his brother, Lord Matthew, were extremely close.

"Are you nervous yet?" Nick asked his cousin.

"Ask me that again in December." Gavin lightly laughed. "I think right now I am still a tad excited."

Nick and Gavin were both twenty-five years of age, Gavin was a couple months older. His cousin was coming up on his first wedding anniversary. Gavin and his wife, Abby, were expecting their first child in December. Nick sighed, he hoped that someday he would have a wife and child as well.

"How is your mother?" Nick really loved his Aunt Caroline.

"She is overwhelmed right now." Gavin took a deep breath. His father's injury had upset the entire household. "As am I."

"Is there anything that I can do to help?" Nick felt helpless just standing around.

"The lookouts reported a rider going into the Eastern Forest between our homes. If you could check that out, I would be forever grateful." Gavin could not leave Ellis Manor right now.

"I chased after a lone rider that was coming out of the forest about an hour ago. Sadly, he got away." Nick assumed that this mysterious rider was the same one the lookouts had seen.

"The lookouts said that the man appeared to be carrying something into the forest." Gavin was greatly concerned over the matter.

"I will check it out right now." Nick was deeply concerned as well, for the rider was not carrying anything when he exited the forest.

Sir Collin and Sir Adam, of the Ellis Manor guard, rode with Nick to the Eastern Forest in case there was trouble. They found the mysterious rider's tracks easily. With extreme caution, the three men entered the forest.

Up ahead, about a hundred yards into the forest, something caught Nick's eye. Sir Collin had noticed it as well and pointed at the mysterious object in front of them.

As they drew closer, Nick realized that the object ahead was a person. He quickly dismounted and hurried toward the man tied to the tree. This must be why the lone rider was in such a hurry to leave Shaw land.

Nick gasped in shock as he now realized that this was a woman and not a man tied up in the trees. He, and both guards, ran the rest of the way to her.

The woman was tied between two trees, with her arms held high above her head. Her feet could not touch the ground. They dangled just inches above the forest floor. Her dress was torn and dirty. Her head, that slouched to one side, was cover with a cloth sack.

Nick wrapped his arms around the woman's waist and held her as the guard cut the ropes. When she was free, Nick sat down on the ground with the woman in his arms. She sucked in a deep breath before crying out in pain. He was grateful to know that she was alive. Slowly, Sir Collin removed the cloth sack from her head.

"Elizabeth!" Nick exclaimed when he saw the woman's face.

Elizabeth's eyes fluttered open when she heard her name. Her left eye was almost swollen shut and the vision in her right eyes was blurry. She could not see him, but still she knew who he was.

"Nick." Elizabeth could barely whisper his name. She went limp in Nick's arms as she fell into unconsciousness again.

With tears in his eyes, Nick held Elizabeth Dawson to his chest. She was the kindest person that he knew. How could she be here like this now? Still holding Elizabeth to him, Nick leaned his head back and let out a blood curly scream that could be heard echoing through the Eastern Forest.

Chapter Two

Sir Collin held Elizabeth and gently handed her up to Nick, after he had mounted his horse. As they exited the forest, Elizabeth whimpered in pain, but she did not open her eyes. Nick was torn between heartache and anger. Elizabeth was more important than his feelings, so he kept his anger at bay, for now.

"We are closer to Kinsley Estate. We will take Elizabeth to my mother." Nick's voice cracked, and he took several deep breaths, as he fought back tears.

"Aye, Sir Nicholas. I think Lady Elizabeth needs to be tended to rather quickly." Sir Collin was near tears as well. Elizabeth had a kind and sweet spirit, even he was heartbroken over the matter.

"We will make sure that you get her there safely." Sir Adam pulled out his pistol as he rode alongside of Nick.

"You ride on ahead and warn Lady Clara that we are coming." Sir Collin, being Captain of the Guard, gave the order to Adam. "I will stay by Sir Nicholas's side." Sir Collin pulled out his pistol as well.

Sir Adam rode on ahead and was waiting for Nick at the gates of Kinsley Estate when they arrived. The guard led them to the side entrance of the estate, where Nick's mother, Lady Clara, and the servants were waiting for Elizabeth.

Nick carried Elizabeth to a spare bedchamber on the first floor that his mother had quickly prepared for Elizabeth. Another piece of Nick's heart tore when Elizabeth gasped in pain as he laid her on the bed.

"Nick?" Elizabeth's voice was weak.

"I'm here." Nick gently held her hand. The cuts in her wrists from the ropes were deep. "You are going to be alright." Nick prayed that his words were true. He had never seen a woman hurt so badly before.

"Send word to Greyham Court that Elizabeth is here." Lady Clara tried to pull her son away from the bedside.

"No!" Elizabeth screamed. Hearing Lady Clara's words caused her to try and sit up.

Nick, as gently as he could, held Elizabeth steady on the bed. He feared that her sudden movements would only cause her more harm. He looked up at his mother, his eyes pleaded with her to help Elizabeth.

"Lady Elizabeth, try not to move for now." Lady Clara was quickly at the young woman's side.

"Do not...tell...home." Elizabeth struggled to speak. The pain in her chest caused breathing to be hard for her.

"Elizabeth, you squeeze my hand if I am correct." Nick had to find a way to communicate with her. "You do not want us to send a messenger to your brother?"

Elizabeth gently squeezed Nick's hand. With her wrists so badly cut, even this small movement was hard for her. She did not have a lot of strength left. Every move she made cause some part of her body more pain. Nick and his mother quickly looked at each other. They both knew, by Elizabeth's request, that something was seriously wrong at Greyham Court.

As the servants entered the room with warm water and medical supplies, Lady Clara pulled her son from the room. Nick protested but his mother won in the end. As much as he hated leaving, Nick would do what was best for Elizabeth.

"Son, you go to Ellis Manor and see if you can get Lady Abigail and Lady Olivia to come here. Both are exceptionally good at treating wounds and Elizabeth is going to need them." Lady Clara remained calm as she spoke to Nick.

"I do not wish to leave her, Mother." Nick really wanted to go back into the room with Elizabeth.

"Sir Nicholas, you remain here." Sir Collin put his hand on Nick's shoulder. "Adam and I will return to Ellis Manor and let Lord Gavin know what has happened. We will make your request for Lady Abigail and Lady Olivia's presence."

Nick was relieved, and grateful, that the guards from Ellis Manor were here with them. Lady Clara nodded her head in approval, and she hurried back into the bedchamber to Elizabeth. She would tend to

Elizabeth the best that she could until more help arrived. By the looks of Elizabeth's wounds, they would probably need Doctor Ramsey as well.

"Make it known to my cousin to not send a messenger to London just yet." Nick escorted the guards out to their horses. "When Elizabeth wakes up, we will find out why she does not want her family to know that she is here."

Both guards agreed to honor Elizabeth's wishes for now. Even they knew that the situation was serious. Sir Collin and Sir Adam mounted their horses and raced toward Ellis Manor. Within an hour or two, help from Ellis Manor would arrive.

Nick hurried back inside the house. He hoped that his mother would have news about Elizabeth's condition by now. As he was walking down the hallway, Nick noticed Lena Norton entering the room where Elizabeth was.

Nick ran to the door. It was bolted shut from the inside. He pounded rapidly, and loudly, on the wooden door with his fist. Someone was going to answer him, or he would break the door down.

"Mother!" Nick shouted, as he continued to pound on the door.

After several minutes, Lady Clara stepped out into the hallway. She pulled the door closed behind her. She remained standing in front of the door, preventing Nick from entering the room.

"Son, you are going to need to calm down." Lady Clara tried to detour Nick away from the room. "Why don't you go and wait in the parlor?"

"I am not going anywhere," Nick declared. "Mother, what is wrong?"

"Elizabeth has been severely beaten. I am sure she has a few broken ribs. When Abigail and Olivia get here, I am sure they can help to ease her pain with those herbal remedies of theirs." Lady Clara told her son all that she knew for now.

"Was she…" Nick felt dizzy and had to brace his hand against the wall. He could not bring himself to say the words.

"No, son." Lady Clara touched her son's arm. "I do not believe that she has been ravished."

9

Nick breathed a sigh of relief. He had to take several deep breaths to clear his mind from the evil thought. His mind could not fully process everything happening right now. He fought to hold his anger at bay, but in the end his anger won the battle.

"Then why do you have a midwife in there?" Nick narrowed his eyes and held his breath as his anger returned.

"Son, Lena was already here and offered her help, after she had delivered Eve's baby." Lady Clara spoke softly to her son, hoping to ease his anger.

"Eve Alton had her baby here?" There was so much going on that Nick could not process it all at once.

"Yes, son. Miss Langley's granddaughter was visiting her in the kitchen today and went into labor. Eve and Dale Alton have a beautiful little girl." Lady Clara smiled at Nick. She had never seen him so distraught before.

In little over an hour, a carriage from Ellis Manor pulled up at the side entrance of Kinsley Estate. One of the servants led Abigail and Olivia to Elizabeth's room.

"How is she?" Abigail asked Nick.

"I do not know. Mother, will not let me inside the room." Nick was growing impatient. He was leaning against the wall, staring angrily at the wooden door across from him.

"That may be for the best right now." Olivia knocked on the door.

Lady Clara was expecting the knock to be from her son once more. She was greatly relieved to see that the wives of her nephews had arrived. Lady Clara ushered Abby and Olivia into the room.

"Mother, may I see her?" Nick grabbed his mother's arm before she could close the door.

"Son, for now you should go with your cousins to the parlor. I will send word when we know more." Lady Clara looked to Nate and Alex for help.

"Come on, Cousin." Alex put his arm around Nick's shoulder. He could clearly see that his aunt was quite distraught and needed help with her son. "Let us go get a drink while we wait."

"Do not fret for Olivia and Abby have excellent doctoring skills." Nate assured Nick as he took him by the arm and led him away.

"But I do not want to leave Elizabeth." Nick had grown weary of protesting by this point. He was not aware that his mother could be so stern.

Reluctantly, Nick went with his cousins, as his mother had suggested. He was too worried to sit down, instead he paced around the parlor. He did gladly accept the glass of brandy that Alex handed him though. Waiting had never been one of his strong characteristics.

With Nick's Uncle Matthew hurt, his cousin Gavin could not leave Ellis Manor. Gavin did not want to send his wife, Abby, to Kinsley Estate alone, so he sent his brother Alex along with her. With a madman on the loose, Nate was not about to let his wife, Olivia, leave the manor without him being by her side.

"We are going to need to find that cloaked rider you chased earlier today." Nate felt helpless just waiting around like this.

"After I know that Elizabeth is going to be alright, we will find him." Nick balled his hand into a fist. He would find this guy no matter how long it took.

"We will get Caleb and track him down." Alex promised as he put his hand on Nick's shoulder. "Whoever this man is, he will pay for what he has done to Lady Elizabeth."

Nick agreed and nodded his head. His younger brother, Caleb, was an excellent tracker. Caleb and Alex were the best hunters in their family. The only problem, however, was finding Caleb. Caleb was not one to sit still for long periods of time. Hopefully, his little brother had not wondered off to London today.

The three men had only been in the parlor for about fifteen minutes when Nick's mother came into the room. Assuming that something horrible was the matter, Nick hurried over to his mother.

"Is she alright?" Nick was anxious for word on Elizabeth's condition.

"I do not know her full report just yet. Abby and Olivia had Lena and I to leave the room." Lady Clara was not comfortable with this arrangement. She now understood how her son felt just a bit.

"May I see her?" Nick asked.

"I am sorry, son." Lady Clara put her hand on Nick's arm. "Elizabeth does not wish to see you."

11

Chapter Three

Nick took a step backwards and shook his head. He felt as if someone had just slapped him across his face. Elizabeth did not want to see him. How could that be? Something was seriously wrong here and he had enough of waiting.

"I think not." Nick narrowed his eyes and walked past his mother.

Nick could not hear his mother and cousins calling after him. His mind had one mission and that was to see Elizabeth. Elizabeth Dawson was his friend, and someone had hurt her badly. His blood boiled with hate and anger over what had happened to her. Nothing, and no one, was going to keep him from seeing her.

Nick's mind could not grasp and place everything that was going on around him right now. Elizabeth would never refuse to see him. Many times, she had even slipped to the stables at Greyham Court to see him. Whatever had happened to her, Nick feared that it was far worse than any of them realized. Perhaps it was even worse than what his mother believed.

Nick pounded on the bedchamber door, demanding entry. Everyone had coddled him enough today. He was going to see Elizabeth. Nate and Alex had caught up with Nick as Olivia opened the door.

Olivia only opened the door just enough so that she could peer out. She stood where no one could see past her into the room.

"Nicholas, we need a little more time with Elizabeth. I will let you know shortly how she is." Olivia spoke softly but she stood firm on the matter. Nick's anger did not frighten her one bit.

"Nate, she is with child." Nick turned to look his cousin in the eye. "Move your wife. I will not ask a second time."

Nate nodded his head at Olivia. Olivia, trying to honor Elizabeth's request, hesitated to open the door further.

"Lady Olivia, I am not asking." Nick's jaw tightened as he tried to hold his anger back from his cousin's pregnant wife.

"Give me one moment, please," Olivia requested of Nick. She looked over at Abby.

"Elizabeth." Abby spoke softly to Elizabeth. She was sitting on the side of the bed applying her grandmother's herbal salve to her wounds.

"I do not want him to see me like this." Elizabeth's voice was weak, and her eyes were filled with tears, even though her left eye was swollen shut.

"Perhaps you could manage just a moment." Abby gently touched Elizabeth's hand. "I can help you to turn onto your side, facing away. Nick needs some peace, or his mind is going to go mad."

Elizabeth agreed and Abby helped her to turn onto her side, facing away from the door. Olivia opened the door wider, to allow Nick to enter the room. Nate quickly pulled his wife out into the hallway and closed the door behind Nick.

Nick approached the bed slowly. His mother and the servants had managed to remove Elizabeth's torn dirty dress. He could see the blue nightdress she wore, as the covers were pulled back enough to expose her left arm. Abby had been applying the herbal salve to the cuts and bruises on her arm and wrists.

"Elizabeth, it is alright. I have already seen the bruises." The image of her beaten face would forever be burned into Nick's mind.

"But I did not know how horrible I looked then." Elizabeth took several jagged breaths as she cried.

"You are going to be alright, Elizabeth." Abby continued to speak softly to her. "You will heal, in time."

Abby looked up at Nick and nodded her head. She wanted him to know that her words were true. Elizabeth's physical wounds should heal within a few short weeks, but her emotional scars would linger for many months, possibly even years.

"I suppose that you want to know who did this." Elizabeth's voice was growing weaker. She was tired and sleepy from the herbal tea Olivia had given her. The tea had an extra herb to help her sleep.

"I want to know how you are." Nick reached over and gently touched Elizabeth's arm. He breathed a sigh of relief when she did not shy away from his touch.

13

"I hate them." Elizabeth whispered. "I hate them all."

Abby quickly looked over at Nick. Stunned, they stared at each other, confused by Elizabeth's words. Up until now, they all had assumed that the lone cloaked rider was the only one involved.

"Do you know who did this to you?" Abby gently brushed a strand of Elizabeth's blond hair away from her face.

"Aye, I do." Elizabeth tried to look at Abby. Her left eye was still swollen shut and the vision in her right eye was blurry.

"If you tell us who did this, I will see to it that they are properly punished." Nick knew his words were a lie. He had full intention on killing whoever had done this to Elizabeth.

"My sister started it. She slapped me first." Elizabeth cried as she remembered that horrid moment.

"Your sister did this to you?" Abby's heart broke for Elizabeth.

"No, Anne just slapped me." Elizabeth turned her left hand over, as an invitation for Nick.

"Who was the rider that left you in the forest?" Nick asked as he gently touched her hand. He closed his eyes tightly when he saw the deep cuts around her wrists.

"After the sack was over my head, I do not know who did what." I just heard their voices." Elizabeth softly gasped.

She was having flashes of memory from what had happened to her. She had not yet fully pieced it all together. Elizabeth's body slightly trembled as she cried. The sound of those horrid voices haunted her mind every time she closed her eyes. If only she could drown them out somehow.

"Do you know who the voices belonged to?" Abby gently applied small amounts of the salve around Elizabeth's left eye.

"Roger Holden and Edmond Prescott." Elizabeth began to cry again.

Nick's entire body went ridged. He fought to hold his anger at bay while he was by Elizabeth's bedside. When he left this room, he would fully explode. He now had an object to focus his anger on.

The very two men that had caused his family the most grief for decades, were responsible for what had happened to Elizabeth. Finally, Nick now had a reason to end both men.

14

"Why do you not want us to send word to your brother that you are here? Was he part of this as well?" Nick was growing angrier by the minute. He liked Samuel Dawson and prayed that he did not have to add the Duke of Greyham to his list.

"Sam is not at home right now. This started at Greyham Court. I do not want to ever go back there. Anne and Evelyn are so cruel." Elizabeth continued to cry.

"Evelyn Cramer was a part of this as well?" Abby had already experienced Evelyn and Anne's cruelty when she first arrived in London a year ago.

"They were plotting together for the party." Elizabeth had to warn Nick. "Do not go to that party, Nick. Promise me that you will not go." Elizabeth was getting sleepier and her voice was fading.

"Anne and Evelyn were plotting something for me?" Nick could not understand why these two would bother with him. He did not hold the family title and both women were after a title.

"Aye, they were." Elizabeth's voice was even weaker now. "And Lord Spencer." Sleep then overtook her.

"We have to warn Maxx." Abby quickly stood up and faced Nick.

Maxwell Spencer was Abby's husband's best friend. Maxx was an ally to the entire Shaw family. Roger Holden had already tried to kill Maxx a few months ago, by poisoning a bottle of wine.

"You tend to her." Nick looked down at Elizabeth asleep on the bed. "I will take care of this."

Something dark and cold overtook Nicholas Shaw as he turned to leave the room. Holden and Prescott had crossed a line this time. Nick was tired of the foolish games that these too men played. If he had to ride straight to Statham Hall and kill Holden on his own front steps, then so be it.

Nick stepped out into the hallway. He looked Olivia in the eye. He had to remind himself that she was not like the rest of her family. Olivia was no longer a Holden. She was now married to his cousin Nathaniel and she was carrying their first child.

"I mean you no disrespect, Lady Olivia." Nick took a deep breath. "But I will personally see to it that your brothers pay dearly for this." With that, Nick walked away.

Chapter Four

Nick's mind was set on revenge as he stormed out the side entrance of Kinsley Estate. Roger Holden could not get away with what he had done to Elizabeth. The snake had always managed to slither out of everything before, but Nick vowed to make sure that he paid for his crimes this time.

"Go, have everyone to search for Caleb, now!" Nick ordered one of the stable boys. The young boy nodded his head and hurried away.

"So, Holden and Prescott are responsible for this?" Nate asked, when he finally caught up with Nick.

"I do not know all the details, but Elizabeth named them both." Nick ran his hand through his hair as he released a deep breath.

"It is long overdue for Holden to answer for the things he has done." Alex would gladly help hunt the snake down.

"Send someone to Hartford and warn Lord Spencer that there is an evil plot brewing." Nick would go himself, but he had a criminal to hunt down.

"What does Maxwell Spencer have to do with this?" Alex froze when he heard Nick's words.

"Abby had given Elizabeth something to help her sleep. She was not able to give me all the details." Nick wanted answers but Elizabeth's health was more important. "Elizabeth did say that Maxx and I should not go to Ms. Rhodes' End of the Summer Party."

"Why can we not just take Roger and Edmond before the king?" Olivia asked.

"Because your brother makes sure that there is no solid proof of his guilt in his shady affairs. One day, I believe that Roger will let Edmond take the blame for everything that they have done together." Nate put his arm around his wife.

"I will warn Maxx." Alex started toward the stables for his horse. He halted when he remembered his promise to his older brother.

"I need you and Caleb to help me track that cloaked rider." Nick caught Alex by the arm. "I have a feeling the rider was Prescott."

"I will ride to Hartford and warn Lord Spencer." Sir Adam, from Ellis Manor, offered.

"I cannot go to Hartford or help you track this man, for I promised Gavin that I would not leave Abby's side." Alex was grateful for the young guards offer. He could not break his promise to his brother, nor did he see how he could help Nick.

Alex shook Sir Adam's hand and sent him on his way. Alex knew that Nick needed him here, he had to find a way to help his cousin. Hopefully, they could find Caleb and track the cloaked rider. He knew, without Caleb, the tracking would fall completely on him.

"I will take your oath and remain by your brother's wife's side." Sir Phillip had just returned from Ellis Manor. "You go and help my sons track this man down."

"Abby and I will stay with Elizabeth. When she wakes up, maybe she can reveal more." Olivia smiled at Nick. She wished that she could offer him more peace, but she could not. She gave Nate a quick kiss and hurried back inside.

"Thank you, Uncle Phillip." Alex shook his uncle's hand and hurried with Nick to the stables. He was grateful that his uncle had returned and offered a solution that even Gavin would approve of.

Nick found his brother Caleb waiting for him at the stables. Thankfully, Caleb was working with the horses when the stable boy arrived. Together, Caleb and Alex should find the rider's trail with ease. Hopefully, by nightfall, they would have the cloaked rider in their custody.

"So, how long have you been in love with Elizabeth Dawson?" Alex bluntly asked Nick the question that everyone at Kinsley Estate had been wondering for the past few hours.

"What?" Caleb looked over at Nick, as they rode through the front gates. "You are in love with the Duke's sister?"

"Elizabeth is my friend." Nick looked straight ahead.

"Sure." Alex smiled. "And a diamond is just another jewel."

"Her family would never approve of such a match." Caleb figured that his older brother was in for a lot of heartache on the matter.

17

"Do you not think that I already know that!" Nick snapped at his brother. "That is why she is just my friend."

"Oh, my dear cousin, you cannot fool me. I have already watched both of my brothers fall in love." Alex knew that when a Shaw fell in love, they fell hard. "And you, Sir Nicholas Shaw, have fallen."

"Nothing can ever come of it. So, let us just leave it be." Nick did not want to talk about the matter.

"You could always approach the Duke and ask for his blessing." Caleb did not think that his suggestion was a bad idea. Samuel Dawson was not as harsh of a man as his father was.

"Her parents wanted her to marry someone of equal status, here in England or possibly in another country." Nick hated the thought of Elizabeth leaving London. "Let us just find the man responsible for hurting her."

Nick and Elizabeth had this conversation many times. Before her father's death, her parents were pursuing marriage contracts for Elizabeth in Spain, Italy, and France. Elizabeth had loudly voiced her disapproval at each suitor.

Her father was going to choose a husband for Elizabeth, before her twenty-first birthday. Elizabeth's father died of heart complications before a decision was ever made. Thankfully, Elizabeth's brother, Samuel, had not followed his father's wishes and pursued the marriage contracts any further. Nick was grateful that his brother and cousin let this matter rest.

Nick showed Alex and Caleb where they had found Elizabeth in the forest. The two easily picked up the cloaked rider's trail. After an hour of following the trail, it was clear to all three men that they were heading straight for London.

***

While Elizabeth slept, Abby and Olivia were able to apply the herbal salve to all her wounds. Abby was sure that Elizabeth had at least one or two broken ribs. Touching her midsection had caused Elisabeth to cry out in pain, causing Abby to stop examining her any further. Elizabeth's wrists had deep cuts and burns from the ropes that had held her up in the trees. The herbal salve should bring Elizabeth some relief in a day or two.

After a couple of hours, Elizabeth woke to find Abby sitting by her bed. Every part of her body screamed in pain as she tried to turn over. Olivia came in with a fresh pot of herbal tea to help with her pain.

"Where is Nick?' Elizabeth asked as Abby helped her to sit up against the pillows.

"Nick is tracking the rider that we think left you in the forest." Abby handed Elizabeth the cup of tea.

Elizabeth's wrists and shoulders were sore from where the ropes had held her to the trees. She whimpered from the pain that holding the teacup had caused. Abby had to take the teacup from her.

"Do you know who left you in the forest?" Olivia asked. She wondered if one of her half-brothers had done the horrible deed, or if they had hired someone else to do it.

"I think it was Edmond Prescott." Elizabeth turned away from the cup of tea that Abby held to her lips. "He spoke while tying me up."

"Do you know what Roger and Edmond are planning?" Abby placed cool cloths over Elizabeth's shoulders and around her wrists.

"To kill the Shaw's." Elizabeth looked down, she could not face Abby or Olivia, for both women were married to Shaw men.

"We know that the Holden's have hated the Shaw's for years." Abby gently touched Elizabeth's arm. She smiled to offer Elizabeth some comfort. This was nothing new to any of them.

"This family feud has been going on long before any of us were even born." Olivia too offered Elizabeth comfort on the matter.

"No. I mean… I know that." Elizabeth was still putting all the pieces of what had happened to her together. "This plot was to have the king execute all the Shaw men."

Abby and Olivia both gasped as they stood up and faced each other. Both ladies had gotten use to the two families arguing and fighting. Execution was a whole new level for Roger Holden.

"We have to warn them all," Abby cried. She placed her hand on her abdomen. Her child's father's life was at stake.

"Their plan has already failed." Elizabeth reached for Abby's hand. She winced, as the movement caused her pain.

"Are you sure?" Abby gently took Elizabeth's hand and sat down on the bed beside her. Olivia sat down the other side of the bed.

"Yes, I am sure." Elizabeth looked between Abby and Olivia. "I did not die."

Olivia stood up again and started pacing around the room. She knew how wicked her older brother's mind was. She could almost picture the evil plan he had concocted for the Shaw family.

"I do not understand." Abby was still in shock. "Part of the plan, was for you to die?"

"Yes. I was supposed to die." Elizabeth cried as she said the hurtful words. It was devastating for her to know that someone wanted her to die.

"Roger and Edmond did this to Elizabeth and left her in the forest between Ellis Manor and Kinsley Estate." Olivia quickly tried to explain what she thought her brothers were planning. "Elizabeth's body was to be found at a place where both Shaw families would be considered guilty of her death."

"They figured that my brother and mother would take the matter before the king." Elizabeth nodded her head at both ladies. Olivia had figured out the main parts of the evil plot against the Shaw's.

"And when no guilty party could be found, to pin the crime on, the king would have all the Shaw men executed to get the guilty one." Olivia finished out the evil plan her brother had set into motion. Once again, Elizabeth nodded her head.

"How does Maxwell Spencer play into this evil plot?" Abby asked, concerned for their family friend.

"I did not get all the details on that matter." Elizabeth thought for a moment, trying to recall what she had heard. "It involves Evelyn Cramer somehow."

"We need to tell Nate, Sir Phillip, and Lady Clara all of this." Olivia started toward the door.

"And send a warning to Maxx and Ellis Manor right away." Abby wanted to know that all the Shaw's and Maxx were safe.

"Do not let them hurt Nick!" Elizabeth exclaimed as she tried to sit up in bed. "Keep Anne away from him!"

"We will do our best to keep Nick, and the others, safe." Abby, as gently as she could, held Elizabeth still on the bed.

Chapter Five

Nick dismounted his horse and walked over to the gate, at the service entrance, to Greyham Court in London. Of all the places to end up, this was not where he had expected. This was Elizabeth's home. How could the rider's trail lead back to here?

"Are you sure about this?" Nick asked Caleb.

"Aye, brother. I am sure." Caleb had no doubts on this. He dismounted and started walking around the estate wall.

"Whoever that rider was, he came here after leaving Elizabeth in the Eastern Forest." Alex was studying the service entrance gate. "There is dried blood here." Alex pointed to the ground.

"I did not notice Elizabeth having any wounds that were bleeding." Nick looked closer at the dried blood splatter on the ground. "Do you think that this is her blood?"

"From the way you described Elizabeth's injuries, I would have to assume so." Alex hated to have to tell his cousin this.

"I have checked every entrance." Caleb returned from his inspection of the estate wall. "Elizabeth was brought out this gate and the rider returned here."

"How do you two track prey so well?" Nick could not understand it. His brother and cousin had extraordinary tracking skills.

"While you and Gavin were busy learning how to run the estates, Caleb and I got to focus on other activities." Alex looked at Caleb, both chuckled.

"There is no way of knowing more until we get inside the gate." Caleb looked toward the servant entrance gate.

"If we go in now, we will tip our hand." Alex grabbed Nick by the arm, before he could pull the cord that would alert the servants to come to the gate.

"What are you suggesting that we do?" Nick would rather go in and drag Roger Holden and Edmond Prescott out. "We cannot let them get away with this."

"We need spies." Alex look up at the Duke's luxurious house.

"Aye, that we do." Caleb grinned as he mounted his horse.

"And just where exactly do we get spies?" Nick had a feeling that he would regret asking this question.

"There is only one place in London that I would trust on the matter." Alex mounted his horse with a grin on his face as well. "To the Blume'N Brew, my dear cousins."

"To the Blume'N Brew." Caleb echoed his cousin's suggestion.

Caleb was tired and ready for a drink. The day had been hot and muggy. Their tracking had been tedious at times once they had reached the city. He was ready for a meal and a brandy.

Nick shook his head and mounted his horse. These two were going to ruin his reputation for sure. What would his mother say when word reached Kinsley Estate that the heir was visiting pubs? So much for being the 'good son'.

After what had happened to Elizabeth, Nick could no longer hide behind the 'good son' imagine any longer. Something dark was hidden inside of him and that darkness would only grow until the day he ended Roger Holden. And end him, Nick would surely do.

To Nick's surprise, they did not tie their horse in front of the Blume'N Brew, like the other patrons did. Instead, Alex and Caleb went around back, to the small stables behind the pub. Nick quickly realized that this was no ordinary pub. He assumed there was more to this establishment, and its little owner, than he had first thought. How could any place that Maxwell Spencer spent a lot of his time, be ordinary?

It was early evening when the three Shaw men walked in the front entrance of the Blume'N Brew. Nick noticed that there were quite a few patrons here already.

There were a couple of tables where men were playing cards. Several more groups of men were laughing and drinking. A tall skinny man was playing a piano in the front right corner. It was a typical looking pub. Nick noticed nothing that made the place so special, as rumors had it to be.

Caleb reached over and tapped Alex on the arm. With a huge grin on his face, Caleb pointed across the pub. There, in the right corner, on a private raised platform section, sat Maxwell Spencer. The Earl of Hartford appeared to be in serious thought.

"Little Man!" Alex patted Maxx on the back as he sat down at the table next to him.

"What's wrong?" Maxx asked as Nick and Caleb joined them at the table.

"What makes you think there is a problem?" Caleb grinned at Maxx. He was always happy to see the little Captain.

"One Shaw is bad enough." Maxx motioned around the table with his hand. "But three Shaw's at one time, that can only mean trouble."

"What are all these papers for?" Alex picked up a few of the papers on the table in front of Maxx.

"These are business logs and work orders." Maxx took the papers away from Alex. "Would you care to help me out with a few of these?"

"Little Man, I never knew that you had a serious side." Alex handed Maxx the last of the papers.

Maxx put his papers away and propped on his forearms on the table. He looked around at the three Shaw's, waiting for an answer. Maxx hated awkward silent moments like this.

"You are right, Lord Spencer." Nick broke the silence. "There is trouble."

"Save the formalities for those dressed up fancy parties." Maxx waved to the bartender for a bottle of rum.

"Speaking of parties…" Caleb turned his head and smiled at the young girl that came to take their drink orders.

"You cannot go to Ms. Rhodes' party on Friday." Alex was serious as he looked Maxx in the eye.

"I have been trying all week to find a good reason to get out of going to that party." Maxx poured himself a mug of rum. "If anyone asks why I did not attend, I can now, with all honesty, say that the Shaw's told me that I could not go." Maxx raised his mug at Alex. "Thank you, my friends."

"And our beloved Maxwell Spencer has returned." Alex waved his hand toward Maxx. Truth be told, he did not care much for the serious Maxx.

For the next hour, the four men discussed what had happened to Elizabeth Dawson, and the plot that Roger Holden was putting together. They all struggled to put the pieces of Holden's plans together. There were a lot of missing pieces to clearly see the plan.

As Maxx signaled the bartender for another bottle of rum, a messenger from Kinsley Estate arrived. Now, with the new information that Elizabeth had given to Abby and Olivia, the four men's hearts gravely fell.

Maxx uncorked the bottle of rum and drank straight from the bottle. It was one thing for Holden to come after him. It was something entirely dark and evil for a man to want an entire family executed.

"You have had enough of this." Alex took the bottle of rum from Maxx.

"I have not had near enough rum for this." Maxx protested as he reached for the bottle of rum.

"You are not going to that party Friday evening either." Miss Nancie sat down on the other side of Maxx, after she had locked up for the night.

"My, are you two not bossy tonight." Maxx was becoming irritated.

"We are only looking out for you." Alex pointed his finger at Maxx.

"I am not the one Holden wants to execute." Maxx snapped at Alex. He did not mean to sound harsh. He just could not lose the Shaw family.

"We do not know what Holden has planned for you." Nick could not figure out how Maxx played into Roger's plans. "All we know is, it involves Evelyn Cramer."

"I will scratch that little demon's eyes out if she harms Maxx in any way." Miss Nancie pounded her fist on the table.

"We need more information." Caleb had not spoken until now. Knowing that someone wanted to have him, and his family, executed had him deeply depressed.

"Maybe Elizabeth can remember more soon." Nick wanted to return to Kinsley Estate to be near her. "Though, I will not push her to remember every horrid detail."

"Are all Shaw men as kind as you are?" Miss Nancie propped her elbow on the table and looked at Nick.

"Nick is the 'good son'." Caleb whispered loudly across the table. "He does no wrong."

"I am far from perfect, little brother." Nick glared at Caleb. "I just do not flaunt my issues openly, as you and Jax do."

"If you two start arguing, I am just going to tie you up to your chairs and gag you both, right now." Maxx pointed between the two brothers. He was not having another incident like what had happened between Caleb and their youngest brother Jax in Nettlesville.

"We need a plan of our own." Nick was not going to blindly walk into Holden's trap.

"We have a plan." Maxx smiled as he leaned back in his chair.

"You want to share that plan with the rest of us, Little Man?" Alex looked at Maxx questionably.

"I know that your mind works in strange ways that I cannot begin to understand." Nick leaned across the table. "But it would be nice to know our parts in this mysterious plan of yours."

"Holden has a trap set for all of you." Miss Nancie grabbed Maxx by the wrist, preventing him from drinking from the bottle of rum. "What are you up to, lil buddy?"

"We are going to spring the trap." Maxx smiled slyly at Miss Nancie.

Maxx was not about to sit around and wait for Roger Holden to come after him again. He would find a way to beat Roger at his own game. Ms. Rhodes' End of the Summer Party should prove to be remarkably interesting this year.

"You are planning on going to that party." Miss Nancie dropped her hand to the table, after releasing Maxx's wrist, and sighed deeply.

"You are not going to that party!" Alex shouted at Maxx, as he stood up. There was no way that he was going to let Maxx walk into a trap.

"I do not take orders from you, Alexander Shaw." Maxx stood up and poked Alex in the chest. "We will discuss the details of the plan in the morning. It has been a long day, gentlemen. I am going to bed." Maxx grabbed the bottle of rum and headed upstairs.

"He is insane." Nick was learning just how odd Maxwell Spencer truly was.

"But he is usually right," Caleb said.

They all watched as Rachel put her arm around Maxx at the top of the stairs before she led him down the hallway. Nick sighed deeply and shook his head. He was not quite sure how they went from looking for spies to send into the Duke's home to plotting with Maxwell Spencer.

"If anyone can figure this out, it will be Maxx." Miss Nancie assured the Shaw's. Nick hoped that the little woman was right.

Chapter Six

The next morning, Nick found Maxx and his first mate, Paul, in Miss Nancie's private dining room. He did not realize that the Blume'N Brew had rooms on the second floor which Miss Nancie rented out to her special guests. Nick had assumed that the second floor was the little pub owners living quarters, until last night.

"Good morning." Nick sat down at the table, across from Maxx.

"After a few more cups, it just might be." Maxx pointed to his cup of coffee.

"You really are not a morning person, are you, Little Man?" Alex sat down at the table, next to Maxx.

"I would be, if it did not come so early." Maxx propped up on his elbow and closed his eyes.

"Perhaps the problem could be all the rum and women that you are so fond of." Nick poured himself a cup of coffee.

Miss Nancie was standing behind Maxx. She wildly shook her head and waved her hands franticly at Nick. It was better to deal with a drunk Maxx, than an early morning hungover Maxx.

Maxx's eyes popped open and he glared across the table at Nick. Alex took an ale mug and quickly filled it with coffee, he added cream and sugar.

"My rum and women are just fine, thank you very much, Sir Nicholas." Maxx was not happy. "You could use a few of both yourself. It might just knock the properness right out of you."

Alex tapped Maxx on the shoulder several times. Maxx snapped his head around at Alex and narrowed his eyes. He had enough of Shaw's pestering him this morning.

"Little Man, you need this." Alex quickly handed Maxx the mug of coffee. "Trust me, Little Man, you *need* this." Alex nodded his head as he spoke.

Maxx closed his eyes as he drank the mug of coffee. Nick watched as the little Earl's facial expression changed to a more

28

peaceful one. He noticed that no one in the room seemed to be breathing as they waited. Nick looked over at Caleb and motioned toward Maxx.

"There is no explaining it." Caleb whispered in his brother's ear. "So, do not even try."

Caleb had already witnessed how people catered to Maxwell Spencer while they were in Nettlesville. It was the darndest thing he had ever seen.

"I like this much better." Maxx smiled up at Miss Nancie as she refilled the ale mug with coffee. "The other cups are too small."

"Thank you." Miss Nancie whispered in Alex's ear, as she refilled his coffee cup. She would make a note to always give Maxx a mug of coffee from now on.

"My pleasure." Alex whispered back at the little pub owner.

"Now, may we discuss this plan of yours?" Nick asked Maxx, as the little fellow started eating the food Miss Nancie had sat before him. Nick was growing impatient.

"The first thing we need to do is move Elizabeth Dawson." Maxx did not look up from his plate of food.

"Are you insane?" Nick snapped.

"On good days, Aye, I am quite insane." Maxx still did not look up at Nick.

"Did you miss the part where she is wounded? Or perhaps, it escaped your mind that she was left for dead yesterday?" Nick could see no reasoning in Maxx's plan.

"Where do we take her?" Caleb smiled up at Miss Nancie as she handed him a plate of eggs and ham.

"You cannot seriously think that moving Elizabeth, in her condition, is a good idea?" Nick grabbed Caleb by his wrist. How could his own brother go along with Maxwell Spencer's madness so easily?

"I am sure that the good Captain has a worthy reason." Caleb pulled his arm away from his brother.

"I know everybody in our family just seems to trust you without question, but I do not agree with this." Nick pointed across the table at Maxx. "Moving Elizabeth could cause her great harm."

"I did not ask you if you agreed or not. I am simply telling you the plan." Maxx looked up at Nick. "And moving Elizabeth, just may save her life."

"Perhaps you should hear Maxx out?" Paul suggested.

Of course, Maxx's first mate would defend him. Nick felt that he was going to regret every part of this ludicrous plan. Reluctantly, Nick gave in and motioned for Maxx to continue.

"It sounds as if a big part of Holden's plan is supposed to play out during Ms. Rhodes' End of the Summer Party. You will need to move Elizabeth the day before the party." Maxx leaned back in his chair and looked calmly at Nick. "She does not need to be at Kinsley Estate or at Ellis Manor on Friday."

"Holden will convince the Duke's mother to send the king's men to both homes." Alex quickly looked over at Maxx. Maxx nodded his head in reply.

"Oh, there are brains in there after all." Maxx patted Alex on the head. Before Alex could respond, Maxx turned back to Nick. "If you cannot figure out another place to take her, then carry Elizabeth to Hartford. My mother and guards will help you to protect her. Or I could put Elisabeth on The Em and carry her to Nettlesville with me Friday night."

"You will do no such of a thing!" Nick roared, as he jumped up from his chair and glared across the table at Maxx.

"I would suggest that you sit back down. It is too early for this kind of attitude." Maxx spoke calmly.

Maxx folded his hands together and placed his chin on top of them, as he propped his elbows on the table. He patiently waited for Nick to sit back down. Nick looked around the room at the harsh stares he was getting from the others. Perhaps sitting back down would be best for now.

"Since Elizabeth did not die, Holden will have to alter his plans." Caleb looked between Nick and Maxx. He figured that someone needed to get the conversation back on the plan, before his brother made enemies out of everyone else in the room.

"Holden is going to be furious when he finds out that another one of his plans have failed." Nick had witnessed Roger's temper tantrums before. He looked over at Maxx. "Do you really think that it is a good idea for you to go to Ms. Rhodes' party."

"Lil buddy, I have a bad feeling about this." Miss Nancie reached over and took Maxx's hand. "Do not go to that party."

"Do not worry about me." Maxx smiled at his little friend. "I will be well protected, at all times." Maxx turned back to Nick. "We need to get to Kinsley Estate today and work out all the details with the rest of your family."

Sensing the urgency in the matter, the men stood up, ready to leave for Kinsley Estate. Nick would be glad to see Elizabeth again. He hoped that moving her would not cause her anymore pain. When they started out the side entrance, Miss Nancie grabbed Maxx by the arm.

"Maxwell, I do not like this plan." Miss Nancie looked as if she were about to cry. "Please reconsider this."

"Trust me," Maxx whispered as he hugged her goodbye. "I will be fine."

"Do not fret, blondie." Alex gave the little pub owner a hug. "I promise you that Maxx will be safe Friday night."

"Maxx does not always think things through, I'm afraid." Miss Nancie tried to laugh but failed to do so.

"I will protect our dear little friend, with my life," Alex promised. Miss Nancie nodded her head and hurried back inside.

✳✳✳

Nick and the others reached Kinsley Estate just before dinner time. While the others joined the family in the dining room, Nick hurried to see Elizabeth. He ran into the maid that his mother had appointed to Elizabeth, outside the bedchamber door. Nick took the food tray from Sarah and dismissed her for a couple of hours.

When Nick entered the room, Elizabeth quickly covered her face with her hands. After setting the food tray on the table, Nick sat down on the edge of the bed.

"You do not have to hide from me." Nick spoke softly to her as he sat down on the edge of the bed. "You never have to hide from me."

"I do not want you to see me like this." Elizabeth was embarrassed. She was glad that Nick had returned to Kinsley Estate though. "I look horrible."

"What happened to you, is horrible." Nick reached up and took her hands in his. "You, my lady, will always be beautiful." Gently and slowly, Nick pulled Elizabeth's hands away from her face.

"I do not agree with you right now." Elizabeth shyly tucked a few strands of her blonde hair behind her ear.

"The herbal salve that Abby and Olivia are using is really helping." Nick put his hand next to Elizabeth's left eye, but he did not touch it. "The swelling is significantly better today. Can you see out of it?"

"It is still blurry." Elizabeth looked over at the food tray. "You should go and dine with your family."

"My family knows how to dine without me." Nick set the food tray on Elizabeth's lap. "I would rather be here with you."

Sarah hurried into the room with another food tray and set it on the table by the bed. The maid smiled at Elizabeth before she scurried back out of the room.

"What are you doing?" Elizabeth asked as Nick pulled the small table closer to him.

"I am dining with you, my lady." Nick smiled slyly. "Is that not obvious?"

"Yes, it is obvious." Elizabeth looked at Nick's tray of food. "But you are having the same foods that I have. I am sure that you need more than broth and bread."

"I will not tease you by eating solid food in front of you." Nick sliced them both a piece of bread.

"Still, you do tease me, Sir Nicholas." Elizabeth blushed as she took the slice of bread from Nick.

"Aye, Lady Elizabeth, that I am guilty of doing." Nick's smile broadened.

Nick wished that they were in another world, one where titles and arranged marriages did not exist. Thankfully, Elizabeth was not bound to a marriage contract yet. He knew that he could not have her as his own, for he held no titles. Still, Nick would enjoy his time with her while it lasted.

"Did you find the cloaked rider?" Elizabeth asked. Thinking of the man made her shudder.

"We tracked him back to your home in London." Nick wished he could tell her that they had captured the man. "Do you remember more about the rider?"

He hated pressuring her for more information. Nick was not sure he wanted Elizabeth to remember all the details of what had happened to her. If she remembered it, then she would have to relive the horrid events that had happened to her.

"He spoke to me in the forest, just before he left." Tears welled up in Elizabeth's eyes. "I think it was Edmond Prescott" Nick thought this as well.

"Maxwell Spencer has a plan that may help to protect you, and my family, from whatever it is that Roger Holden has plotted against us. I personally think that the little Earl of Hartford is completely insane." Nick sighed and shook his head. "He wants us to move you to another safe location, if we can find one, in two days' time."

"I will be ready." Elizabeth touched Nick's hand. "And I may know of a safe place where we can go, at least for a while anyway."

Chapter Seven

The day before Ms. Rhodes' End of the Summer Party, Nick walked Elizabeth to the side entrance of Kinsley Estate. Elizabeth rode in the family carriage, with Nick's parents, to Ellis Manor. From Nick's uncle's home, everything would drastically change for everyone.

Surprisingly, Elizabeth was doing very well with traveling. Nick was sure that the carriage ride would not be too rough on her. However, he was concerned about what would happen once they changed to riding on horseback.

Elizabeth wore a large hat that Nick's mother had given to her. Lady Clara added a cloth veil under the left side of the hat, to help conceal Elizabeth's black eye. The swelling was all but gone but the bruises remained. Her vision was clearing up a little more each day.

Most of the family gathered in the sitting room at Ellis Manor. Nick's father hurried upstairs to visit with his older brother. Lord Matthew's leg was broken in three places and his wife refused to let him go downstairs until he had healed a bit more.

"Does everyone understand your parts in the plan?" Gavin asked as he looked around the room.

"I am not sure that I agree with this plan." Nick looked at his cousin, with a concerned look on his face.

"Your part is simple." Maxwell Spencer was sitting in the big chair by the window. "You go with Elizabeth and protect her."

"Is Lady Elizabeth really in that much danger?" Gavin's sister, Dani, asked.

Dani was fond of Elizabeth. Elizabeth had always been kind to Dani and her family. She was nothing like her cruel sister, Anne.

"Holden wanted her dead. So, he is going to be looking for her, to either kidnap her or to finish what he started." Gavin put his arm around his little sister. He was not trying to upset Elizabeth, but everyone needed to know just how serious the situation was.

"Our plan is to hide Elizabeth, while we try and spring the trap that Holden and Prescott have set." Alex tried to ease his little sister, and the other ladies in the room minds a bit.

"If we can catch Holden red handed in a crime, it may be enough for the king to charge him and imprison him for a long time." Nate like this idea.

"But Maxx is the one in the most danger." Dani protested their plan, once again. She did not like the idea of Maxx walking into a trap.

"I agree with my daughter." Lady Caroline walked over to Maxx. "There has to be another way. Roger Holden has already tried to kill you once. You do not need to go to this party."

"I will not leave Maxx's side, Mother." Alex took his mother's hand. "I promise you, Little Man, will be well protected tomorrow night."

"Elizabeth, this is Rosa." Abby led the maid over to Elizabeth. "She will be going with you. Rosa will take great care of you. You will find that she is much more than a lady's maid." Abby hugged Rosa.

"Harper and Caleb will also go with you." Gavin put his hand on Nick's shoulder. "More men from Hartford will arrive in a few days."

Nick looked over at Maxwell Spencer. Maxx raised his glass of brandy to Nick and nodded his head. Clearly the little Earl had thought his wild plan through more than Nick had realized. Maxx was offering his own guards to protect Elizabeth. Perhaps Nick had judged his cousin's friend a bit too harshly.

"The Em will set sail for Nettlesville tomorrow night. Depending on what Holden does at Ms. Rhodes' party, we may need to leave rather quickly." Paul stood by the window, next to Maxx.

"If that happens, you go with Maxx." Gavin told Alex.

"That is not necessary." Maxx leaned forward in his chair.

"It is absolutely necessary." Lady Caroline pointed her finger at Maxx as she spoke sternly to him. "Alex vowed to not leave your side and he will honor that, or we change this plan right now. Do you understand?"

"Yes, ma'am." Maxx leaned back in his chair and narrowed his eyes at Alex. Several of the family members silently chuckled.

After a light luncheon, everyone gathered out on the front steps of Ellis Manor to see Nick and Elizabeth off. Up until this point, Elizabeth was not nervous. She placed her arm protectively across her midsection as she looked at the horses waiting in the drive. Hopefully, this ride would not jar her ribs too badly.

"Since your ribs are broken and your shoulders and wrists are still sore, we think that it is best for you ride with me today." Nick led Elizabeth over to his horse.

"Is that really a good idea?" Elizabeth hesitated. "I can try to ride."

"It will be alright, my dear." Lady Caroline gently hugged Elizabeth. She understood Elizabeth's concerns. "The only people that will know of this, are on these steps. You do not need to worry for your reputation will be safe with us."

"You stay close to my sons, my dear, they will protect you." Lady Clara hugged Elizabeth as well. "You come safely back to us when this is all over with." Elizabeth nodded her head at Nick's mother and hugged her once more.

"It is best that you do not try to lead a horse just yet, Lady Elizabeth." Rosa gently patted her on the arm. "If this move was not important, you would not even be traveling this soon."

Elizabeth thanked everyone and allowed Nick to help her up onto his horse. Nick and Caleb told their parents goodbye, while Rosa said goodbye to Abby.

"You stay safe, my friend, and hurry back to us." Abby hugged Rosa. "Even though I have a feeling that you are about ready to leave our service soon."

"Aye, my lady. I am." Rosa looked over at Paul and smiled. "But I cannot go until this little guy makes his entrance into the world."

"So, you believe that I will give birth to a son?" Abby and Rosa both touched Abby's growing belly.

"I do, my lady." Rosa smiled and looked over at Paul again. She hated the moments when they had to part company.

"All I want is your happiness." Abby held Rosa's hands in hers. "Now, go over there and tell Paul goodbye." Both ladies smiled. Rosa hurried over to hug Paul goodbye.

"If there is any trouble, my men will get you all safely to Hartford." Maxx shook Nick's hand, after he had mounted his horse. "My mother has already been sent word and will be ready to assist you, if you need her."

"Thank you, Maxx." Nick felt bad for doubting Maxx in the first place. "You stay safe, and hurry back from Nettlesville with my little brother."

"When it is safe for you to return, we will send word." Gavin shook Nick's hand and bid his cousin farewell.

Nick and Elizabeth left the safety of the fortress wall of Ellis Manor. He was glad to be protecting her, but Nick was nervous about what lay ahead for them.

There were still so many unanswered questions. There were many more 'what if' scenarios that were driving Nick mad. He was amazed at the bravery of Maxwell Spencer. Maxx was a strange little fellow, but he was risking his own life to discover Roger Holden's plot against the Shaw family. For the first time, Nick realized that his cousin had a true and loyal friend.

Nick was glad to have his brother Caleb and Harper, one of Maxx's loyal men, along for extra protection. Hopefully, they would not need it. Rosa was greatly needed to help tend to Elizabeth and to treat her wounds. Abby and Olivia had given Rosa the herbal salve and tea that had been helping Elizabeth heal so quickly.

"I hope that this ride will not be too difficult for you." Nick whispered in Elizabeth's ear.

"I will make the best of it." Elizabeth leaned back against Nick. Truth be told, she rather liked being this close to Nick. She would deal with her sore ribs later.

"How long of a journey do we have ahead of us?" Nick asked.

"We should reach the Summer Cottage in about two or three days." Elizabeth loved her family's cottage.

Hopefully, they could wait things out there until the matter with Roger Holden was settled. The cottage was well hidden and very few people knew of its exitance. It was the safest place that Elizabeth could think of it hide for a few weeks.

It was sad to Elizabeth that her family had not visited the cottage for many years now. It was a beautiful and peaceful house, nestled in the forest near a small private lake. When she was little, the Summer Cottage was her favorite place to visit. Her father was always a different person during their summer visits. He was free from the worries that troubled him as the Duke of Greyham. Elizabeth hated that those same worries now fell upon her younger brother, Samuel.

"Are you sure that you do not mind sleeping in a tent for a couple of nights?" Nick smiled. He could not imagine the Duke's sister sleeping outside.

"I guess I will have to learn how to 'rough it'." Elizabeth laughed at the thought. This was a whole new experience for her, but it was one that was designed to save her life.

Chapter Eight

The first day of traveling on horseback was not too rough on Elizabeth. However, Nick could tell that the second day had worn more on her than she had admitted. He could hear Elizabeth groan in pain as Rosa applied the herbal salve to her wounds, inside the tent.

Nick admired Elizabeth's courage. He had not expected her to brave through 'roughing it' in the open like this. Elizabeth was sweet and innocent. She did not deserve any of this hardship that was now thrown upon her.

Elizabeth had lived her entire life behind walls of protection. Her days were spent being tended to by maids, and protected by armed guards, up until now. Nick wondered, where were the Duke's guards on the day that Elizabeth was taken?

Tomorrow they would reach the Duke's Summer Cottage. It would be much easier to protect Elizabeth when they got there. Tonight, Nick, along with Caleb, Harper, and Rosa, would be closely guarding Elizabeth while their family and friends went up against Roger Holden.

"She is resting, if you would like to go in and see her now." Rosa smiled at Nick as she sat down next to him by the fire.

"Thank you, Rosa." Nick got up to go see Elizabeth. He was grateful for the maid's help. He could already tell that Rosa was no ordinary lady's maid. Leave it to Maxwell Spencer to train a maid to fight.

"Where is Caleb?" Rosa did not see him in the campsite.

"Caleb is taking first watch." Harper went over to his bedroll and laid down. He covered his face with his hat. He would be taking the second watch.

"We figured that Holden probably knows by now that Elizabeth did not die in the forest. He is probably already searching for her." Nick looked around the campsite. "We marked a perimeter just a few feet out, around the campsite."

Rosa looked up at Nick and nodded her head. She would be sleeping inside the tent with Elizabeth again tonight. Rosa doubted that any of them would sleep well this night. She would have her pistol and knife hidden within the covers, by her side, just in case.

Nick went inside the tent and sat down next to Elizabeth. Rosa had a single lantern dimly burning between their bedrolls. Elizabeth kept the veil, that his mother had made for her, over her left eye. As concerned as Elizabeth was about the way her eye looked, Nick assumed that she would keep it covered for a week or two, until the bruises were all but gone.

Elizabeth smiled when she saw Nick. She started to sit up, but she was too sore to do so. Nick reached over to hold her still on her bedroll. Her weary smile could not hide the fact that she was in pain.

"Tomorrow night you will be able to, once again, sleep in a nice comfortable bed." Nick hated seeing her so uncomfortable.

"If my ribs were not so sore, I would probably be enjoying this more." Elizabeth laughed lightly.

"Perhaps we could do this again someday. When you are feeling better, of course." Nick also laughed. "We would have to camp on the lawn of Greyham Court. But if we did that, I do believe that your brother would kill me in the night."

"No!" Elizabeth exclaimed as she quickly sat up. She put her arm across her midsection. The sudden movement caused her great pain.

"It's alright." Nick gently grabbed Elizabeth by her upper arms to steady her. He was cautious to not touch her wounded shoulders.

"I am not going back to Greyham Court!" Elizabeth was terrified, and with great reason. Rosa had heard her shout and hurried inside the tent.

"Are you alright, My Lady?" Rosa gently touched Elizabeth on her arm.

"I cannot do it." Elizabeth covered her mouth with her hand. "Please do not make me do it." Elizabeth laid down on her bedroll and cried.

"Sir Nicholas, out!" Rosa ordered as she pointed toward the tent entrance.

"I…" Nick was at a loss for words.

When Nick tried to protest further, Rosa narrowed her eyes at him and continued to point toward the tent entrance. Not wanting to cause Elizabeth any more grief, Nick did as Rosa asked. Elizabeth's wellbeing was more important than what he wanted right now.

"What happened?" Harper was standing by the tent with his sword in his hand.

"It's alright." Nick held his hand up as Caleb came running into camp. "I teased her, and it caused her to become hysterical."

"She has been through a nightmare." Caleb looked sternly at his older brother. "Teasing, may not be a good idea for quite a while yet."

"She was fine up until I mentioned Greyham Court." Nick was a little defensive.

"That is understandable." Harper went back to his bedroll, near the fire. "She was hurt at Greyham Court."

"So naturally, she is going to resent the place for a while." Caleb thought that this should have been an obvious fact to his brother.

Nick knew that his brother and Harper were right. He should have known better than to tease Elizabeth to begin with. Surely Elizabeth knew that he did not mean to cause her more grief. All he could do for now was to sit down and wait while Rosa comforted Elizabeth. He would rather be the one comforting her.

"She is asleep now." Rosa joined Nick by the fire again.

"I did not mean…" Nick was deeply sorry for upsetting Elizabeth.

"Even Elizabeth knows that you did not intend her any harm." Rosa sat down on the log by the fire. "I am afraid that she will have moments like that for a while."

"Do you think that Maxx is alright?" Harper looked at Rosa.

"Hopefully, we will receive word in a few days." Rosa sadly dropped her head.

*** ***

While Nick and Caleb were protecting Elizabeth Dawson, the rest of their family was preparing for Ms. Rhodes' End of the Summer

Party. Extra guards were placed at both estates, and in London, to help once Roger Holden's plan was set in motion.

Most of the Shaw family did not attend Ms. Rhodes' party this year. Alex made the excuses for his family. His mother, Gavin and Abby had remained at Ellis Manor because his father, Lord Matthew, had been severely injured. Nate and Olivia remained at the manor under the pretense that Olivia's pregnancy had her extremely tired. Lady Caroline was not about to let her only daughter, Dani, travel to London without her parents.

Nick's parents did attend the party, to help keep suspicions down. If anyone acquired of Nick and Caleb's whereabouts, the family was saying that they were preparing to go with Lord Spencer to Nettlesville to get their brother Jax. They told a few of the young ladies at the party that Nick and Caleb may drop in on the party later.

True to Maxx's belief, the king's men paid a visit to both Shaw estate homes that day. Lord Matthew was not going to allow his family to be found guilty of lying to the king. When Captain Cromwell, of the king's men arrived, he was escorted to the Earl of Claybourne's private study on the second floor. The Shaw family explained the situation to the Captain. They all prayed that the king's Captain would hear them out.

"So, I do have your word that Lady Elizabeth Dawson is alive and safe?" Captain Cromwell was not happy about the situation.

"Aye, Captain. You have my word." Lord Matthew nodded his head. "Until we clear the matter up, and find the Duke of Greyham, we will keep Lady Elizabeth safe."

"We do not know who all is involved in the matter just yet." Gavin stood before Captain Cromwell, pleading their case. "Will you help us?"

"Naturally, I am going to do all that I can to protect the Duke's family. I will send messengers to find the Duke at once." Captain Cromwell stood up to leave. "Sadly, Lady Elizabeth having that sack over her head, makes nothing that she said useful in incriminating the Earl of Statham. I cannot arrest Roger Holden on any of it."

"We were afraid of that." Nate put his arm around his wife. No one in their family would be safe until Olivia's brother was arrested.

Gavin and Lady Caroline walked Captain Cromwell to the front door of Ellis Manor. They all were relieved to have the help of the King's Captain.

"Thank you, Captain." Gavin shook the man's hand. Captain Cromwell halted at the door.

"So, the Earl of Hartford, Lord Maxwell Spencer, is about to walk into a trap tonight at Ms. Rhodes' party?" Captain Cromwell looked deeply concerned.

"If Lady Elizabeth's information is correct, Aye, Captain, I am afraid that he is." Lady Caroline, with tears in her eyes, looked away.

"My men and I will hurry back to London then." Captain Cromwell nodded his head at Gavin.

"Sir, even if you rode through the night, you would not make London until daybreak." Gavin wished the king's men could get there sooner.

"Then my men and I will arrive at daybreak. I have grown quite fond of that little lad." Captain Cromwell turned to go.

Lady Caroline smiled as Gavin put his arm around her. Hopefully, Maxx and Alex would not need the help of the king's men but they both were relieved to know that help was on its way.

Chapter Nine

Sir Phillip and Lady Clara arrived at Ms. Rhodes' party at sunset. Maxx and Alex waited until after dark before they entered the ballroom. Paul had men patrolling around Ms. Rhodes' London home for Roger Holden and Edmond Prescott. They all were as prepared as they could be, for whatever this trap was that Roger Holden had planned for this night.

"Have you seen anything yet?" Alex whispered to his uncle. Sir Phillip shook his head.

"Anne Dawson and Evelyn Cramer are across the room. They have not moved all evening." Lady Clara spoke softly to Maxx and Alex.

"No sign of Roger Holden yet." Sir Phillip smiled politely and led his wife out onto the dance floor.

Maxx and Alex casually looked around the room. They spotted Anne and Evelyn whispering in the corner on the far side of the room. The smiles on their faces let Maxx know that these two conniving women were about to set their plan into motion.

"Do you want a drink? I sure could use a drink." Alex asked as he continued surveying the room for Holden. He hated to admit it but this trap, whatever it was, had him a bit nervous.

"No, I do not want a drink." Maxx looked up at Alex as if he had lost his mind. "Nor do I want anything to eat from here."

"Right. That is probably for the best tonight." Alex was sure that Maxx would probably never drink in public again, after being poisoned by wine a few months ago.

"I have a meal, and a bottle of rum, waiting on the ship." Maxx noticed that Evelyn and Anne were now walking toward them.

"Did Miss Nancie send you roast beef and vegetables?" Alex also noticed the two women coming toward them. Maxx looked up at Alex with a surprised expression on his face. "What? Miss Nancie always fixes you that meal."

"You are right on that." Maxx nodded his head and pretended to be enjoying the party.

"What do we do?" Alex whispered. Anne and Evelyn were almost to them now.

"Normally, I would say run, but we need to spring this trap." Maxx was dreading having to speak with these two evil women. "So, I guess we will have to play along, my friend."

"Lord Spencer. Lord Alexander." Anne Dawson greeted them. "It is a lovely evening, is it not? Is Sir Nicholas with you?"

"It is a lovely evening indeed, Lady Anne." Alex faked a smile. He noticed that Anne continued to watch the door. Both women truly disgusted him.

"Lord Spencer, forgive me for being so bold." Evelyn Cramer batted her eyelashes at Maxx. "But would you care to dance."

"Of course, he would love to dance." Alex nudged Maxx toward Evelyn.

Maxx looked up at Alex like he wanted to punch him. Alex only smiled and nodded his head. Alex thought that perhaps there was some fun to be had in this night after all. Maxx would probably not forgive him for this, but it was amusing to watch.

"Lady Anne, why don't you dance with Lord Alexander until Sir Nicholas arrives?" Maxx suggested as Evelyn pulled him toward the dance floor.

Anne Dawson seemed to love the idea. She grabbed Alex by the arm and pulled him onto the dance floor. Maxx smiled up at Alex with an 'I got you' grin. Alex would have to remember to punch Maxx later. That was, if they managed to wiggle out of the trap these two women were helping Roger Holden with.

"What are you thinking about?" Evelyn asked, as she and Maxx moved around the dance floor.

"Leaving," Maxx mumbled. This dance made Maxx want to lose his stomach.

"What a wonderful idea," Evelyn exclaimed happily. Evelyn quickly pulled Maxx outside to the garden.

"Mind if I cut in?" Sir Phillip ignored Anne's protest as he stepped in and took her away from Alex.

Alex happily handed Anne over to his uncle. He was not sure how much longer he was going to be able to look Anne in the face without saying something that would insult her. With Anne taken care of, he could now go and help Maxx.

Lady Clara quickly led Alex to the exit doors at the flower garden, where Evelyn had taken Maxx through. Alex was grateful for his Aunt and Uncle's help tonight. Having the extra eyes in the ballroom proved beneficial tonight. He would have never seen where Evelyn had taken Maxx without his aunt's help.

Alex hurried outside. He did not see Maxx and Evelyn on the terrace that overlooked the gardens. Franticly, Alex searched through the flower garden for Maxx. Finally, at the center of the garden, Alex found Maxx, fist fighting with a man dressed in black. Evelyn stood to the side with her hands over her mouth. She made no attempt to call for help, so Alex assumed this was part of the trap.

Evelyn screamed out for help when she looked over and saw Alex approaching. Alex knew that this was for his benefit rather than an actual call for help. If Evelyn were not a woman, he would surely punch her in the face right now.

"Oh, Lord Alexander, do not fret. I am sure that Lord Spencer will be alright." Evelyn tried to prevent Alex from passing. "This man came out of nowhere." Evelyn's theatrics was annoying.

Alex could not get past the little evil woman. He hated what he was about to do but she had to be moved. Hopefully, his mother would not flog him later for this. Alex grabbed Evelyn by her arms and shoved her into the man dressed in black, before the man could take another swing at Maxx. The man and Evelyn stumbled and fell together, into the garden fountain.

"How dare you assault my daughter!" Evelyn's father shouted as he ran around the corner of the house.

Several men were now running toward the fountain behind Evelyn's father. Alex and Maxx assumed Mr. Cramer was part of the plot tonight since he was so readily nearby.

"Time to go!" Maxx shouted.

Maxx grabbed Alex by the arm and pulled him toward the exit off the gardens. Paul was waiting for them with their horses. The shouts of the men, and the screams from Evelyn, grew louder as more men joined the chase. Alex, Maxx, and Paul quickly mounted their horses and raced toward London Harbor.

Lord Benjamin Mason, the Earl of Huntington, was waiting for them at the docks. His guards would be taking their horses to the stables behind the Blume'N Brew.

"Glad you made it out of there, young man. I must say that I was deeply concerned." Lord Mason handed Maxx the documents that he was sending to Nettlesville.

"Is everything loaded and ready to sail?' Maxx quickly took the papers. He and the others were looking over their shoulders for their pursuers.

"Aye, it is. And I will make sure that Sir Phillip and Lady Clara get safely to Kinsley Estate tomorrow." Lord Mason could hear the shouts coming toward the docks.

"I am afraid that we have a mob behind us." Maxx hurried on board The Em, behind Paul and Alex.

"Do not fret, Lord Spencer. My men have this under control." Lord Mason waved farewell as The Em pulled away from the dock.

Lord Mason nodded his head at his Captain of the Guard, Sir Charles. Sir Charles gave the order and Lord Mason's men toppled the crates and barrels at the main entrance to London Harbor, preventing the mob that was chasing after Maxx and Alex from entering the dock area.

Maxx laughed so hard that he had to lean over the ship's railing for support. Paul shook his head and laughed as he patted Maxx on the back.

"Do you do this kind of stuff often?" Alex looked from Maxx to the chaos happening on the docks.

"Only on good days." Maxx could not stop laughing.

"You cannot condone this?" Maxx looked at Paul. How could Maxx's first mate approve of him being in situations like this?

"Maxx is safe and alive." Paul looked seriously at Alex. "That is my only concern. And I will help make sure that Maxx stays safe and alive, no matter what."

How had his brother Gavin survived nine years by Maxx's side? His brother's little friend was now a mystery to Alex. He had heard the wild tales of the many adventure that Lord Maxwell Spencer had gotten into, but never had he realized how great the chances were, that the little Earl had been taking, until this night. Maxx seemed to love the thrill of it all.

"You, Little Man, are going to be the death of me." Alex continued to watch the chaos happening on the docks as they sailed away from London Harbor.

"You know, I have said that very same statement about your family for years." Maxx looked up at Alex. "Now, my friend, I need that drink."

"Did he…?" Alex's eyes widened as he watched Maxx walk away.

"Promote you to friend?" Paul raised his eyebrow. "I do believe so."

Alex and Paul followed Maxx below deck to the Captain's quarters. They all were ready for a fine meal and a stiff drink. Hopefully, Lord Mason and Sir Phillip would be able to figure out the full extent of Roger Holden's trap.

Alex now realized that Maxx was not planning on sticking around tonight for the outcome of that plan. Maxx only wanted to spring the trap tonight. He apparently did that in Ms. Rhodes' garden, with Evelyn Cramer's help.

"Are you sure that my aunt and uncle will get home safely after the chaos we just left behind tonight?" Alex asked. He hated leaving them behind at the party.

"Aye. Lord Mason's men escorted them from Ms. Rhodes' house the moment we left the ballroom." Maxx leaned back in his chair and stretched out his legs. "They may not be too comfortable with their lodging arrangements for the night, but they are indeed safe."

"What did you do with my aunt?" Alex stared at Maxx.

"Your aunt and uncle are in the safest place in London tonight. Trust me, no one will find them tonight." Paul handed Alex a glass of brandy. Maxx slyly grinned at Alex.

"You sent my aunt to the Blume'N Brew!" Alex was shocked. "How could you do that? My aunt is a gentle woman."

"Your aunt is made of tougher stuff than your entire family is aware of." Maxx opened a bottle of rum.

"My father is going to kill us both when we return." Alex shook his head and pointed at Maxx. "That is the last time that I let you plan anything by yourself."

"I had help in the planning part. Lord Mason is handling everything in London tonight. Trust me, all is well." Maxx was not worried over the matter.

"No! What you did, was tell everybody what to do and they all rushed to do it. And I will never figure out how you come up with these ludicrous ideas to start with." Alex threw his hands in the air. It was pointless to try and understand how Maxx's mind worked.

"What is even more surprising is, somehow all of his ludicrous ideas seem to work out for the better." Paul laughed as he sat down at the table.

"What do we do now?" Alex held his hands out, as he gave up protesting the matter.

Alex blamed himself for the mayhem that just happened tonight. He should have gotten all the details of Maxx's plan from the beginning. After tonight, he would not make that mistake again.

"We deliver the supplies, and documents, to Nettlesville for Lord Mason, and we bring your cousin, Jax, home." Paul uncovered the meal on the table that Miss Nancie had sent on board.

"And we keep a look out for the Duke of Greyham along the way." Maxx sat down at the table.

"Where do you think the Duke is?" Alex joined Maxx and Paul at the table. "He sure is gone a lot."

"That is a mystery in itself." Maxx looked between Alex and Paul. "We will do what we can to find Samuel Dawson. Let us hope that Nick and Caleb can keep Elizabeth safe and alive until the Duke is found."

Chapter Ten

Nick, Elizabeth, and the others arrived at the Duke's Summer Cottage, midafternoon on the next day. Elizabeth's face lit up when she saw the cottage as it came into view. Nick was glad to see her smile again. This was the first time that Elizabeth had truly appeared to be happy since he had found her in the Eastern Forest.

"This is a cottage?" Caleb whispered to Rosa as they dismounted their horses in front of the house.

The cottage was beautiful and well kept. The gardens were lovely and maintained with great care. The house was nestled in a large clearing in the forest. The small lake even connected to the river that they had been following for the past couple of days. Caleb was amazed for the Duke's cottage was almost the size of Kinsley Estate.

"Lady Elizabeth, we were not expecting you." The butler, Mr. Hayes, hurried out to greet them.

"We do apologize for the inconvenience, but this is an emergency." Elizabeth spoke politely to the elderly gentleman.

"Lady Elizabeth, I am afraid that it is us that will inconvenience you." Ms. Colby, the housekeeper, escorted everyone into the parlor.

"Ms. Colby is right, My Lady." Mr. Hayes was concerned. "There is only the six of us here at this time."

When the Summer Cottage was not in use by the Duke's family, only a minimum staff resided at the house. There was the butler, the housekeeper, the cook, two stable hands, and the groundkeeper that lived here year-round.

"Rosa is a lady's maid." Nick was now by Elizabeth's side. "You and the other staff members can help Rosa take care of Elizabeth. The rest of us know how to take care of ourselves."

"We should round the staff up and explain to them what has happened." Caleb stood watching out the parlor window.

So far there were no signs that anyone was following them. However, dealing with Roger Holden, Caleb was not taking any chances. There was a lot of forest surrounding the cottage. This was something that they had not planned on. The forest would be a perfect place for slimy men, like Holden and Prescott, to hide and attack them when they least expected it, if they were to let their guard down.

After the servants were informed of the situation, Harper and the two stable hands took their horses to the stables, once everything was unloaded. Arlo Perry and Dean Tinley were both in their early forties and had worked for the Duke's family for over fifteen years. Nick was relieved to hear that both men had been trained as guards as well. Arlo and Dean were outraged over what had happened to Lady Elizabeth. Both men would help guard the house until the men from Hartford arrived.

After a bath and an early dinner, Rosa helped Elizabeth prepare for bed. Elizabeth was glad to be in a regular bed once again. The past two nights of sleeping in a tent, had opened her eyes to a world she had never known before. Under different circumstances it would have been quite the adventure.

Elizabeth had never looked down on the lower-class people, as her sister Anne had. Even her own mother had spoken harshly about the poor on several occasions, but never in front of her brother Samuel. Elizabeth's heart had always wanted to help the poor somehow. She vowed, when and if, she ever returned to London, she would find a way to help others.

Elizabeth woke before dawn and grabbed her robe. She went downstairs to get a bite to eat. As she descended the stairs, Elizabeth saw Nick watching out the window by the front doors. Nick was standing next to the doorway, leaning against the wall. He turned and smiled when he saw her. She was not sure how Nick had heard her so easily.

"Good morning." Elizabeth spoke just above whisper.

"You should be resting." Nick was glad to see her though.

"Trust me, I have rested." Elizabeth stepped beside Nick, as she looked out the window.

There was a full moon that illuminated everything outside. A light fog was flowing in from the lake. Everything looked still and calm to

Elizabeth. She was not sure if it was the memories of the view before her that warmed her spirit, or if it was because of Nick.

"I am glad, My Lady." Nick took Elizabeth by the arm and gently pulled her away from the window.

"Is something the matter?" Elizabeth tried to peep out the window again. Had she missed something?

"All is quiet outside, for now." Nick did not want to alarm her. "Still, it is best to stay away from the windows as much as possible." Elizabeth understood and nodded her head.

"Would you like some tea?" Elizabeth asked.

"You, Lady Elizabeth, know how to make tea?" Nick teasingly smiled at her.

"Aye, Sir Nicholas, I do know how to make tea." Elizabeth playfully curtsied. Nick liked seeing her this way again.

Elizabeth hurried to the kitchen and started making the tea. Hearing someone moving about in the kitchen alerted the cook, Ms. Graham. The frightful woman was relieved to find Elizabeth in the kitchen rather than a prowler.

"Lady Elizabeth, let me help you with that." Ms. Graham took over and made coffee as well. "Might as well get breakfast going while I'm here."

Elizabeth thanked Ms. Graham and carried a tray with coffee and tea to the front parlor. She found Rosa waiting in the parlor. She should have known that there was no slipping anything past a maid that had once worked for Maxwell Spencer. The past two days had already proved to her that Rosa was not just a lady's maid.

"You are a sly one, Lady Elizabeth." Rosa handed Elizabeth a cup of tea for Nick. "I will have to watch you a tad bit closer, I think."

"Forgive me for not waking you. I could not go back to sleep." Elizabeth apologized.

Elizabeth woke to find Rosa sleeping on a cot in her room. She knew that Rosa was as tired as she was, so Elizabeth let her rest.

"It is quite alright." Rosa nodded her head toward the front doors. "You go on and take that tea to Nick." Elizabeth was happy to do so.

"The sun will be up soon." Elizabeth spoke softly as she handed the cup of tea to Nick. "What shall we do today?"

"You, My Lady, will remain hidden from view of the outside world as much as possible." Nick was not taking any chances with her safety.

"What?" Elizabeth did not understand. "You mean that I am to be a prisoner in my own home?"

"I did not mean it as harshly as that." Nick knew that she would not like this plan. "Until the guards from Hartford arrive, I think that it is best for you to remain inside the house."

"And after the guards arrive?" Elizabeth folded her arms across her chest.

"We will wait and see." Nick stood firm on his decision.

"I see." Elizabeth narrowed her eyes at Nick as she held her head high.

"It is for your protection." Nick pleaded with her to understand.

"I am not as delicate as what you and everyone else believes." Elizabeth was deeply offended.

"Let us hope that we do not have to find that out." Nick looked out the window again.

"I mean it…" Elizabeth did not get to finish her protest.

Nick quickly pulled her behind him and put his finger to his lips to silence her. Something had moved in the shadows outside. After several minutes, the man moved again. Nick breathed a sigh of relief.

"It is only Caleb." He turned to face Elizabeth again. "Let us just take this day by day and see what we can do."

Elizabeth nodded that she agreed before dropping her head and looking away. She hated that everyone treated her as if she was porcelain. She was not as uppity as her mother and sister were. Elizabeth had always believed that she had more of a free spirit, like her father and brother had.

"I will not let anything happen to you ever again." Nick spoke softly as he took a step closer to Elizabeth.

"I feel safe just knowing that you are my protector." Elizabeth looked up at Nick. She could clearly see his deep brown eyes in the moonlight.

"I wish…" Nick reached out his hand to touch her face.

"I wish that too." Elizabeth took his hand in hers before Nick could touch her.

"You do not know what I was going to say." Nick took another step closer to her.

Elizabeth's breath caught for a moment. One more step, just one more step and she would be next to Nick. She would be able to touch his chest and put her arms around his neck. Could she take that step? Did she dare to make that move? Did Nick wish for that final step to be taken as well?

"You do not have to say what my heart already knows," Elisabeth whispered.

The sound of the kitchen door opening, and closing, snapped them both back to the real world. Elizabeth backed away from Nick. She could not look him in the eye. She had spoken too boldly, and a lady was not to do such a thing with a man.

Elizabeth wanted to be more than a friend to Nick, but that was not possible. Before the tears in her eyes could become noticeable, Elizabeth turned and hurried upstairs to her room.

"I do not know why you two fight what is obviously between you." Rosa stepped into the foyer.

"I have no title." Nick still looked up at the stairs, even though Elizabeth was no longer in sight.

This was the only reason he envied his cousin Gavin for being next in line for the title of Earl of Claybourne. A title would mean that he could safely approach the Duke of Greyham and ask for Elizabeth's hand in marriage.

"There are greater things than titles." Rosa told him.

"I would sure love to know what those things are." Nick looked over at Rosa. She could clearly see how much he loved Elizabeth.

"Those things are already here. It is only a matter of time before they make themselves known." Rosa nodded her head and went to the kitchen, leaving Nick to ponder the meaning of her words.

Chapter Eleven

Elizabeth Dawson was a sweet and kind young woman. She had always had a loving heart toward others. She was a model for all the ladies in London's society to follow, which few rarely did. That was, before the past five days of keeping her confined within the walls of her family's Summer Cottage.

"You cannot keep me inside like this!" Elizabeth shouted at Nick.

"Until I know that it is safe, I most certainly will keep you inside." Nick was not backing down on his decision.

Elizabeth folded her arms across her chest. With a deep huff, she stamped her foot and abruptly turned away from Nick.

At the beginning, this idea being protected by Nick had sounded great to her. Now, knowing that she was not allowed to go outside was wearing greatly on Elizabeth.

"You said that I could go outside once the guards from Harford arrived." Elizabeth spoke a tad bit calmer, but she did not turn to look at Nick.

"So far, there have only been five guards to arrive." Nick pleaded with her to see reason. "There is a lot of forest here for us to keep watch over."

The five guards from Hartford had taken over the night watch so that Nick and Caleb could get some much-needed rest. Five more guards were on their way and were scheduled to arrive sometime today. Nick was grateful for the help, but he had thought that Maxwell Spencer would send more than ten men total.

"Then perhaps we should not have come here." Elizabeth sounded more hurt than mad.

Nick fought to hold back a smile. He was deeply concerned for Elizabeth's wellbeing, but she reminded him of his little cousin Dani when she pouted. He, Jax, and Caleb had no little sister, so they became protective over their little cousin, from the moment she was born. Dani had often pouted like this when she was younger.

55

"Rosa, would you please give us a moment?" Nick moved from standing in front of Elizabeth's bedchamber door so that Rosa could pass.

"Speak to her softly. She is not like most women of her status." Rosa whispered to Nick, as she stepped outside the door. Nick nodded his head and closed the door behind her.

"I do apologize that you are so extremely unhappy." Nick walked over to stand behind Elizabeth. "But everything that I am doing is for your safety."

"I know." Elizabeth sighed deeply.

Of course, she knew that Nick was doing everything that he possibly could to protect her. She did not realize how hard sitting still would affect her. Elizabeth was used to moving about Greyham Court, without difficulty and constrictions.

"This is a huge house. Perhaps you and Rosa could explore some of it together." Nick needed to find a way to keep Elizabeth calm, yet busy at the same time. "Once the other guards arrive, perhaps we can find a way to let you go outside for a few minutes."

Nick hated making her a promise like this. If the news the guards brought from London was not good, he knew that he could not keep this promise to Elizabeth. She deserved honesty on the matter, but he could not give it to her until they knew more.

"Fine." Elizabeth turned to face Nick. Her expression clearly showed that she was still upset over the matter.

"Sir Nicholas." Rosa opened the door and stepped inside the room. "The other guards have arrived. Doug is waiting for you in the parlor."

Doug, one of Maxwell Spencer's most loyal men, brought the good news that Maxx was alright. The Em had set sail for Nettlesville, to bring Nick and Caleb's brother Jax back to London. Gavin and Lord Mason were working together to try and uncover exactly what Roger Holden's evil plot was.

"So, everyone is alright?" Elizabeth walked into the parlor. She and Rosa were listening to the men talk from the foyer.

"Everyone is alive." Doug looked over at Nick. "We are not sure if everyone is going to be alright."

"What exactly does that mean?" Rosa was concerned and pushed for a better answer.

"Evelyn Cramer's father has gone to the magistrate. During the party, while Maxx and Alex were escaping, Evelyn was knocked into the garden fountain." Doug looked at Rosa with a grim expression on his face.

"Who cares if Evelyn Cramer fell into a fountain?" Elizabeth thought that it was exactly what the evil woman deserved.

"We are sure that they are twisting the story." Doug held his hat in hand. "We are not sure yet, if they will charge the Captain and Lord Alexander when they return to London."

"And we have no way to warn them." Rosa closed her eyes and dropped her head.

"I am sure that Gavin and Lord Mason will have everything figured out before The Em returns to London Harbor." Nick tried to sound hopeful.

Roger Holden's plan seemed to revolve around trapping Maxwell Spencer somehow. His original plan was to have all the Shaw men executed for Elizabeth's death. They all knew that Holden would have to revise his evil scheme when the snake discovered that Elizabeth Dawson had not died in the forest. Now, it looked as if Nick's cousin Alexander was going to take the blunt of the blow that Holden was throwing at their family.

"I do not like this. I do not like this at all." Caleb angrily walked away.

Caleb had become good friends with Maxwell Spencer while they worked together in Nettlesville. It was not right for Alex and Maxx to be charged when it was Roger Holden that had plotted against the Shaw's in the first place. Maxx seemed to always be in harm's way here lately.

"We should get everyone settled in." Elizabeth batted back tears as she started out of the room. She hated that good people were now in great trouble because of her.

"Right." Rosa took a deep breath and nodded her head. She knew that wherever Maxx was, Paul would loyally be by his Captain's side. "After dinner we can create a plan on what to do next."

"Everything is going to be alright." Nick gently took Elizabeth by the arm before she could leave.

"Everyone is in danger because of me." Elizabeth quickly looked away. "How can any of it ever be alright?"

Nick turned her to face him. Her blackened eye had almost healed. She no longer wore the dark veil that his mother had made for her. He hated the hurt that he saw in her precious hazel eyes.

"None of this is your fault," Nick assured her.

"He is right, My Lady." Rosa put her arm around Elizabeth. "All of this is because of an evil man." She then led Elizabeth out of the parlor.

It ripped Nick's heart out to see Elizabeth so sad. As he watched her go up the stairs with Rosa, Nick formed a surprise for her in his mind. Hopefully, he could pull it off later this afternoon. Right now, he needed to find his brother and make sure that the house and grounds were protected.

***

That afternoon, before dinner, Nick put a cloak over Elizabeth and led her out to the stables. He remembered how much she loved horses. The Summer Cottage now had more than two horses stalled here. Nick thought that this would be a wonderful treat for them both. Of course, he had Caleb to ensure that it was safe to have this little outing before he attempted it. He hoped that these few minutes would be enough to calm Elizabeth's restless spirit for a while.

"This is perfect." Elizabeth smiled as she petted Nick's horse, Toby.

"I am glad that you are pleased." Nick leaned against the stall as he watched Elizabeth give Toby an apple.

"They all are magnificent." Elizabeth walked around to each stall and gave an apple to each horse, from the basket that Ms. Graham had given to her.

"And before you ask, No, we cannot go for a ride." Nick smiled at her.

"I know." Elizabeth laughed and walked over to Nick. "I do apologize for my behavior earlier today."

"No need to apologize." Nick gently touched her cheek. He knew that it was not proper for him to do such a thing, but his need to touch her was too great.

"But there is a need." Elizabeth took a step closer to Nick.

There was a need, a great need between them but it was one that could not be satisfied. She felt it deeply in her heart and she knew that Nick felt it too.

Nick closed his eyes for a moment. He dreamed of a world where he could be part of Elizabeth's life. He wanted it and he knew that she wanted it too. However, the rules of their births did not allow for such a dream to happen.

Nick tenderly kissed Elizabeth on her forehead. He would not be the one to defile her and ruin Elizabeth's chances of having an honorable husband. She deserved to have a loving marriage someday. It was only a matter of time before her brother chose a husband for her. Even though he could not have her, Nick wanted nothing but happiness for Elizabeth.

"I best be getting you back to the main house." Nick put the cloak over her again.

"Perhaps you are right." Elizabeth pulled the cloak tighter around herself.

Elizabeth felt the same cold and loss that Nick was feeling. Their friendship had bordered on something more for years now. Because of their difference in society statuses, their hopes of something more could never happen. Her family would never approve of a marriage between them. Sadly, their love had to be denied to them.

Chapter Twelve

Over the next week, everyone at the Duke's Summer Cottage settled into a routine of guarding the grounds and protecting Elizabeth. For Nick, the daily functions became an easy duty. His father had trained him, from his youth, on how to run and manage an estate. Nick was sure that when the time came for him to run Kinsley Estate that he could handle the task with ease.

Elizabeth had taken Nick's advice and started to explore the rooms of her family's Summer Cottage. While in her brother Samuel's room, Elizabeth sent Rosa to get the housekeeper.

"Ms. Colby, who has been using this room?" Elizabeth looked around her brother's room.

"I beg your pardon, My Lady?" Ms. Colby was nervous.

"Someone has been using this room." Elizabeth was sure of the matter. "Who was it?"

Elizabeth had not been to the Summer Cottage in years, but she knew this house and this room. She and Samuel were close when they were younger. They would sit on his balcony and talk for hours. Samuel's room was different now. The decorations had changed, along with some of the furnishings.

"Lady Elizabeth, perhaps you are mistaken." Ms. Colby could not look Elizabeth in the eye.

Ellen Colby had come to work for the Dawson family the year before Samuel was born. For twenty-four years she had been the housekeeper at the Summer Cottage. Elizabeth was sure that the woman was hiding something from her.

"Has my brother been here?" Elizabeth knew that Ms. Colby was fond of her brother.

"I do not know what you mean, Lady Elizabeth." Ms. Colby chanced a look in Elizabeth's direction. The expression on her face gave her away.

"It is alright, Ms. Colby." Elizabeth smiled. "My brother's secrets are safe with me."

"This must be where your brother goes when he is not in London." Rosa opened the balcony doors. The view of the gardens and lake were breathtaking from the Duke's balcony.

"Sam has not been home in weeks. If my brother comes here when he is not in London, then where is he now?" Elizabeth wondered. She looked at Ms. Colby again. "Do you know where my brother is?"

"No, Lady Elizabeth. I do not know where the Duke goes when he is not here." Ms. Colby looked away again. She felt bad for betraying the Duke's trust.

"Has Samuel brought a woman here?" Elizabeth was curious.

"Lady Elizabeth!" Ms. Colby was shocked at the bold question. "Never has the Duke brought a woman here."

"I guess all the romantic rumors of my brother courting a beautiful woman are simply not true." Elizabeth giggled when she thought about those rumors.

The gossip from all the young society girls had reached Elizabeth's ears long ago. Young girls in love with the thoughts of romance and marriage had quite the imaginations. Elizabeth now knew where her brother went to hide when he wished to escape all the society nonsense. Perhaps he would let her join him sometime.

"Are you sure that my brother has not brought a woman here?" Elizabeth asked again.

"I am quite sure, Lady Elizabeth." Ms. Colby's lips tightened.

"But he is in love with someone, is he not?" Elizabeth could see how nervous Ms. Colby was.

"Lady Elizabeth, I beg you to leave it be." Ms. Colby fought to hold her composure.

"Do you know who she is?" Elizabeth walked over to the housekeeper. "Do not fret, Ms. Colby. You have my word. I will not betray my brother."

"I do not know her name, Lady Elizabeth. I just know that he loves her dearly." Ms. Colby was almost in tears. She hated betraying the Duke, even if it was to his sister.

"I am glad that my brother has found love." Elizabeth walked out onto the balcony. She saw Nick talking with guards from Hartford. "It is sad that we all cannot marry for love."

When Elizabeth came back inside, Rosa closed and locked the balcony doors. Elizabeth took one last glance around her brother's room. She wished she knew where Samuel was. She missed her brother greatly. If Sam was here, he would take control of things and settle the matter quickly.

When Sam became Duke of Greyham, after their father's death, her brother had entered a new world in which she could not follow. Rules, protocols, and the demands of Sam's new station in society demanded all his time here lately.

Through it all, somehow, Sam had managed to find love. Elizabeth hoped, that someday, Sam would make that love known to their family. Whoever this woman was, she must be someone that their mother would not approve of, or the family would already know this woman's name. Elizabeth liked the woman already.

Sam was a strong and brave man. He no longer took orders from their mother, nor did he tolerate rudeness. Elizabeth smiled as she closed the door to her brother's bedchamber. She would let Sam have his secrets and privacy, if it meant that he had love and peace.

Rosa went downstairs with Ms. Colby, while Elizabeth explored her father's room. This room was exactly how she remembered it. She sat in her father's big chair and cried as she remembered the times they shared here as a family.

For the first time, Elizabeth realized that the happiest moments she had as a child, were here at the Summer Cottage, with her father and brother. Up until this moment, she had not realized that their mother and Anne were never part of her fondest family memories.

Her mother was a stern woman that rarely smiled. Obviously, Anne had followed in their mother's footsteps. The only time that Anne seemed to laugh and be happy was when she was plotting one of her horrid schemes.

Her father's room revealed no secrets to Elizabeth. She wondered if her mother's room would be any different. Elizabeth walked to the west wing of the house. For some reason, her mother's and Anne's rooms were not on the same wing of the house as the rest of the family's rooms were. Elizabeth realized that there had to be some hidden secrets within her parent's marriage for her parents to have separate rooms like this.

***

After two weeks at sea, The Em docked in Nettlesville. Alex and Maxx were surprised to see that Captain Sayer and The Raven were docked here as well. Hopefully, Captain Sayer had not made Nettlesville and Bryson's Landing one of his base ports.

They found Jax at Pete's Pub, sitting alone at Maxx's favorite table, in the far-right corner. Captain Sayer and his misfits of pirates were a couple of tables away.

Jax and the rest of the pub patrons were extremely glad to see Maxx and Alex. Captain Sayer and his crew never said a word but watched them with interest.

"I thought that the lot of you had forgotten me." Jax laughed as Maxx and Alex joined him.

"That is not possible." Alex patted Jax on the back.

"Your mother was not about to let that happen." Maxx kept his eyes on the pirates.

"Have they been here all this time?" Alex followed Maxx's gaze over to the pirates.

"They come and go regularly." Jax waved to Pete for a round of drinks.

"Have they caused any trouble?" Alex was surprised that Captain Sayer liked Nettlesville so much. This was a struggling village that had just started making progress a year ago, when his brother Nate was here.

"They come here and eat at Miss Margaret's restaurant. They have stayed a few nights in Ms. Dudley's inn. They will sit here in the pub for hours." Jax looked over at Captain Sayer. "But they have not caused one problem. In fact, their trades with the businesses here, have helped tremendously. They have even brought back requests from some of the business owners."

"Are you sure that he is a pirate?" Alex asked Maxx.

"He is a pirate. He attacks and burns ships until they sink." Maxx refused the bottle of rum that Pete brought to their table.

"Who has ever heard of a good pirate before?" Alex was baffled.

"It is not our concern what the pirate does, as long as he is not causing us and this island any trouble." Maxx stood up.

"Sit back down and have a drink. You just got here." Jax lifted his mug of ale to Maxx.

"We cannot stay. In fact, you need to go get your things for we sail for London as soon as the ship is unloaded." Maxx started to walk away.

"What is the hurry?" Jax shouted.

"There is trouble afoot at Greyham. Now, I need to take these documents to Marty Dudley. I suggest that you go and get your things." Maxx stood by the door, waiting for Jax and Alex.

"Did something happen to the Duke?" Jax asked Alex.

"The Duke's sister has been badly hurt." Alex quickly downed his drink.

"Which sister?" Jax finished his drink as he stood up.

"Lady Elizabeth." Alex headed for the door.

"We sail!" Captain Sayer stood up and shouted to his crew. "France awaits!"

Captain Sayer walked past Maxx and nodded his head. Maxx nodded his head to the pirate as he walked out of the pub. Maxx motioned for Jax and Alex to hurry up.

"Hey, Maxx, ask Miss Margaret for some of her butter rolls for the voyage." Jax hurried across the street to the inn.

"Why don't you ask her?" Maxx shouted.

"She likes you better." Jax disappeared into the inn to get his things.

In less than an hour, The Em set sail for the return trip to London. The Raven, and her notorious Captain Sayer, had left dock about half an hour before them. The crew of The Em watched diligently throughout the night but there was no sign of the pirate ship. Still, no one on board The Em would rest easily until they were safely docked in London Harbor.

Chapter Thirteen

As the month of September came, the fall season started to set in a bit early. Nick and Elizabeth had been at the Summer Cottage for nearly a month now, with no outside issues.

Nick thought that since things had been calm all this time that they could enjoy a short walk together, to allow Elizabeth to get out of the house for a few minutes. Of course, Caleb and the guards were hiding in the forest, watching them, just to be on the safe side.

Nick watched the road, every day now, for a messenger to arrive from his cousin Gavin. Sadly, no one had shown up yet to tell them that it was safe to return with Elizabeth. Everyone at the cottage was wondering if Alex and Maxx were alright. The past few weeks here had been peaceful, but Nick felt as if they were completely cut off from the outside world.

"Do you think that Roger Holden has given up?" Elizabeth asked, as she and Nick started walking away from the lake.

"I have never known the Earl of Statham to give up before." Nick figured that Roger Holden was hiding somewhere while licking his wounds. Roger would soon come up with another plan, but he would never give up.

"Thank you for today." Elizabeth smiled up at Nick. She had genuinely enjoyed their walk today.

The cool autumn air felt nice on Elizabeth's face. She treasured moments like this with Nick. She held tightly to his arm as they walked back from the lake. Even though it was only for a few minutes, it was minutes that would be cherished in years to come. She felt safe by Nick's side. Elizabeth knew that this was where she truly belonged, even though her world would not allow it.

"I wish that we could take walks more often." Nick would enjoy it more if he were not so concerned with what could be lurking out there in the forest.

"I have found something that Rosa thinks I should show to you." Elizabeth opened the kitchen door and stepped inside the cottage.

"Why don't you go get whatever it is, and I will meet you in the upstairs sitting room." Nick noticed that Caleb was hurrying toward them.

Elizabeth hurried away as Nick waited for Caleb outside the kitchen door. Elizabeth's discovery had him intrigued but Caleb's urgency had him deeply concerned.

"We had some movement on the west side of the cottage. Doug and a few guards have gone to check it out." Caleb spoke quickly. "Harper and I are on our way to make sure that they do not need help."

"Very well, brother." Nick was greatly alarmed. This was the first movement they have had in a month. "I will keep Elizabeth inside and away from the windows."

Nick hurried upstairs and found Elizabeth waiting for him in the private sitting room. He went over and pulled the thick curtains closed before he turned to face her.

"What has happened?" Elizabeth quickly stood up. She was deeply alarmed by Nick's actions. She could see the worried look on his face. "We should not have taken that walk today, should we?"

"It may be nothing." Nick held his hand out in front of him, he hoped to keep Elizabeth calm. "Caleb and some of the other guards have gone to check it out."

"Where is Rosa?" Elizabeth had not seen the maid in a while.

"Rosa is out in the hallway, guarding the stairs." Nick walked over to Elizabeth. She was standing in the middle of the room. "What do you have here?" Nick looked down at the wooden box in her hands.

"I found this hidden in the bottom of my mother's wardrobe." The wooden box shook in Elizabeth's hands.

Nick took the box from her and looked it over. It was beautifully crafted with leaves; the carvings were all around the box. It was too long and narrow to be a lady's a jewelry box. He noticed that the latch was broken.

"You opened it?" Nick asked as he raised the lid.

"Rosa helped me to break the lock off." Elizabeth started toward the window.

"Of course, she did." Nick chuckled. Rosa had surprised him on several occasions the past few weeks.

"Rosa has many skills." Elizabeth smiled. "I am sure that Maxwell Spencer trained her himself."

Inside the box, Nick found three scrolls. Each scroll had the king's seal on them. They looked old and none of them had been opened. It was quite peculiar for Elizabeth's mother to have such documents in her possession. He could understand the former Duke having these but not his wife.

"I wonder what these are?" Nick carefully placed the scrolls back into the wooden box.

"I do not know." Elizabeth thought better than to open the curtain and peep out. She walked back over to Nick. "Rosa thought it best to not open them."

"I think that Rosa is right on that matter." Nick handed the wooden box back to Elizabeth. "It would be best to let your brother take these to the magistrate and have them officially opened."

"I highly doubt that Sam even knows that these papers exist." Elizabeth looked up at Nick. "They were well hiddened."

"Do you know of a safe place where you can hide them, until you can show them to your brother?" Nick asked.

There was nothing on the outside of the scrolls to indicate what they contained. Nick sensed that they were important documents of some kind, or they would not have been hidden like they were. It was best to keep them secure and protected, for now.

"I know a place." Elizabeth nodded her head.

"Have Rosa go with you and quickly hide it." Nick led her out into the hallway. "I will help guard the doors."

After hiding the wooden box, Rosa led Elizabeth downstairs to one of the servant quarters. Nick and Rosa had prepared this room in case of an emergency. The butler, housekeeper, and cook were already inside the room.

With everyone now safely inside the room, Rosa bolted the door shut. She pulled out her pistol and stood guard at the door. The two stable hands and the grounds keeper, Mr. Blackwood, were stationed within the cottage, armed with pistols as well.

For several hours, nothing outside the cottage moved. Finally, Doug and several of the guards came into sight. As the guards carried the horses to the stables, Doug rushed inside to talk with Nick.

"We watched two men on horseback riding north, over the ridge and out of sight." Doug spoke quickly. "We found their camp. Caleb, Harper, and a couple of the guards are now tracking the two riders to see if there is a larger group is nearby."

This report was greatly alarming. Nick hoped that Caleb would return soon and tell him more. Were these two men just passing by, or were they spies for Roger Holden. Nick had to calm his own racing heart before he would be able to explain this situation to Elizabeth and the house staff.

"Do you think that they were Holden's men?" Nick had a feeling that there were more to these two riders than just passing by. "Do you think that they know we are here?"

"We are not sure just yet. Your brother did give me new post positions to station the guards at for now." Doug started for the kitchen door of the cottage. "He said to tell you, to keep everyone else inside the house until he returns."

Nick understood his brother's orders. This was still a questionable situation, but it was alright for now to let the staff go about the house. He hurried downstairs to share this news with Elizabeth and the others. He released them from their hiding place, but he gave strict orders for everyone to stay inside the house and away from the windows.

"Do you think that these men are a threat to us?" Elizabeth had remained behind in the room. She wanted to speak with Nick alone.

"It is too early to tell, but we must treat it as a threat for now." Nick wished that he had a better answer for her.

"Thank you for protecting me." Elizabeth spoke softly as she stepped closer to Nick. This incident made her realize that every moment with Nick was a precious gift to her.

"I will always protect you." Nick vowed to Elizabeth as he looked into her eyes.

Nick's eyes locked with hers. Elizabeth's hazel eyes had golden steaks that glistened when light hit them. Her eyes had always dazzled him. When she smiled, her eyes seemed to dance with excitement. To him, Elizabeth Dawson was absolutely perfect.

"I know that you will." Elizabeth took the final step to close the distance between her and Nick.

She placed her hands against Nick's chest and looked up at him tenderly. His brown eyes tugged lovingly at her heart. Elizabeth reached her hand up and ran her fingers through his wavy brown hair. She had wanted to touch Nick's curls like this for years.

"My Lady." Nick gently grabbed her wrist. His breath caught and his heartbeat quickened as he looked lovingly into her eyes.

Elizabeth's boldness grew as she placed her finger to his lips to prevent Nick from protesting further. She could no longer control her own breathing. Each heartbeat pulled her deeper into the passion building between them.

She would not let Nick protest her actions today. He would be honorable and say that this was wrong. They had this conversation many times over the years. Of course, she knew that her mother and the society set would say that this was wrong.

Nick was born of a lower status than herself and the women in the higher society statuses would shun her for wanting Nick. None of that mattered to her right now. The only thing that mattered to Elizabeth was the love she felt for Nick.

"I do not care anymore about what the world thinks." Elizabeth blinked several times to fight back the tears that had welled up in her eyes.

"You have to marry of your own status." Nick hated saying the words. If only she could be his.

"Then I will denounce my status." Elizabeth placed her palm against Nick's cheek.

"I will not let you do that." Nick swallowed the lump that was stuck in his throat. "You simply cannot do it."

"You cannot stop me from doing so." Elizabeth refused to be talked out of it this time.

69

"You deserve a great life." Nick tried to step away, but Elizabeth took the step with him. "You deserve far more than I can ever offer to you."

"I will have no great life without you in it." A tear slide from Elizabeth's eye. "You are everything that I wish for."

Nick used his thumb to wipe the single tear from her cheek. The look in Elizabeth's eyes pleaded with him to not refuse her. How could he refuse her? She meant more to him than life itself. He was beneath her in birth ranking, but he loved her with all his heart.

Nick gently cupped Elizabeth's face in his hands. She stood here before him declaring that she would step away from the higher society life to be with him. Only a fool would refuse her, and he was no fool.

"And you are everything that I wish for, you are everything that my heart desires." Nick could not deny his feelings for her.

Nick lowered his head and gently pressed his lips to hers. He was not expecting what happened next. Elizabeth stood on her tiptoes and put her arms around his neck. She wanted this, he wanted this, and there was no denying it any longer.

As their hearts quickened, the love between them could no longer be denied because of rules and protocols. It no longer mattered what anyone else thought. All that mattered to Nick was the woman in his arms. He had no right, except by the right of love, to claim her. She belonged with a man far greater than him. However, now that his lips had touched hers, he would never give her up.

No longer would Nick be able to push Elizabeth away and hold her at bay for the sake of her society reputation. No longer would he deny his love for Elizabeth. It no longer mattered what anyone thought. Nick was never going to let Elizabeth go. Nick would fight to keep what was now rightly his.

Chapter Fourteen

Caleb and Harper returned in time to join everyone for dinner. Nick would have preferred hearing their report in private, rather than in front of everyone. He was trying his best to not upset Elizabeth if it could be helped.

"We followed their trail for almost two hours. We saw no sign of a larger camp." Caleb sat next to Nick.

"Do you honestly believe that they were just passing by?" Rosa had an uneasy feeling on the matter. Perhaps it was all the training she had while working for Maxwell Spencer, but she sensed that something was off here.

"No, I do not believe that." Caleb sighed deeply and shook his head.

"You do not have to speak cautiously around me." Elizabeth looked across the table at Caleb. "I would rather know the truth."

Nick reached over and gently squeezed Elizabeth's hand. He admired the strength that she tried to show. He knew, deep down, that she was terrified, and with good reasons.

Roger Holden was a vicious man. His hate for the Shaw family ran deep. Nick, nor his brothers, understood why Roger attacked their family every chance he got. Holden was also a coward that hid behind others so that he would not be caught and held accountable for his actions.

Rosa and Caleb had noticed the sweet exchange between Nick and Elizabeth. They smiled across the table at each other. Both pretended to be more interested in the food on their plates than the romance that was blooming between the couple.

Rosa was thrilled that Nick and Elizabeth were finally following their hearts. The path ahead of the young couple would not be an easy one but she knew they had the strength to see it through. However, Caleb was concerned that his brother would not think clearly if he were focused too much on a relationship with Elizabeth right now.

"What are you not telling us?" Nick turned back to his brother. He hoped his brother's news would be something that Elizabeth could handle.

"I believe that they camped down river for at least a couple of nights, maybe more." Caleb had checked the camp again before returning to the cottage. "There were a lot of tracks in and out of the river. It was too many for two men to have stayed for only one night."

"But there were only two men. We are sure on this." Harper completely agreed with Caleb's findings.

"What does this mean?" Elizabeth did not understand.

"They were using the river to try and throw off the trail of their movements." Nick rubbed his forehead and released a deep breath.

He and Caleb had seen this tactic many times when they were in the military. This was not the activities of someone just passing by. Nick was now greatly concerned. This meant that Elizabeth was in greater danger than they first believed.

"That river connects to the lake outside." Caleb looked Nick in the eye, hoping he would understand his meaning.

"So, does this mean that Roger Holden now knows that we are here?" Elizabeth tried to not sound as alarmed as she truly was.

"That is a seriously strong possibility." Caleb was not sure that telling Elizabeth everything was a good idea.

Elizabeth had lived a pampered lifestyle, up until a few weeks ago. She had now experienced a traumatic situation that was bound to have changed her forever. Still, she was sweet, and Caleb did not wish to darken her spirit any more than necessary.

"What do we do?" Elizabeth jumped up from the table.

"Do not worry so much." Nick walked over and held her by her upper arms. "If it comes to it, we all will protect you."

"How did he find us?" Elizabeth was frantic. "Very few people know where this house is."

"Your sister knows." Caleb leaned back in his chair. Nick shot him a stern look.

"Of course." Elizabeth threw her hands in the air. "Anne would tell Roger Holden about this house. She and Evelyn were really cozy with Roger in the parlor at Greyham Court that day."

"There are not enough men here for us to continue tracking those riders and to protect this house at the same time." Caleb folded his arms across his chest.

"We could take Lady Elizabeth to Hartford," Rosa suggested. She wondered if this was what they should have done in the first place.

"Holden would not dare cross onto Hartford land." Harper would prefer to be on his homeland if a battle were to come of this.

"It would be too much of a fight for Holden if he crossed our borders." Doug stated this fact proudly.

"Brother, I do have to say, that I like the idea of having more help." Caleb gave his opinion, but he knew his brother's mind all too well.

"We are well hidden here." Nick took Elizabeth's hand in his. "I would hate to move Elizabeth, if it were not absolutely necessary."

"Then Harper and I will take James with us at first light and follow the trail a little further." Caleb did not like his brother's decision on this, but he would honor it just the same.

The tension for the rest of the meal was strained for everyone. Caleb offered no more suggestions to his brother. He and Harper quickly finished their dinner. The two men went to bed early so they could rest and be ready to leave first thing in the morning. Even Rosa was disappointed in Nick's decision, but she remained quiet on the matter as well.

That night a guard was placed in the hallway, outside Elizabeth's door. Rosa moved her cot over next to the window. She would keep a check outside when she was not sleeping. She had a feeling that sleep would be lost to them all tonight.

"Rosa?" Elizabeth looked at Rosa in the mirror, as the lady's maid helped her prepare for bed.

"Is something the matter, Lady Elizabeth?" Rosa continued brushing Elizabeth's hair.

"You are much more than just a lady's maid." Elizabeth was already convinced of this fact. Even Abby had said this to her.

"Thank you, My Lady." Rosa pretended to not understand Elizabeth's intent.

"Of course, I meant that as a compliment, but I know that Lord Spencer has trained you in more ways than that of just a maid." Elizabeth was not going to let Rosa push the matter aside.

"Aye, My Lady." Rosa's eyes met Elizabeth's in the mirror.

"Will you teach me?" Elizabeth asked.

Rosa tied a blue ribbon in Elizabeth's hair. She walked over and pulled back the bed covers as she pondered Elizabeth's request. Elizabeth walked over beside the bed and gently touched Rosa's arm.

"You want me to teach you how to fight?" Rosa was unsure of the matter. "What will Nick and the Duke say?"

"It does not matter what they will say." Elizabeth was not going to give up. "I want to know how to defend myself."

"Well." Rosa thought for a moment. "I guess showing you how to defend yourself is not the same as training you on how to actually fight a battle."

"Yes, that is truly what I meant to say." Elizabeth giggled. "Will you teach me how to defend myself?"

"We will start tomorrow." Rosa loved Elizabeth's spirit. "For now, it is bedtime, My Lady."

Elizabeth settle under the covers as Rosa doused the lights in the room. She was happy that Rosa had agreed to help her. She had already decided that if Rosa had refused, that she would have asked one of the stable hands here at the Summer Cottage to teach her. Both men were loyal to her brother and she was sure that they would honor her request. She hoped that this idea of hers would not be a mistake later. If Nick found out, he was bound to object, but she was tired of being helpless all the time.

✳✳✳

The Em docked in London Harbor shortly after sunrise. Jax was eager to get home to Kinsley Estate. Maxx was concerned about what they would find in London. Hopefully, Lord Mason had everything under control here by now. He and Alex did leave with chaos erupting between Ms. Rhodes' house and the docks about a month ago.

As they were leaving the dock area, Alex and Maxx were surrounded by the king's men. Their hearts sank when they saw the soldiers. Paul became greatly defensive and stepped in front of Maxx and Alex.

"Good day, Captain Cromwell." Paul was not happy with the situation already.

"I need to speak to Lord Spencer and Lord Alexander." Captain Cromwell was stern. "Kindly step aside."

"It is alright, Paul." Maxx took Paul by the arm and pulled him back.

"What have you two done?" Jax leaned over and whispered to Alex.

"I need both of you gentlemen to come with me." Captain Cromwell spoke to Maxx. "We have some questions for you, about the events that transpired at Ms. Rhodes' End of the Summer Party a month ago."

"Just questions?" Paul narrowed his eyes at the King's Captain of the Guard.

"Their answers will determine if both men are to be arrested." Captain Cromwell was not happy in having to do his duty today. "As of this moment, I am afraid that Lord Alexander *is* under arrest."

The king's men surrounded Alex and pulled him away from the others. Paul grabbed Maxx by the arm to keep him from being arrested as well, for protesting Alex's arrest.

"What is going on?" Jax bellowed.

"You go with Ollie to the Blume'N Brew. He and Miss Nancie will explain everything." Paul put his hand against Jax's chest to keep him from advancing on Captain Cromwell. "I will go with Maxx and Alex."

"Something is not right here!" Jax pointed his finger at Captain Cromwell. Jax was highly upset over the situation.

"Causing a scene will only make it worse for your cousin." Paul whispered to Jax.

"Send a message to Ellis Manor. Let Gavin know that we may need him." Alex told Jax, just before the king's men led him away.

"I will stay with him," Maxx promised to Jax. "Send someone to Lord Mason as well. He should have had this all handled by now."

Jax watched as the king's men took Alex and Maxx away. Ollie grabbed him by the arm and started pulling Jax toward the Blume'N Brew. The situation was dire and there was not a moment to spare if they wanted to help Alex and Maxx.

Chapter Fifteen

At daybreak the next morning, Nick walked with Caleb and Harper to the stables. Arlo Perry and Dean Tinley had their horses ready and waiting.

"I thought James was going with you." Nick did not see the guard from Hartford anywhere.

"I have sent James on ahead for the moment." Harper mounted his horse.

"If we are not back in four days, you should assume the worst and move Elizabeth on to Hartford immediately." Caleb mounted his horse as well.

"Let us hope that is not the case." Nick did not want to believe the worst just yet.

"We all knew that it was only a matter of time before they found us here." Caleb wished his brother would listen to him.

"Perhaps you should go ahead and make preparations to be able to leave a moment's notice." Harper had to agree with Caleb on the matter. "Just in case."

"I will get Doug to help me plan that out." Nick hated having to admit that he could be wrong on this matter.

"Keep my brother safe." Nick shook Harper's hand.

"What are you talking about?" Caleb laughed. "I am the one keeping him safe."

Nick watched as Caleb and Harper rode out of sight. Hopefully, the Duke of Greyham would return soon and put an end to the evil plots of Roger Holden. Until then, he would do his best to protect Elizabeth. Nick hurried back to the main house to find Doug so they could put an emergency escape plan into place.

When Nick entered the door near the kitchen, he found Elizabeth and Rosa in the kitchen with Ms. Graham. It was surprising for him to see Elizabeth in an apron. He smiled as he watched the cook show her how to make bread. Seeing the flour on her face made him chuckle.

"I am glad that I amuse you." Elizabeth looked up at Nick and smiled.

"I am glad to see that you found something to keep you busy." Nick leaned against the doorframe.

"Are you implying that I was bored?" Elizabeth began kneading the dough on the table.

"I would never imply such a thing of a lady." Nick could not help but to tease her.

"Has Caleb and Harper left yet?" Rosa was making tea.

"Aye, they have." Nick took the tea Rosa offered to him. "I need to find Doug." He quickly drank the tea.

"Doug is guarding the front doors." Rosa took the empty teacup from Nick.

Nick excused himself and hurried upstairs. Elizabeth quickly moved and let the cook take over making the bread. Rosa checked to make sure that Nick was busy upstairs. They had to be cautious today. Their plans would be halted if Nick caught them.

"Are you ready?" Rosa asked when she returned to the kitchen.

"I am ready." Elizabeth dried her hands. She was eager to get started.

Elizabeth followed Rosa to the servant's room at the far end of the corridor. Rosa spent the next hour teaching Elizabeth how to defend herself with a dagger and a small knife. These weapons were small enough that Elizabeth could easily keep them hidden in her skirts.

They made sure to limit their lesson times to no more than an hours' time, so that they would not alarm Nick to their activities. They both were sure that Nick would not agree with these lessons.

For two days, Elizabeth and Rosa slipped away every chance they got to have their self-defense lessons. Elizabeth talked Rosa into including the house staff as well. She was sure that the grounds keeper and the stable hands were able to defend themselves, but the inside staff needed to know more on the matter.

In the evenings, Elizabeth would spend time with Nick in the upstairs sitting room. She was careful to not mention how she and

Rosa spent much of their days here lately. After two days of doing this, idle chit chat with Nick was becoming a chore for Elizabeth. She had never like hiding things. Her secret was starting to wear on her emotionally.

"Any word from your brother yet?" Elizabeth was sure that if Nick had heard from Caleb that he would have already told her.

"Caleb and Harper were going to follow the trail for two days. I am sure that they are already on their way back here by now." Nick knew the schedule, but he was growing concerned for his little brother.

"I am sure they will return soon." Elizabeth walked over to the window, where Nick was peeping around the curtain every few minutes.

"I hope that you are right." Nick had not noticed that Elizabeth had moved from her chair.

Elizabeth gently touched Nick on his arm. He quickly turned around to face her. Elizabeth placed her palm against his cheek. She knew that he was deeply worried about his brother.

"I wish that I could relieve your worries." Elizabeth spoke softly.

Nick reach up and took her hand that was against his cheek. He brought her hand to his lips and gently kissed the back of it. His free hand went around Elizabeth's waist as he pulled her closer to him.

"Knowing that you are safe, relieves my worries greatly." Nick whisper next to her ear.

The feel of his breath against her skin sent a warm feeling through Elizabeth. She closed her eyes as she leaned closer to Nick. She rested her head against his broad shoulders as she wrapped her arms around him. This was the safest place on earth for her right now.

For years she had dreamed of holding Nick like this. She had wanted to be more than friends with him for a long time now. Before she was attacked, Elizabeth did not dare voice what her heart felt for Nick. Now, everything was different for her. She no longer lived in a pampered and sheltered world.

Elizabeth looked up at Nick. He hid it within his words, but the worry in his mind clearly showed in his eyes. He was tired, but she knew that he would never admit it. Nick was a man bound by duty and honor. He would not abandon his post. Nicholas Shaw would protect her, even with his own life if it were necessary.

"Kiss me," Elizabeth whispered.

"My Lady?" Nick had never expected to hear her say such words to him. He greatly admired her boldness.

"Kiss me," Elizabeth softly repeated.

Nick smiled as he put his arms around her and pulled her closer to him. His eyes locked with hers. Slowly, very slowly, Nick lowered his head. His lips were just above hers. He paused and waited. Elizabeth could hear her own heart beating as she waited with anticipation for Nick's kiss.

After a moment of teasing her like this, Nick closed his eyes and gently pressed his lips to hers. Elizabeth wrapped her arms around his neck and began to kiss him with a hungered passion. She had read about romantic and passionate kisses before. Never had she realized what passion truly was until this moment. Here in Nick's arms, she found a passion that no book could have ever prepared her for.

Elizabeth would gladly trade her higher status life for the world Nick lived in. He did not need a title for her to love him. Somehow, someway, she would be by Nicholas Shaw's side, no matter what. She had no problem with setting London on its ear. She would fight to stay beside Nicholas Shaw forever.

Chapter Sixteen

Shortly after lunch, the next day, Nick stepped out the back door of the Summer Cottage. He watched as a flock of ducks flew over and landed in the small lake. The fall wind had a bit of a chill to it today. Leaves were already changing colors and starting to fall to the ground.

This was his mother's favorite season. She was always excited to change the colors of their house decorations. At his mother's request, the kitchen staff would bake special treats, throughout the season, that made Kinsley Estate smell wonderful.

Nick was snapped back to the present by an uneasy feeling. The horses in the stables behind the cottage, neighed loudly. Nick had watched Arlo Perry enter the stables, as he was coming out the back door of the main house. To Nick, the horses appeared to be a bit restless today. To others, this might seem normal as any other day was. Due to their situation, the horse's actions caused Nick to become more alert.

There was something more hanging in the fall air today. Nick wondered if this was the feeling of great urgency that Caleb had always talked about. Caleb could never find the right words to explain his feelings, but he always had a keen sense for when something was out of sorts. Nick strongly felt that something was greatly out of sorts right now.

Nick went back inside the back door and bolted it shut. He hated to lock the stable hands out of the main house like this. He quietly signaled to the staff and guards within the cottage. Each dropped what they were doing and went to their assigned places in the house.

"Where is Elizabeth?" Nick asked Mr. Hayes.

"We are here." Rosa spoke before the butler could reply. Doug had signaled the warning to Rosa from the stairs.

"Nick." Elizabeth quickly hugged him. She no longer cared who saw them together.

"Stay close to Rosa." Nick gave her a quick kiss on her forehead before he hurried up the stairs to the main floor of the house.

He found Doug guarding the front door. Nick noticed that the guards on this floor were already in position to protect the house. He was amazed at how well-trained Maxwell Spencer's men were. To look at the little Earl of Hartford, you would not expect his men to be trained this well. Not once, in all the years that his family had known Maxx, had he seen a guard in uniform around the little Earl.

"Have you seen anything?" Nick asked Doug.

"Not yet." Doug looked at Nick from the corner of his eye. "What did you see?"

"I saw nothing." Nick looked out the window. "But I felt it."

"Now you sound like your brother and cousin." Doug had seen Caleb and Alex track before. The two were hardly ever wrong.

There was no movement on the front side of the cottage, except for the wind. Nick turned when a shot was heard from the back side of the house. He left Doug and quickly hurried to one of the servant rooms downstairs. Through the window he could see several men moving around the stables.

Caleb was right, he should have moved Elizabeth to Hartford days ago, now it was too late. Nick watched in disbelief as the doors to the stables flung open and all the horses came running out. His first thought was that the stable hands were fools. They had just released their only means of escape. It was then that he noticed the flames inside the stables. Someone had set the stables on fire and the stable hands were saving the horses. He could not fault them for that.

Soon, and very soon, these men would be forcing their way into the house. He had to get everyone out, but how? Nick hurried to the servant's room where Rosa was supposed to take Elizabeth and the house staff.

When Nick saw Elizabeth, he quickly pulled her into his arms. The terrified look on the faces of the staff tore at his heart. They all had depended on him and he had failed them.

"Somehow, I have to get all of you out of here and safely to Hartford." Nick sighed deeply.

"There is a hidden exit on the east wing of the house." Mr. Hayes told Nick.

"And you forgot to share that information with us until now?" Nick could not believe the butler's reluctance to share this with him before now.

"The Duke added that exit a few years ago and said that we were to only use it in an emergency." Ms. Colby sounded defensive.

"Well, I would definitely call this an emergency." Nick looked between the three servants. "Lead the way."

Nick sent one of the guards up to tell Doug, and the other men from Hartford, their plan. Soon all the guards in the house met Nick, Elizabeth, Rosa, and the staff members at the east wing servant's hall.

"I smell smoke," Ms. Graham said.

"They have set the stables on fire." Doug said to the cook.

They all were shocked, but no one had time to say so. Nick opened the hidden door. He was amazed when they stepped out into an area that was well hidden by the tall shrubs that were planted on the east side of the house. Nick had seen this area from the outside many times. He was totally unaware that a door was hidden within. The Duke had planned a great escape if it was ever needed.

"Glad to see that you all made it out." Mr. Blackwood was waiting for them on the outside. Of course, the groundskeeper would know of this door, Nick thought.

"Good of you to be here." Nick was irritated. He now realized just how loyal this staff was to their young Duke.

"We need to hurry or is it our plan to sit here in the shrubbery?" Rosa was also irritated with the Duke's staff.

"We go through here." Mr. Blackwood held the branches of one of the shrubs aside.

Nick looked through the opening the groundskeeper just made. Tall, tree like, shrubs were planted in two rows from the house to the forest. These shrubs made a path that they could take, without being seen. From the outside, these thick green trees looked as if they had grown together to create a privacy wall for the backyard flower garden.

Nick was amazed at the detail that the Duke had put into this escape route. He wondered why the Duke had thought of this in the first place. Had their family been threatened before and it was never made public knowledge? Whatever the reasons were, Nick had to commend Samuel Dawson for creating this escape route.

Later, Nick would still scold the Duke's staff for keeping this hidden route from him until now. He had a feeling that if Elizabeth were not here with them, the staff would have never disclosed this hidden exit. Whatever their reasons were, Nick was grateful that this hidden path now allowed them to get Elizabeth safely out of the house unseen.

At the other end of the hidden path, Arlo Perry was waiting for them. Nick took Elizabeth's hand in his as they followed the stable hand through the forest. They soon came to a small clearing where Dean Tinley had all their horses waiting for them. Nick would have to ask later how the stable hands hand managed this task.

The stable hands took the housekeeper and the cook on their horses with them. Since the Duke only had the two horses stabled here at the Summer Cottage, Rosa gave her horse to the butler, while she rode with Doug. Nick kept Elizabeth with him. Soon they rode out of the forest and onto the road, heading for Hartford.

Nick breathed a sigh of relieve. They had made it safely out of what was an impossible situation, thanks to the Duke's careful planning. He would have to personally thank the Duke one day.

Before joy and excitement could overtake them, the men that attacked the Summer Cottage were chasing after them. Nick made the mistake of looking back over his shoulder. He was caught off guard when a man dropped out of the tree branches that hung over the road.

The man landed on Nick and Elizabeth, knocking them to the ground. Doug slowed his horse to allow Rosa to jump down. As Nick fought the man that had dropped from the tree, Rosa grabbed Elizabeth's hand and led her through the forest. Rose kept Elizabeth within the safety of the trees as they ran, following the river.

A man rushed out from behind a tree and tackled Rosa and Elizabeth to the ground. Elizabeth slide down the hill toward the river. She saw Rosa fighting with the man, just before she fell down a steep drop, into the bushes that were overgrown at the water's edge.

As she landed, Elizabeth heard Rosa scream. Next, her ears were filled with the sound of a single gunshot. Elizabeth covered her mouth with both her hands to keep herself from screaming. Elizabeth could not stop her tears. Rosa had just lost her life protecting her.

Chapter Seventeen

Everything was happening so fast that it caused Elizabeth's mind to spin out of control. She was alone here in this dark and damp place near the river, and she did not know what to do. When a man's body slid down the hill and landed at Elizabeth's feet, she knew she had to move.

She did not wait to see if the man was alive or dead. Elizabeth pushed her way through the brush overgrowth and started running down the edge of the river. She had not gotten far when a man grabbed her by her arm and forcefully pulled her to him.

"You are a nuisance!" Edmond Prescott growled in her ear. "You should have died weeks ago!"

"Let her go, Prescott!" Nick was standing a few away with his sword pointed at Edmond.

Edmond quickly pulled Elizabeth in front of him, to shield himself from Nick. Elizabeth cried out in pain as Edmond twisted her arm behind her back.

"You cannot seriously be willing to die over this useless little twit." Edmond slyly smiled at Nick.

"My brother will see to it that you are hanged for this." Elizabeth snapped at Edmond. She cried out again as Edmond tightened his grip on her arm.

"You let her go now or the Duke will miss his chance to hang you." Nick threatened, as he stepped closer.

"If you come any closer, I will kill this frilly little thing right here!" Edmond took a step backwards, toward the river, pulling Elizabeth along with him.

"You are the one that is going to die here today, if you do not release her now!" Nick's eyes bore into Edmond's.

"Come a little closer, Shaw, and I will wipe her blood on your face as I kill you as well." Edmond growled.

"Nick, please." Tears filled Elizabeth's eyes.

"Aw, so you want this little twit for yourself." Edmond laughed when he saw how Nick looked at Elizabeth. "You, like every other Shaw before you, have always taken what is not yours!"

The hate that Edmond Prescott had for Nick ran deep. The two men had been fighting since they were in school together. The last fight between them at school had gotten Edmond expelled. Edmond had loudly made it known, as they were escorting him out of the school, that the only reason Nick had not been expelled was because his father was a knight and his uncle was the Earl of Claybourne.

"I will not ask you again to let Elizabeth go." Nick was ready to advance on Edmond.

"Nick, look out!" Elizabeth shouted when she saw the man approaching Nick from behind.

Elizabeth was too late with her warning. The man swung a fallen piece of tree branch and hit Nick on the side of his head. Nick stumbled to the ground. At the same time, Elizabeth remembered something that Rosa had taught her. She reached up with her free hand and managed to poke Edmond in the eye with her thumb. Edmond screamed out in pain. Edmond's face flared with anger as he flung Elizabeth into the river.

"No!" Nick shouted as he struggled to get to his feet.

Nick used his shoulder to knock Edmond to the ground as he ran pass the horrible man. Nick would stop and kill Edmond now, but Elizabeth needed help. Nick, without a second thought, jumped into the river to save Elizabeth. The water quickly carried them down stream.

The river was wider and deeper here than it was back near the Duke's Summer Cottage. Several more streams had connected to the river by this point, causing the river's flow to move much faster. Nick quickly caught up with Elizabeth and pulled her to the riverbank.

"Are you hurt?" Nick held Elizabeth by her shoulders.

"I am alright." Elizabeth reached up and touched the side of Nick's head. "You are the one that is hurt."

Nick gently grabbed Elizabeth's wrist and pulled her hand away. His head did hurt, and he was sure it was bleeding. He was sure that touching it would only make it hurt worse right now. Needing to hold her, Nick wrapped his arms around Elizabeth and pulled her to him. He was thankful that she was once again safe.

Nick and Elizabeth could hear the shouts of men cheering up on the road. Elizabeth helped Nick to stand up. She was sure that the blow to his head had him dizzy. Nick's head was throbbing with pain. Elizabeth was relieved to see Caleb running toward them.

"Let us get you up to the road." Caleb put his arm around his brother and helped him up the hill.

"What has happened?" Nick asked as they reached the road.

"The Hartford guard has shown up to help us." Caleb helped Nick over to his horse. He pulled out a cloth from one of the saddlebags and held it to the side of his brother's bleeding head.

"How did they know?" Elizabeth took the cloth from Caleb and applied pressure to Nick's head.

"When we left, three days ago, Harper sent James on to Hartford for help." Caleb handed Nick his water canteen. He was now glad that they had not asked his brother for permission and sent for help anyway.

"I am sorry that I doubted your judgement, brother." Nick blamed himself for what had happened here today.

"Do not be too hard on yourself." Caleb put his hand on his brother's shoulder. "They only hand about twenty men total, and it is handled now."

"Prescott was here." Nick had to forgo fighting his long time enemy to save Elizabeth.

"I know. He and a few more got away." Caleb knew this was not the last they would see of Edmond Prescott. "The Hartford guard took care of the rest."

"Rosa!" Elizabeth exclaimed.

"I am sure that Rosa is fine." Nick squeezed Elizabeth's hand.

"Rosa is dead." Elizabeth was shaking her head.

Nick pulled Elizabeth into his arms as she cried. She and Rosa had grown close over the past month. He was sure that the maid's death would leave a huge hole in Elizabeth's heart. Nick did not want to have to face Maxwell Spencer, or Paul, over losing Rosa.

"You might want to come over here and clear this up." Caleb look over Nick's horse to the other side of the road and smiled.

"Clear what up?" Rosa asked as she walked over to where Nick and Elizabeth were.

"Rosa!" Elizabeth exclaimed as she wrapped her arms around the maid. Rosa groaned in pain. "Oh, please forgive me." Elizabeth quickly released her.

Rosa had splints and a sling around her left arm. Elizabeth covered her mouth with her hand. Rosa's arm was broken but she was here and alive.

"I apologize that we got separated." Rosa took Elizabeth's hand in hers.

"I heard the gunshot. I thought…" Elizabeth could not finish her sentence. The thought that they had lost Rosa was too overwhelming for her.

"It was not I that was shot, My Lady." Rosa briefly smiled. The pain in her arm was great and she could not pretend to be happy for too long.

"They set the stables at the Summer Cottage on fire." Nick had almost forgotten about this.

"We know." Caleb helped Rosa onto the horse with Harper. "About twenty men have gone to put it out if they can. If they cannot, they will do their best to keep it from reaching the house."

The Duke would be furious over the loss of his stables. Nick hoped that Sam would not treat them too harshly over the matter once he realized that they had saved Elizabeth's life today. If it had not been for Caleb and Harper thinking ahead, they would have surely lost the battle here today. This was a humbling experience for Nick and one that he would make sure never happened again.

"The rest of us are to journey on to Hartford." Harper was glad to be going home. Hartford Manor would offer more protection than the Duke's Summer Cottage ever could.

"Was Holden with them?" Nick put his hand to his throbbing head. He had only seen Edmond during the battle.

"That snake is not about to get his hands dirty in a fight like this." Caleb helped Elizabeth up onto Nick's horse.

"Thank you, brother." Nick was grateful for all that Caleb had done. "Let us hope we find rest at Hartford."

"Lady Spencer is already waiting for us." Caleb helped Nick up on his horse. "Lady Elizabeth, can you lead for a while?" Caleb handed her the reins. He was sure that Nick's headache would cause his vison to be blurry for bit.

"Aye." Elizabeth smiled as she rubbed the horse on his neck. "I got Toby."

Chapter Eighteen

Nick was relieved when they reached Hartford Manor. His little brother had annoyed him greatly over the past few days. Caleb was concerned about Edmond Prescott returning, so he had pushed them hard on the road. They had made the journey from the Duke's Summer Cottage to Hartford Manor in only two days' time. Everyone was extremely tired, but they all had agreed that they needed to get to the safety at Hartford as soon as possible.

Lady Spencer had rooms prepared and waiting for them when they arrived. The staff at Hartford Manor was very welcoming. The servants helped them all to get cleaned up from their journey and sent them to rest before dinner.

"You have a very lovely home, Lady Spencer." Elizabeth was amazed at the beauty of Hartford Manor.

"I sure never expected Maxwell Spencer to live in a house as grand as this." Caleb was in awe as he looked around the dining room.

"Maxx is an Earl." Nick elbowed his brother in his side. He did not want to offend Lady Spencer.

"It is alright, gentlemen. I have known for years, that if it were possible to do so, Maxx would prefer to live on that ship." Lady Spencer lightly laughed.

"Have you heard from Maxx?" Nick sat next to Lady Spencer.

"Maxx is in London." Lady Spencer sighed deeply. "He will not leave until he has found a way to get your cousin, Alexander, released from prison."

"Evelyn Cramer got what she deserved for setting Maxx up like that." Elizabeth would have loved to have been the one to push that hateful woman into the fountain at Ms. Rhodes' house.

"Let us hope that your brother can help Lord Alexander somehow." Lady Spencer smiled at Elizabeth.

"My brother?" Elizabeth was stunned. "Does this mean that Sam in back in London?"

"Aye, your brother has returned to Greyham Court." Lady Spencer assure Elizabeth.

"Are you sure that the Duke has returned to London?" Nick asked. He wondered what would happen to Elizabeth when her brother showed up here at Hartford Manor.

"Our sources say that the Duke was seen entering Greyham Court about three days ago." Lady Spencer was sad. She looked away for a moment. "Maxx has been trying for days now to get an appointment to speak with the Duke."

"I see that your guard, here at Hartford, keeps you well informed, Lady Spencer." Nick admired the strength that Maxx's mother tried to display.

As Lady of the Manor, Lady Spencer was a strong and amazing woman. She managed her household with a smile and the staff appeared to love her greatly. As a mother, Nick knew that her heart was breaking for her son. He assumed that his aunt, Lady Caroline, felt the same pain over her son Alex. Hopefully, his cousin would be released from prison soon.

"Where Maxx is concerned, I make sure that they keep me well informed." Lady Spencer stood up from the table and led her guests to the sitting room.

"Will we have the pleasure of meeting your daughter while we are here?" Caleb asked as he sat down.

Nick tapped his bother on the back of his head, while he politely smiled at Maxx's mother. It was clear that Lady Spencer was upset and worried about Maxx. Caleb did not need to pester the woman about meeting her daughter. Caleb rubbed the back of his head as he narrowed his eyes at Nick.

"It is possible that you could meet Emily. That will depend on a few things." Lady Spencer looked around the room as she smiled sweetly at her guests.

"Such as?" Nick was now curious about Emily Spencer. Did Maxx and his mother keep Lady Emily hidden from the world for some reason?

"It will depend on how long your stay is here and if Emily returns in time." Lady Spencer folded her hands on her lap.

"Does your daughter travel as Maxx does?" Elizabeth would very much like to meet Lady Emily.

"No. Emily went with the midwife to one of our farmers homes. Sybil Darcy is in labor and is having a hard time of it." Lady Spencer genuinely smiled at Elizabeth. She loved the young woman's sweet spirit. "Now, if you all will excuse me, I need to speak with the cook. Rosa and Ms. Duncan will see to it that you are taken care of for the evening."

Lady Spencer left the siting room. She released a deep breath once she was out in the grand hallway. She was not used to having guest from London here at Hartford.

"How long do we have to keep these airs up?" Harper escorted Maxx's mother to the kitchen.

"We will have to as long as the Duke's sister is in this house." Lady Spencer quickly looked over the cook's menu for the next couple of days. The kitchen staff had made the necessary changes that would accommodate their new guests.

"I do not think that Lady Elizabeth would mind if we were not so formal." Harper did not believe that Elizabeth cared much for the formal matters of things. He had seen how well she had adjusted to a simpler life at the Duke's Summer Cottage.

"We cannot take that chance." Lady Spencer approved the menu and retired to her room.

Since it was still early evening, Nick and Elizabeth enjoyed a walk in Lady Spencer's gardens. Being safely behind a fortress wall and having armed guards stationed around the manor, allowed them both to relax tonight. Nick wished that they had been able to take walks like this back at the cottage.

"What do you think my brother will do?" Elizabeth had her own opinions on the matter. She did not like her own thoughts on this.

"Rest assured, Sam will get to the bottom of things and he will do so quickly." Nick had seen how stern the Duke was on several occasions in the past.

"Do you believe that he will come here to Hartford?" Elizabeth nestled closer to Nick's side as they walked through the beautiful garden.

"Your brother will find you, no matter where you are." Nick had no doubts on this.

"I do not want to go back to Greyham Court." Elizabeth sighed deeply.

"You will have to tell Sam everything that happened to you and exactly how you feel about the matter." Nick wondered if she was ready to recall everything that had happened to her.

Nick hoped that when Elizabeth told her brother what she had gone through, that it would be enough for the Duke to honor Elizabeth's wishes somehow. The trouble with her request was, just where was Elizabeth supposed to go? Her home had always been at Greyham Court. Could she manage to live anywhere else?

"If Sam forces me to go back to London, I am afraid that I will have to do something drastic." Elizabeth was determined to not return to that house and the presence of her sister Anne.

"Just what are you planning?" Nick stopped and quickly turned her to face him.

"I will simply do what I must to not have to go back to Greyham Court." Elizabeth could not look Nick in the eye.

"No, My Lady." Nick was upset. "You are planning something."

"I will not go back there." Elizabeth looked up at Nick. "Sam cannot force me to."

"What are you planning?" Nick held Elizabeth by her upper arms as he asked her the question again.

"I have planned nothing," Elizabeth fought to remain calm and strong, but it was hard for her to lie to Nick.

"I do not believe you." Nick slowly shook his head at her.

Elizabeth had never been able to tell a lie without giving herself away. There was no doubt in Nick's mind that she was hiding something from him now.

"It does not matter if you believe me or not." Elizabeth looked away. Nick had always been able to read her well. This time was no different.

Nick did not wish to argue with her. He would find out soon enough what Elizabeth was up to. No doubt that Rosa would know of her plans. He would find the maid and question her later. For now, he would let Elizabeth keep her secrets. He did not wish to lose this peaceful night with her by asking a lot of questions.

"I apologize, my dear." Nick pulled Elizabeth into his arms. "I have a fear of losing you and doing so would destroy me."

"I never want to lose you either." Elizabeth wrapped her arms around Nick as she rested her head on his chest. She was relieved that he let the matter rest.

The truth was, she had been forming a plan on what she should do, but she had not decided on exactly what that was just yet. She would stand her ground though, even with her brother. She was not going back to Greyham Court if Anne was there.

After everything that had happed to her, Elizabeth no longer trusted the staff and the guards at Greyham Court to keep her safe anymore. For now, she would enjoy her time here with Nick. With her brother back in London, things should progress rather quickly.

"You have had a trying few days, my dear." Nick kissed the top of her head. "Why don't we get you upstairs so you can rest."

"How can we rest until this matter is resolved?" Elizabeth held Nick tighter. She was not ready to let him go just yet.

"Something tells me that the hidden pieces of the matter are about to come to light." Nick was sure that the Duke would not rest until he had uncovered everything.

Elizabeth tilted her head back enough to look up at Nick. He had found her in the forest in time to save her life. He had risked his own life over the past few weeks to protect hers. Nick had been her friend for years. Now, he was all that she wanted.

Elizabeth hated keeping secrets from Nick. Until she had decided on what path she was going to take, it was best to keep Nick in the dark about her plans. Hopefully, however things ended, she prayed that she would be by Nick's side. She was not sure if her brother would believe that a life with Nick was the best thing for her, but she would not dwell on that tonight.

Elizabeth put her arms around Nick's neck and pulled him closer to her. She did not care that she was being bold in this moment. What she cared about was this man in her arms. She loved him and nothing was more precious to her than that.

Nick did not fight against her actions. How could he resist her? The moment that her lips touched his, Nick wrapped his arms around her and deepened their kiss.

Chapter Nineteen

For two days, Maxwell Spencer sent requests to Greyham Court. For two days, his requests, to have an appointment to speak with the Duke of Greyham, went unanswered. On the third day, Maxx had enough of waiting. He was not going to let Samuel Dawson push him aside any longer.

Angrily, Maxx stormed up the steps at Greyham Court and loudly pounded on the front door. When the butler, Mr. Walter Reed, opened the door, Maxx pushed past the man.

"Lord Spencer, wait!" Mr. Reed shouted, as he hurried down the hall behind Maxx.

"I have waited long enough!" Maxx shouted over his shoulder.

"This may not be the best plan of action here." Paul was still trying to protest Maxx's decision to push into the Duke's home, like he had been for over an hour now.

Maxx went straight to the Duke's private study and flung the doors wide open. He was not letting the Duke put him off any longer. He found Samuel Dawson sitting at his huge fancy desk. The Duke's mother jumped from her chair and screamed when Maxx entered the room.

"Lord Spencer, how kind of you to visit us today." Sam leaned back in his chair and stared at Maxx.

"How dare you intrude on our home in such a manner!" The Duke's mother spat at Maxx. Maxx ignored her.

"I am fully aware that you wish to see me." Sam also ignored his mother. "I have a family situation and once I have gathered all the facts on that, I will gladly speak with you, Lord Spencer."

"You will speak with me today!" Maxx pointed his finger at Sam.

"If I desire to do so, I will speak with you today." Sam remained calm and unmoved.

"Lord Spencer, you should calm down." Anne Dawson walked into the room.

"Maxx, we should go." Paul took Maxx by the arm.

"I rather hoped that you would stay and join me for tea." Anne gently placed her hand on Maxx's arm. She smiled sweetly at Maxx and batted her eye lashes.

"Are you insane?" Maxx jerked his arm back, as he quickly stepped away from Anne. The vile woman had no boundaries.

"Enough, Anne." Sam shot his sister a stern look. "Why don't you take Mother and go enjoy your tea together."

Anne started to say something, but she thought better of it and quickly closed her mouth. She knew not to test her brother's patience too much. She had worked hard to get into Sam's good graces over the past couple of days. She could not afford to mess that up now. So, as Sam had requested, she and the dowager duchess left the room, to go have their tea together.

"You do need to calm down." Paul whispered in Maxx's ear.

"Now, Lord Spencer, I am quite aware of Lord Alexander Shaw's current situation. I assume that is the matter in which you are here to ask my help with." Sam folded his arms across his chest.

Maxx was still looking at the closed door of the study, which Anne had just exited. He looked back at Sam in disbelief of what he had just witnessed. How could the Duke sit here so calmly? How could he be nice to his evil sister like this?

"I do wish to speak to you, but I will not do so here." Maxx no longer felt comfortable discussing any matter with the Duke in this house. "I am afraid that your house has been greatly compromised."

"That is a rather peculiar thing to say." Sam rested his arms on his desk and looked Maxx in the eye. "How do you know what goes on in my home?"

"If you want to know the answer to that, you know where to find me." Maxx turned and left the Duke's home without saying another word.

"I do not get it. You bust in there to speak to the Duke, then you refuse to speak to him when you got the chance." Paul mounted his horse. Nothing that Maxx had done over the past few days had made much sense to him.

"Something is amiss in that house." Maxx thought on the matter as they rode through the streets of London. "Either Roger Holden's plot runs deeper than we originally thought, or our dear little Duke is a complete and utter idiot."

"I do not see either of those situations being the case." Paul understood Maxx's frustrations and confusion on the matter though.

"Let us hope that the Duke shows up soon." Maxx dismounted his horse outside the Blume'N Brew pub. "Gavin and Lord Mason could sure use Sam's help today."

Gavin and Lord Mason had an appointment with the magistrate later in the afternoon. With any luck, their requests would be honored today or perhaps Alex's case would be carried on to the king for a final decision. Having the Duke of Greyham standing with them, should give Alex a better advantage.

After waiting nearly an hour, Maxx had almost given up hope. Finally, the Duke walked through the doors of the Blume'N Brew. Miss Nancie let them use her private parlor, on the second floor, so that they would not be disturbed.

After telling the Duke everything he knew, Maxx opened a bottle of rum and poured himself a drink. Samuel Dawson sat quietly for a few moments as he pondered over all the new information that Maxx had just given to him.

"I was already aware that the corruption in my own home was severe." Sam grabbed the rum bottle and poured himself a drink as well. "I am sorry to say that I did not realize before just how deep and dark that corruption truly ran."

"That is a polite way of putting it." Maxx said flatly, as he poured another drink.

"If I were to help Alexander Shaw, I will expect some things in return." Sam smiled slyly at Maxx.

"Somehow, I knew you would say that." Maxx was sarcastic as he leaned back in his chair.

"Are you absolutely sure that you are willing to offer your services to me, to ensure Alexander Shaw's freedom?" Sam's smile grew broader. This day just might end on a good note for him after all.

"What do I have to do?" Maxx asked as he stared straight ahead.

Maxx closed his eyes as he listened to the Duke's terms. Sam was quite thorough as he gave Maxx his list of conditions. After the Duke left the Blume'N Brew, Maxx opened another bottle of rum and quickly drank the contents straight from the bottle.

Maxx walked to the doorway and took the bottle of rum from Miss Nancie's hands. She was the only one that was permitted to enter the room while the Duke was present. She stood there frozen and unable to speak. Miss Nancie had heard the last part of Maxx's conversation with Samuel Dawson.

"It was not right for you to have to agree to all of that just to ensure the Duke's help." Miss Nancie found her voice again as she helped Maxx down the stairs and to his favorite table in the pub.

"Do not fret, my friend. All is well in the world." Maxx flopped down in the chair.

"All is not well." Miss Nancie folded her arms and stared at Maxx. "I fear that you have made a great error today. Is Alexander Shaw really worth all that?"

"Carter!" Maxx pointed at the man sitting at a table not far away. "Music, my good man. And make it a lively tune!"

Will Carter was a little man that always wore a large hat, which was way too big for his head. He got up and went to the piano in the front corner of the pub. The few patrons in the pub seemed to not mind the change in the atmosphere of the room.

"Do not do this to yourself. There is too much at stake here." Miss Nancie pleaded as she sat down next to Maxx. "Perhaps the Duke will let you take it all back."

"It's done." Maxx looked straight ahead, not really focusing on anything. "You should get things ready. I am sure that Gavin will want to have his brother cleaned up before he carries him home to their mother."

Miss Nancie let the matter drop for now. She paused at the stairs and looked back at Maxx. This was the first time that she, or anyone else, had ever seen a defeated Maxwell Spencer. To her, Alexander Shaw's freedom came at too high of a price. Maxx greatly valued his friendship with the Shaw family. She prayed that it did not cost Maxx his life in the end.

A couple of hours later, Gavin walked into the Blume'N Brew with his brother Alex. Neither of them was prepared for the sight before them. Mr. Carter was still playing the piano and needed a break. Maxx twirled Rachel around near his private table in the back corner. Something was amiss here at the Blume'N Brew. They had never seen Maxx act like this before.

"I sit, for days, in a prison and you are here, drinking and dancing with women?" Alex sat down at the table as he stared in disbelief at Maxx.

"I guess that is how you would see things." Maxx picked up the bottle of rum from the table and drank what was left of it.

"Whoa there, Little Man. You have had enough rum." Alex took the new bottle of rum that Maxx had reached for.

"I have not had near enough rum." Maxx unsuccessfully tried to take the bottle of rum from Alex.

"How many bottles has he had?" Gavin asked Miss Nancie.

"Sadly, five." Miss Nancie handed Maxx a new bottle of rum.

"And you are giving him more?" Gavin took the new bottle away from Maxx before it could be opened. "Three is more than enough for him."

"Captain, the horses are ready." Paul spoke loudly, as he interrupted everyone.

"You cannot seriously be putting him on a horse in his condition!" Gavin shouted at Paul. "He cannot even walk straight!"

How was it that the people who were supposed to be looking out for Maxx were failing miserably today? Miss Nancie usually cut Maxx off on his rum at three bottles. Today, the little woman was giving Maxx all he could drink. Now, Paul, the one man that had always stayed by Maxx's side, was letting the little guy get on a horse. In Maxx's present condition, he would get hurt.

"It is alright, my friend." Maxx patted Gavin on the back. "I do not walk on a horse, I sit."

Paul took Maxx by the arm and started leading him toward the side door of the pub. Alex quickly caught up with them. He grabbed

Maxx by the arm and turned Maxx to face him. The movement caused Maxx to stumble.

"What has happened to you?" Alex did not understand Maxx's actions.

"You need a bath." Maxx patted Alex on the arm while nodding his head. Maxx then followed Paul out the door.

"How could you let him get like this?" Alex turned his anger onto Miss Nancie.

"After today, Maxx deservers whatever he wants!" Rachel shouted at Alex.

Miss Nancie snapped her fingers and pointed upstairs. Rachel glared at Alex for a moment before she dropped her head. She angrily stomped upstairs and out of sight.

What does she mean by that?" Gavin wanted some answers.

"Your brother is free." Miss Nancie had the same expression Rachel had, as she looked Gavin in the eye. "I guess that is all that matters."

"Alex was granted his freedom because the Duke stood with us and gave the report of his findings on the matter to the king." Gavin told Miss Nancie what had happened today at their meeting.

"The Duke is a demon!" Miss Nancie shouted.

"Samuel Dawson is stern, but I would say that calling him a demon is a tad harsh." Gavin did not understand the little woman's outburst.

Something was truly off on this entire matter. Gavin had never seen Miss Nancie, or Rachel, act like this. The little pub owner had been stern with customers on many occasions, but she had never treated him this way before.

"Today, Maxx finally got to speak with the Duke, here in the pub. It was just hours before your appointment with the magistrate." Miss Nancie looked from Gavin to Alex. "Enjoy your freedom, Lord Alexander, for it came at a great price."

"Something tells me that our little friend is in deep trouble." Alex looked over at his brother as Miss Nancie walked to the bar. "What do we do? How do we help Maxx?"

"First, you go up and get that bath. Next, we see our parents for a moment." Gavin did not like his best friend being taken advantage of like this.

"Then we ride to Hartford?" Alex wanted to get to the bottom of this.

"Then we ride to Hartford," Gavin agreed.

Alex hurried upstairs to the room where his bath waited for him. Somehow, he and Gavin would get Maxx out of whatever mess he had gotten into. Alex knew that it was on his account that Maxx was now in trouble.

"I am sure you two can show yourselves out." Miss Nancie said to Gavin, as she walked past him.

"How much do we owe you, Miss Nancie." Gavin hated that the little woman now seemed to hate him and his brother.

"Do not trouble yourself with that, Lord Gavin. Maxx already paid for that too." Miss Nancie walked away leaving Gavin to sit alone at a table, while he waited for his brother.

Chapter Twenty

Elizabeth and Nick stood on the front steps of Hartford Manor and watched as her brother, the Duke of Greyham, followed Lord Maxwell Spencer through the front gates. Elizabeth reached over and squeezed Nick's hand as she looked up at him nervously.

Lady Spencer gasped and ran down the steps to Maxx, when he all but fell off his horse. Paul quickly dismounted and helped to carry the Earl of Hartford into the manor. They had ridden straight through the past two nights from London to Hartford. Maxx, having had five bottles of rum before leaving the Blume'N Brew pub, did not fare well on the journey.

A part of Elizabeth dreaded seeing her brother. She had no idea what he would do about their sister Anne, or what he would say about her loving Nicholas Shaw. Still, a bigger part of her was happy to see her little brother again.

Elizabeth laughed, and burst into tears of joy, as Sam hurried up the steps and wrapped his arms around her. She hated that he traveled so much. Perhaps now, Sam would stay in London a bit more.

"I am so grateful that you are safe." Sam cupped Elizabeth's face in his hands as if she were a little girl.

"It is grand to see you, brother." Elizabeth smiled up at Sam.

"We have much to talk about." Sam hugged her again. He looked over Elizabeth's head at Nick. "I hear that I owe you much thanks."

"You owe me nothing." Nick shook the Duke's hand.

"Your Grace, if you will follow me, I will escort you and Lady Elizabeth to a private study, where you will not be disturbed." Rosa motioned toward the manor doors. She still had her left arm in a sling.

Sam sat next to Elizabeth on the small sofa in the study, as he listened to her recall to him what had happed to her. Sam had refused to let Nick, or anyone else, be in the room with him and his sister. Sam's heart broke, many times over, as he listened to Elizabeth.

Anger and something dark, and deeper than hatred, ran through Sam. A wicked spirit had been roaming through the halls of Greyham Court long before he was even born. His father had felt it but sadly he could never prove it. He had warned Sam about it many times over the years. His father had urged Sam to stamp the evil out once the source was found. It troubled Sam to know that the source of evil in his home was linking back to members of his own family.

"I do not wish to return to Greyham Court." Elizabeth wiped the tears from her cheeks.

"I understand your reluctance in wanting to go back but we must confront our sister on this matter." Sam held Elizabeth as she cried while telling him her story.

"No. I mean it, Sam." Elizabeth sat back and shook her head. "I am not going back. I never want to see Anne again."

"I will deal with Anne." Sam got up and started walking toward the door. "Tomorrow morning, you will journey with me, back to London."

"I will not!" Elizabeth jumped up, as she shouted to her brother.

"You will return to London with me. I will not debate that with you." Sam opened the study door. "Now, will you send in Nicholas Shaw?"

"I am sure that you know how to request Nick's presence yourself." Elizabeth was heartbroken. She hurried past her brother and did not stop to speak to Nick in the hallway.

Nick stepped forward when he saw Elizabeth rush from the study. He reached out to stop her as she hurried on past him. He dropped his hand and let her go on her way when Rosa shook her head at him. Rosa, being partly a lady's maid, had a keen sense when a lady needed to be alone. Then again, Rosa could have been giving him a warning, for the Duke was watching from the doorway.

Nick entered the study and gave the Duke an account of everything that had happened, from the moment he had seen the cloaked rider exiting the Eastern Forest, up until they had arrived at Hartford Manor. Sam Dawson was not an easy man to read. Nick was sure the young Duke was listening to him, but whatever Sam's thought were, Nick could not be sure of.

"We have to do something about Roger Holden and Edmond Prescott." Nick paced back and forth across the study.

"We will have to proceed cautiously on that." Sam leaned back in his chair.

"What more do you need?" Nick was becoming frustrated with the Duke. "Surely you know that neither man will stop."

"Roger Holden is an Earl." Sam watched Nick closely. "Catching him red handed will be hard, yet it is something that must be done."

"That snake has always covered his tracks well." Nick sighed deeply. He already knew this to be true.

"Now, leaning on Prescott, that just might prove beneficial and it could lead us to Holden in the end." Sam smiled slyly at Nick.

Nick tilted his head and narrowed his eyes at the Duke. This was the first sign that Sam had shown to Nick that proved he was not a fool. Was it possible that, together, they could form a plan that would trap both Prescott and Holden?

"What is to become of Elizabeth?" Nick bravely asked.

"My sister will return to London with me in the morning." Sam stood up and started for the door.

"But Elizabeth does not wish to return to Greyham Court." Nick was sure that this was why Elizabeth had been upset earlier.

"I understand, Sir Nicholas, that you care for my sister." Sam stopped and looked Nick in the eye. "I will decide what is best for my sister. Right now, I have decided that she needs to return to London with me. I hope I have made myself clear on the matter."

"Quite clear, Your Grace." Nick almost spat the words at Sam.

Before his anger overtook him, Nick left the study. He had to find Elizabeth. Nick was sure that she was upset and probably crying over her brother's decision.

One by one, the Duke questioned everyone that was involved in protecting Elizabeth over the past few weeks. He had already sent men to the Summer Cottage to start rebuilding the stables. He would be sending the staff back to the cottage in the morning, with a company of armed guards that would remain at the cottage to keep them all safe.

Rosa took Nick to where Elizabeth had sought refuge in Lady Spencer's garden. When Nick had entered the study earlier, Rosa had followed Elizabeth to make sure that she was alright. Rosa had Elizabeth to remain in this private spot in the garden, until she could bring Nick to join her. Rosa had grown fond of Elizabeth and only wanted her happiness. It was clear to everyone at Hartford that Nick was Elizabeth's happiness.

When Elizabeth saw Nick, she ran into his arms. Nick held her tightly for a long time without saying a word. Words were not needed when your heart loved this strongly. Elizabeth did not cry anymore. Nick was sure that she had already cried enough today.

Nick's heart broke for Elizabeth. Telling her brother what had happened to her meant that she had to relive those horrors. He was sure that it had shattered her world when Sam told her that she would be returning to London with him tomorrow.

"I will not go back there." Elizabeth was determined to not return to Greyham Court.

"I wish there was something that we could do." Nick was trying to come up with an alternative plan that the Duke would approve of. "But your brother does not appear to be listening on the matter."

"Will you stay here with me for a while?" Elizabeth held Nick tighter. "Rosa will have a meal brought out to us. I am not ready for this to end."

"I will stay with you for as long as you wish." Nick held her at arm's length so that he could look Elizabeth in the eye. "I do not wish for this to end either."

Elizabeth reached up and placed her palm against Nick's cheek. Her hazel eyes never left his deep brown eyes as her hand moved up to run her fingers through his wavy hair.

"No matter what tomorrow brings, or how long it will be until I see you again, never forget that I love you." Elizabeth smiled up at Nick.

"And I love you." Nick softly pressed his lips to hers.

In his mind, Nick vowed to himself, and Elizabeth, that one day he would find a way to convince the Duke of Greyham that he, a knight without a title, was worthy of Elizabeth's love.

That evening, Gavin and Alex showed up at Hartford Manor in time to have dinner with Lady Spencer and her guests. Maxx was still exhausted, so his mother refused to let the Earl leave his room. After speaking with Gavin and Alex, Lady Spencer had little respect for the Duke of Greyham. She was glad that His Grace would be leaving Hartford first thing in the morning.

Lady Spencer helped Rosa to keep the Duke occupied through dinner so that Nick and Elizabeth could enjoy their last evening together. Rosa had the staff carry out a dinner tray to the garden. This was the greatest gift that she could give to the young couple tonight.

After dinner, Gavin and Alex tried to get Sam to tell them about the deal that Maxx had made with him. Whatever this deal was, it had Miss Nancie and Rachel furious with them both. This deal had helped Alex to be granted his freedom and they wished to know what price their friend had paid for it. The Duke would not discuss the matter with anyone.

Everyone at Hartford Manor went to bed either frustrated or heartbroken. Hopefully, morning would bring a kinder spirit into the house. Nick was sure that it would not though. He escorted Elizabeth up to her room. She seemed distant and he understood that.

Nick kissed Elizabeth outside her door. He no longer cared if the Duke approved of their relationship or not. He loved Elizabeth and she was all that mattered to him. When her door closed, Nick stood there, staring the wooden door for several minutes. He hoped that they would see each other again very soon.

Chapter Twenty - One

A couple of hours past midnight, Elizabeth quietly entered the stables at Hartford. She quickly found Nick's horse and saddled him. She whispered sweetly to Toby as she prepared him to ride.

"I bid you goodnight and you decide, out of the blue, to steal my horse?" Elizabeth jumped when she heard Nick's voice behind her.

"I..." Elizabeth had no words. She was caught red handed.

"My, my, Lady Elizabeth." Nick walked closer to her. "Just what am I going to do with you?"

"I can explain." Elizabeth held her hands out.

"I would love to hear your explanation, my dear." Nick took the reins from her. "But there is just not time for it."

"Nick, please. Just hear me out." Elizabeth wanted to explain her actions.

"Oh, you will get your chance to explain." Nick looked into her eyes. "You do know that horse theft is a serious offense, do you not?"

"Yes, but I can explain." Elizabeth tried to step away, but Nick caught her by her waist.

"Explain later. Right now, there is not the time for it." Nick lifted Elizabeth up onto Toby's back.

"What are you doing?" Elizabeth asked as Nick tied her satchel onto the saddle with his.

"I am going with you." Nick led Toby out the back door of the stables.

After they had safely exited the servant's entrance gate, Nick mounted his horse and quickly headed for the forest. His goal, for now, was to get them out of sight of Hartford Manor. Hopefully, the guards and lookouts had not noticed them leaving.

Once they were out of sight of Hartford Manor, Nick made his way back to the road, so they could travel farther and faster for a while. Before daybreak, he led Toby back into the forest so they could travel on unseen. Nick stopped at the river long enough to let Toby rest and to feed him some oats.

"I have apples." Elizabeth pulled an apple from her satchel.

"At least you did think to provide some type of food for my horse." Nick lightly chuckled. "Other than that, did you have a plan, besides stealing Toby and just running?" Nick sat down next to Elizabeth on a nearby log.

"I will have to admit, I did not think that far ahead." Elizabeth handed Nick a slice of bread.

"We are in so much trouble here." Nick sighed as he handed her his water canteen.

"Do you think that my brother will catch us?" Elizabeth walked over and petted Toby.

"Eventually, Aye, I do." Nick tucked a lock of Elizabeth's long blonde hair behind her ear.

"But rather than stopping me, you decided to come with me, knowing that we would be caught?" Elizabeth now regretted leaving for Nick's sake. She was sure that Sam would go hard on Nick.

"Well, I was up for an adventure today." Nick smiled.

Nick gave Elizabeth a quick kiss before he helped her up on Toby. He quickly looked around the forest. It was still early and the only thing he saw moving among the trees were the animals. Soon, and very soon, Samuel Dawson would realize that his sister had ran away. Chaos would erupt at Hartford Manor and the hunt for him and Elizabeth would begin.

It was too late to worry about all that now, for the deed was done. Once they were caught, Nick had no doubts that the Duke would have him arrested for this. He could possibly even be charged with kidnapping.

If somehow, he managed to bypass the arrest, Maxwell Spencer would flog him for starting this irrational adventure from his home, Hartford Manor. Nick thought the arrest sounded more pleasant than facing Maxx.

Nick led Toby back to the edge of the forest. It was now daylight and they had to be careful to not be seen by travelers. He knew of a place where they could rest for the night. Hopefully, they could get there without being caught today. The tree line of the forest would be out of sight of the road for most of the day. They would ride next to the forest and could duck into the safety of the trees if it were necessary. Nick quickly mounted his horse and hurried toward a possible refuge for the night.

✳✳✳

About eight in the morning, everyone at Hartford Manor was waiting in the sitting room for breakfast to be served. Before Maxx could enter the room, Paul and Rosa grabbled him and pulled him into his private study.

"We cannot find Nick or Elizabeth." Rosa was frantic.

"Nick's horse is gone too." Paul was also alarmed over the matter. This reckless move of Nick's would surely infuriate the Duke.

Maxx sighed deeply and shook his head. He would expect a move like this from every Shaw but this one. Nick had always done things the proper way. He listened to his father's teachings and honored every request that his parents had given to him. Nicholas Shaw was the good and proper son that other families wished that they had.

"Have the servants to bring in a cart of coffee and tea to the sitting room." Maxx gave instructions to Rosa. "Tell the kitchen staff to delay breakfast for at least an hour and a half, two hours if they can manage it."

"I do not understand, but it will be done as you ask." Rosa looked from Maxx to Paul. She hoped that Maxx knew what he was doing here.

"You are buying them some time." Paul smiled for he realized Maxx's plan right away. This brought a smile to Rosa's face as well.

Maxx's smile broadened as he put his finger to his lips to shush Paul and Rosa. Rosa kissed Maxx on the cheek before she hurried to the kitchen.

"I may be bound to our dear little Duke, but it does not mean that I have to make sure that everything runs smoothly for him." Maxx was pleased with how this morning was starting out.

111

"So, it's what the Duke does not know that does not hurt you?" Paul smiled and shook his head.

"So right you are." Maxx patted Paul on the back.

Maxx straightened himself up and wiped the grin from his face. With a devastated expression on his face and laughter in his heart, Maxx entered the sitting room. It was time to give his guests the awful news of the problems in the kitchen that would delay their morning meal for just a bit. Word was even sent to Maxx's mother to delay her coming downstairs to signal that breakfast was served.

The kitchen staff had managed to hold breakfast for a little over an hour and a half. Lady Spencer entered the sitting room to announce that breakfast was ready. Gavin did not know anything about Maxx's plan, but he conveniently kept Samuel Dawson engaged in conversation for most of the morning. After ten minutes at the table, no one had mentioned Nick or Elizabeth.

"Rosa, will you please go up and see what is taking Lady Elizabeth so long?" Lady Spencer thought that it was best to say something before the Duke caught on to their little ruse.

Rosa curtsied to Lady Spencer and left the dining room. She took her time going up the stairs to Elizabeth's room. She waited another fifteen minutes before going back down to the dining room.

"I am sorry, My Lady, but I cannot find Lady Elizabeth." Rosa stood next to Lady Spencer.

"What do you mean, you cannot find my sister?" Sam was greatly upset. He looked around the table. "And where is Nicholas Shaw?"

"Rosa, do have the servants to go out and check the gardens." Lady Spencer tried to stall for more time. "Perhaps Nick and Elizabeth wanted to have breakfast alone." Rosa nodded her head and hurried away.

"I am sure that it's nothing." Gavin assured the Duke.

"Search the grounds, now!" Sam shouted to one of his own guards.

After thirty minutes of searching, it was determined that Nick and Elizabeth had left Hartford Manor. Maxx, along with his entire household, appeared greatly distraught over the matter.

"They could not have gotten far." Gavin told Sam.

"You will track them and help me bring my sister home." Sam demanded to Caleb.

"Wait. You want me to track my own brother?" Caleb was appalled.

"I do believe that is what I just said." Sam was growing impatient.

"What are you planning on doing when you find them?" Lady Spencer asked.

"I will have Nicholas Shaw arrested and then I will take my sister home!" Sam snapped.

"Whoa there, little Duke." Maxx stepped in front of Lady Spencer. "You have a right to be upset, but you, Your Grace, do not have a right to speak to my mother in such a manner and in my home!"

"My apologies, Lady Spencer." Sam nodded toward Maxx's mother. It was not his intent to insult the Earl of Hartford's mother.

"I am not tracking my brother, for you or anyone else." Caleb pointed at Sam as he walked away.

"Then you track them!" Sam looked over at Alex.

"Me?" Alex agreed with Caleb on this. He did not wish to have any part in tracking his own cousin.

Before anything more could be said, Maxx stepped in between Alex and the Duke. He hated what needed to happen here, but this was an opportunity that they could not pass up. This could partly free them from the Duke of Greyham.

"If Alex does this, then he is free of any and all debt owed to you." Maxx stood firm before Sam.

"Looks like I underestimated you, Spencer." Sam looked away as he thought on the matter for a moment.

"You made a deal that bound me to the Duke?" Alex grabbed Maxx by the arm and turned him to face him.

"I did what had to be done to get you out of that dreadful place." Maxx spoke softly so the others could not hear.

"Alright, Spencer. You win on this one." Sam hated giving in like this, but he needed a good tracker. "If Alex finds my sister, he is free, but you, however, are not."

"I am already aware of that fact." Maxx glared at Sam. He turned back to Alex. "Track them."

"You and I," Alex motioned with his finger between him and Maxx, "We will talk about this later."

"Let us just get you free of this demon first." Maxx whispered as he walked away.

Chapter Twenty-Two

That night, a few hours after dark, it started to rain. It had taken them longer than Nick had hoped, but they finally made it to the old, abandoned stables, not too far from the lands that were owned by his family. His father and uncle were looking to purchase this forgotten little farm to bring it into their estate. The house roof had caved in years ago and was not livable. The stables had held up well enough and should provide them a safe and dry shelter for the night.

Nick cleared an area in the stables to build a small fire. They had been riding in the rain for a little over half an hour. He helped Elizabeth hang their cloaks and bedrolls over the stall railings to dry. Elizabeth pulled dry clothing from her satchel and hurried to the back stall to change out of her wet clothes.

"How are you holding up?" Nick asked when she returned.

"I am making the best of it." Elizabeth sat down on a small stool by the fire.

"This is not a life for you." Nick hoped that she would see his words as truth.

"It will not be like this forever." Elizabeth did not want to admit that running away had been a horrible idea.

"This is something that we both can rightly agree on." Nick hurried to the back stall to change out of his wet clothes as well.

It was only a matter of time before the Duke found them. He should have stopped Elizabeth from running away. Nick had to admit that he was caught up in doing what Elizabeth had wanted at the time. However wrong this was, Nick would not give her away to her brother. So, the only thing he could think to do, at the time, was to go with her. There was no telling what kind of troubles that would have befallen Elizabeth if she had struck out on her own.

Would the Duke ever see that him going with Elizabeth was to keep her safe? It was doubtful but Nick could not allow her to leave alone. Whatever punishment fell upon him for keeping Elizabeth safe, would be a burden that he would gladly bear.

After their bedrolls had dried, Nick carried them up to the loft. With Toby settled for the night in one of the stalls and the fire put out, Nick pulled the ladder up into the loft with him and Elizabeth. He had positioned his bedroll near the small door of the loft so that he could keep watch for a while.

Elizabeth did not wish to sleep alone, even though she was only a few feet away from Nick. She pulled her bedroll over next to him and settled down against Nick's side.

"Is this a wise decision, My Lady?" Nick asked as he put an arm around her.

"I think wise decisions were thrown out the window hours ago." Elizabeth looked up at Nick.

With the rain clouds overhead, the moon was hidden tonight. Still, once her eyes had adjusted to the darkness, Elizabeth could make out the outline of Nick's face. Her heart allowed her to seem him clearly in her mind.

"That is a true statement for sure." Nick smiled and leaned his head down to kiss her.

The cool damp night air no longer chilled Elizabeth's skin. The warmth she felt from being next to Nick soothed her tired spirit. Finding this moment of comfort let Elizabeth know just how tired her body was as well. She closed her eyes and nestled closer to Nick's side. She could no longer fight to stay awake, within minutes sleep found her.

Nick looked down and smiled at the sleeping woman at his side. They should not be here like this but holding Elizabeth was the rightest thing that he had ever done in his life. This run a way adventure was bound to destroy Elizabeth's society reputation. Somehow, he figured that her brother would make all the rumors of this scandal go away.

For a while, Nick watched out the loft door as the rain steadily fell outside. The sound the rain made on the roof was comforting to him. This rain shower would either be a blessing or a curse to him and Elizabeth. Their tracks could be washed away in the night, or they could highlight a clear path to where they were. He could not help but wonder if the Duke was forcing his brother Caleb to track them. If so, Nick was sure that they would be found very soon.

***

Before the rain had set in, Gavin convinced the Duke to stop and set up camp for the night. Gavin had hoped to return to Ellis Manor after leaving Hartford, to be with his pregnant wife and his injured father. However, he could not let his little brother and his best friend go it alone with the Duke.

Usually, Samuel Dawson was a calm and levelheaded man, but today, the Duke of Greyham had lost his temper more than once. Gavin understood how the Duke felt though. Last year, he was out of his mind when Abby and Dani had been kidnapped by Roger Holden. Sam had been the one to get Gavin's wife and little sister safely away from Roger Holden that night.

"I believe that your brother is leading us on a wild goose chase." Sam was frustrated with how the day had turned out.

"Alex would not do that." Gavin pleaded with Sam to see reason. "My brother knows how important this is."

"Then your cousin is a madman! This trail makes no sense!" Sam threw his hands up. "If any harm comes to my sister because of him…"

"Nick cares deeply for Elizabeth." Gavin interrupted the Duke. "He would never let anything happen to her."

"If that were true then your cousin would have never taken my sister!" Sam shouted.

"Why don't we save all the anger, accusations, and threats until we have found them?" Gavin was becoming irritated with the Duke.

"You go tell your little brother that if he fails me, I will double his and Maxwell Spencer's payment." Sam angrily pointed his finger at Gavin.

Gavin, not wishing to make matters worse for his brother or Maxx, nodded his head and left the Duke's tent. He hurried across the camp, in the rain, to the tent he shared with Alex, Maxx, and

Paul. Gavin thought it was time that his little friend came clean on what this deal was that he had made with the Duke.

When Gavin entered the tent, he took off his wet cloak and hurried over to his cot. The tent was large enough for the four of them to share, but there was not much room for moving around. Maxx had opened a bottle of rum and turned the bottle up.

"I will take that." Gavin took the bottle of rum from Maxx's hands.

"Hey!" Maxx sat up on his cot.

"This seems to get you into too much trouble here lately." Gavin held the bottle away from Maxx. "Like this mysterious deal you made with the Duke."

"I was sober on that." Maxx laid back down on his cot.

"Do you want to share with us exactly what this deal is?" Alex wanted answers on this.

"No, I do not." Maxx put his hands behind his head and stared up at the tent ceiling. "Just find Elizabeth Dawson and you are free of it."

"That's another thing." Alex grabbed Maxx by the arm and pulled him up to a sitting position. "How could you make a deal that bound me to the Duke?"

"You want to kindly let him go?" Paul grabbed Alex by the arm.

"You are the most loyal first mate that I have ever seen in my life." Alex narrowed his eyes at Paul as he released Maxx's arm.

"I am sure that you had good reasons for making this deal." Gavin sat down on his cot. "I would just like to know what those reasons were."

"The Duke only asked for a favor in return from Alex." Maxx laid back down. "I never expected Alex to have to actually do the favor. My men and I were going to carry out whatever request the Duke made to Alex."

"That was very noble of you to work as hard as you did to gain my brother's release." Gavin knew Maxx well. "But this deal you made, has me deeply concerned for you."

Over the past nine years, Maxx had become part of Gavin's family. Maxx had done what any true friend would have done in his position and that was everything. If the situation were reversed, somehow Gavin would have done everything that he could have to save Maxx.

"You never expected the Duke to ask Alex to track someone." Paul understood all too well what Maxx had done and why.

"This is a simple deed, but it is one that I am not good at. It is a horrible situation, I know, but this will free you from the Duke." Maxx looked over at Alex.

"What about you?" Alex hated that Maxx was trapped. "And what about Nick?"

"Do not worry about me, I will get free of it someday." Maxx looked between Alex and Gavin. "And as far as Nick goes, that is why some of my men are here with us as well. We will not allow the Duke to take Nick."

"Sam will kill you!" Alex grabbed Maxx by the arm again.

"Then, I too, will be free of the Duke." Maxx pulled his arm back. He turned over and pulled his blanket over him. He had talked enough for one day.

Chapter Twenty-Three

The next day, Nick managed to keep his and Elizabeth's whereabouts hidden within the forest. The river here was narrower and shallow, which allowed him to walk Toby in the water at times. Nick took every precaution he had learned in the military to conceal their tracks. Caleb was the best tracker that Nick had ever known. All his tricks would not fool his little brother for too long.

The sky remained overcast all day. Thankfully, the rain that threatened had held off for the day. It had been dark for hours now and Nick had to find shelter for the night. There was only one place that he could think of, but it would be very risky to go there. There was not much choice in the matter, so it was a chance they would have to take.

Just before midnight, the first drops of rain began to fall as Nick led Toby through the servant's gate. Elizabeth frantically shook her head. Panic set in for she knew that this was a bad idea. Nick only put his finger to his lips to signal her to remain quiet.

When they had safely entered the back of the stables at Kinsley Estate, Nick helped Elizabeth down from his horse.

"We will leave before daybreak, if that is still your wish." Nick took her hand in his.

"You want me to stop running." Elizabeth dropped her head.

"I want what is best for you." Nick tilted her face up so that he could look into her eyes. "If you wish to keep going, then we will keep going."

Nick softly pressed his lips to hers. He wrapped his arms around Elizabeth and held her close. He did not wish to keep running with her like this, but he would not betray her trust. The longer they stayed on the run, the harder it was going to be when the Duke finally caught up with them.

"Sir Nicholas? Is that you?" The sound of the stable boy's voice startled Nick and Elizabeth.

120

"Yes, Finley, it is I." Nick turned to face the young lad.

Finley Thompson was only about fifteen years of age and had already been working in the stables at Kinsley Estate for two years now. On many occasions the young boy had rode with Nick when he surveyed the estate lands. Nick had grown fond of the boy from the moment they first met.

"I will let them know at the main house that you are home, Sir." Finley turned to leave.

"No!" Nick stopped the boy. "I need your help, Finley, but I need you to keep quiet about it. Do you understand?"

Nick explained as much of their situation as he could to Finley. Thankfully, the young lad agreed to help them. Finley took them to the spare servant's quarters in the back of the stables.

While Nick and Elizabeth slept, Finley gathered the list of supplies and food that they had asked for. About an hour before daybreak, the stable boy woke them up. Finley helped Nick saddle Toby for the hard ride that was ahead of them today.

Elizabeth smiled and shook Finley's hand before Nick helped her up onto his horse. Finley walked beside Nick to the servant's entrance gate.

"When the Duke shows up here, make yourself scarce so that he cannot question you." Nick would hate to see the young boy lose his job and be punished for helping them.

"Do you think that the Duke will figure out that you were here?" Finley asked.

"Caleb is an excellent tracker." Nick hated that his own brother was having to track them. "I have no doubts that he will find our trail with ease."

"Sir Caleb is not tracking you." Finley opened the gate. "Your brother is at Ellis Manor, helping Lord Nathaniel until his brothers return. I am afraid that Lord Alexander is the one that is being forced to track you."

Nick shook Finley's hand and rode away from Kinsley Estate. It was good news that Caleb was not the one tracking them. The bad news was that his cousin Alex was the tracker. Alex was just as good

121

as Caleb at this task. It was only a matter of time before he and Elizabeth were caught by the Duke.

Nick decided to try and think about something else rather than who was tracking them. There were many more obstacles ahead for him and Elizabeth today. It was going to be a hard ride to reach shelter for the night. Elizabeth would hate where he was taking her, but Nick could think of no other safe place to go.

As the day wore on, Elizabeth realized where they were heading. Once again, fear rose in her heart as she questioned Nick's choice of direction.

"We are heading to London." Elizabeth looked over her shoulder at Nick, as the city came into view.

"I know a place where we can rest tonight and from there, we can figure out our next step." Nick spoke next to her ear.

"Is London really a good idea?" Elizabeth had not been back to London since she was attacked.

"It is about as grand of an idea as all the other ones that we have had over the past two days." Nick chuckled lightly.

Elizabeth decided to trust Nick on this, and she let the matter drop. That was until Nick rode into the small stables behind the Blume'N Brew pub. Thankfully, it was dark and after hours, so no one had seen them stop here.

Nick knocked on the side entrance to the pub. To his surprise, Miss Nancie herself opened the door. Without saying a word, Miss Nancie grabbed Nick by the arm and quickly pulled him inside.

Rachel and Jerry Griffin, the pub bartender, helped Elizabeth and Nick get cleaned up, while Miss Nancie fixed them a proper meal. As they sat down in the private dining room, Elizabeth started to relax a little. This little pub was not what she had expected from a drinking establishment.

The little pub owner was an even bigger surprise to Elizabeth. Over the years, she had heard stories from the servants at Greyham Court about this pub and Miss Nancie. She had always assumed that Miss Nancie was an older woman, but that was not the case.

Miss Nancie looked to be no more than thirty years of age, at the most. Elizabeth wondered why a young woman would be running such an establishment. Still, there was something about the little woman that Elizabeth instantly liked. Perhaps it was Miss Nancie's desire to protect others or maybe it was her boldness to speak her mind. One thing was for sure, Miss Nancie truly protected Maxwell Spencer.

"Where will you two go from here?" Miss Nancie joined them at the table.

"We have not decided on that just yet." Nick took the glass of brandy that Miss Nancie offered to him.

"Thank you for helping us." Elizabeth smiled at the little pub owner.

"You two are not going to get far if you do not come up with a better plan." Miss Nancie poured Elizabeth, and herself, a cup of tea.

"I know that running away was a horrible idea." Elizabeth looked down at her plate. "But it was better than being forced to return to Greyham Court."

Miss Nancie smiled when Nick put his arm around Elizabeth. She knew that this relationship would ruffle the Duke's feathers. She had no problem with seeing Samuel Dawson's feathers ruffled. There had to be something more that she could do to help Nick and Elizabeth.

"Have you decided to return to your family then?" Rachel now joined them at the table.

"That will depend on my brother." Elizabeth smiled at Rachel.

Elizabeth had heard the stories of Maxwell Spencer's women for years. She had never expected to ever meet Rachel. The young woman was very pretty. Her long brown hair flowed perfectly over her shoulders. Rachel was sweet and caring. This was not how she pictured a kept woman to act. Elizabeth genuinely liked Rachel and she wished for a world where they could be friends without the ridicule from those in society.

"Do you wish to talk with Sam?" Nick asked Elizabeth questionably. He was sure that the past few nights had been hard on her, perhaps she was ready to return to the comfortable life she knew.

"I am afraid that Sam has made up his mind." Elizabeth folded her hands on her lap. "For some reason, my brother is determined that I return to Greyham Court. That is something that I cannot do."

"I had always thought that the Duke was a reasonable man, until now." Jerry now joined them. He too was not happy with the deal that the Duke had forced upon Maxx.

"Whatever you decided, my dear, I will be by your side." Nick took Elizabeth's hand in his. "But Miss Nancie is right, we need to come up with a better plan."

"I left a letter for my brother with the stable boy at Kinsley Estate." Elizabeth looked up at Nick. She knew she should not have kept this from him.

Nick and everyone else's mouths dropped open as their eyes widened in shock. Nick leaned his head back and sighed deeply. He thought that it was best for them to just go on and give up now, but he would not force that upon Elizabeth. Whatever they did from here, would be her decision.

"Was that wise?" Rachel gently touched Elizabeth's arm.

"If Sam will not force me to go to Greyham Court or near our sister Anne, ever again, then I will stop running." These were the only terms that Elizabeth would agree to.

"But where will you go if you do not return to Greyham Court?" Rachel was concerned for Elizabeth.

"Oh, do not fret. The Duke has several houses throughout England. I am sure that Lady Elizabeth would be taken care of at any one of those houses." Miss Nancie could not understand why the Duke did not agree with this idea. It seemed the obvious solution for Elizabeth.

"We still need to come up with a plan until you have a reply from your brother." Nick hoped that a good night's rest would help him come up with their next step.

"I might have an idea." Miss Nancie smiled at Nick. "I think I know of a place where you can rest safely and wait for a reply from the Duke."

"Thank you, Miss Nancie." Elizabeth was grateful for the pub owners help.

"How will you get a reply from your brother if you are on the run?" Rachel asked.

"Sam can post his reply." Elizabeth nodded her head at Rachel.

"You mean, in the paper?" Rachel was confused for she had never heard of anything like this before. Elizabeth nodded her head again.

"The ways of the rich will never cease to amaze me." Jerry got up and went to the stables.

Jerry moved Nick's horse to the private side of the stables, that was not visible to other guests. This would help keep anyone from knowing that Nick and Elizabeth had been to the Blume'N Brew. Maxx had thought of this idea a few years ago. It was a safety precaution in case the little captain ever needed to hide his whereabouts.

"Now, off to bed with you two." Miss Nancie hurried Nick and Elizabeth to their rooms. "We can talk more about a plan in the morning."

"Why are you helping us like this?" Nick asked before he went to his room.

"Would you believe that it's because I care?" Miss Nancie asked.

"Oh, I know that you care." Nick looked the little woman in the eye. "About what that is, other than Maxwell Spencer, I am not all too sure of."

Miss Nancie smiled, refusing to give her secrets away. Nick laughed and escorted Elizabeth to her room. This was the last place he wanted to bring her to, but it was the only one that he could think of that the Duke would not expect. Whether his decision on this was for better or worse, it was one that kept Elizabeth safe and had her sleeping in a bed, rather than on a bedroll in the forest.

Chapter Twenty-Four

Late the next afternoon, Alex followed Nick and Elizabeth's trail to the servant's gate at Kinsley Estate. Alex, along with everyone else in their party, had grown irritated with the Duke's demands by this point. Sensing that they all needed a rest, Alex ignored the tracks that had led back out the gate.

"Now I know that you are not being truthful! What kind of fool do you take me for?" Sam pointed his finger at Alex. "Why would your cousin come to his own home?"

"If you will calm down and stop shouting at everyone, perhaps we can find out." Alex snapped at the Duke.

"Maybe Nick and Elizabeth are still here and waiting for you." Gavin offered a suggestion that seemed to quieten Sam down for now. He hoped that his cousin had come to his senses by now.

The tracking party left their horses at the stables and hurried up to the main house to see Sir Phillip and Lady Clara. Sam hoped that Gavin was right, and he would find his sister waiting inside Kinsley Estate. The servants led the Duke to the family sitting room.

"We have not seen Nick and Elizabeth since they left for the Summer Cottage." Sir Phillip told the Duke. "Why would you think that they are here?"

"Your nephew says that their trail leads to your servant's gate." The Duke sat across the sitting room, glaring holes into Alex.

"Is our son in some kind of trouble?" Lady Clara stood behind her husband's chair.

"Your son has my sister." Sam spoke calmly to Lady Clara, he would not disrespect her, even though his patience was wearing thin with the Shaw family. "I would like her to be returned to me at once."

"I am sure that there is a good explanation as to why they are together and on their own like this." Lady Clara forced a smile at the Duke. She was deeply worried for her oldest son.

Lady Clara was sure that it was an explanation that the Duke would not wish to hear. It was obvious to her, and everyone else, while Elizabeth was at Kinsley Estate, that she and Nick loved each other.

"The longer they run, the harder it will be for your son. I would rather not have to take Sir Nicholas before the king." Sam politely threatened.

"We will have a room prepared for you for this one night, Your Grace. I will ask, since you are threatening my son, who happened to have saved your sister's life, will you kindly leave Kinsley Estate tomorrow morning after breakfast?" Sir Phillip stood up and left the room. He did not like his family being threatened, and in their own home.

At breakfast the next morning, the atmosphere at Kinsley Estate had not changed. Sir Phillip and Lady Clara were deeply worried about what was going to happen to their oldest son, once the Duke had his sister back. They both had always respected the young Duke of Greyham, and they hoped that he could be reasoned with today.

"How is your father and the rest of your family?" Sam asked Gavin, who was sitting next to him.

Gavin had returned to Ellis Manor, for the night, to see his pregnant wife and to check on his father's condition. He hated leaving his family this morning, but he was not going to leave Alex and Maxx in the hands of the Duke right now.

"Doctor Ramsey gave father a good report yesterday. His leg is mending nicely. Although, there will be no more horse training for my father in the future. Caleb is helping Nate and Dani with father. Abby and Olivia are great support for mother, plus they are managing the household for now." Gavin spoke kindly to the Duke.

"I take it that Lady Danielle is faring well?" Sam smiled when he mentioned Dani. This was an action that had not gone unnoticed by Maxwell Spencer.

"Lady Danielle is faring *very* well." Maxx smiled as he raised his coffee cup at the Duke before he pretended to be interested in the food on his plate.

"That is my sister." Alex elbowed Maxx in the side as he whispered sternly to him.

"I am well aware of who she is," Maxx whispered back.

Maxx chanced a look at Sam across the table. Samuel Dawson was glaring at him, while he tapped his fingers lightly on the table. Maxx was pleased that he now had a matter in which he could regularly irritate the Duke with.

Everyone noticed as one of the footmen carried in a letter and gave it to Sir Phillip. Sir Phillip listened as the footman whispered something in his ear. Before he could be questioned, the footman hurried out of the dining room.

"Your Grace, it appears that our cook found this letter on the preparation table in the kitchen just now." Sir Phillip passed the unopened letter to Sam.

After reading the letter, Sam tossed the piece of paper on the table and sprang to his feet. His anger was at a full boil and his patience was finally at its end.

"You all must take me for a fool!" Sam shouted.

"Well," Maxx leaned back in his chair. "If the shoe fits."

"I swear, Spencer! That mouth of yours is going to cause me to kill you one of these days!" Sam angrily pointed his finger at Maxx.

"No one here believes that you are a fool." Gavin, who had been trying to keep the Duke calm all morning, stood up and drew Sam's attention away from Maxx. "Would you kindly explain to all of us just what that letter is about?"

"This!" Sam picked up the letter and waved it at Gavin. "This is from my sister! You lot are hiding them from me!"

"I am sure that there has been a misunderstanding here somewhere." Gavin tried to calm the Duke down but failed to do so.

"I will say this clearly, to ensure that there are no more misunderstandings." Sam pointed at Alex. "You will find them and soon, or I will double your debt!" Sam then pointed at Maxx. "And that little weasel will never be free until the day I kill him myself!"

"Oh dear," Lady Clara gasped as her eyes widened in horror.

"Your Grace, I assure you that we are not hiding your sister from you." Sir Phillip stood up and started toward the door. "I will go and question the staff immediately."

"And I will go and speak with our cook." Lady Clara hurried down to the kitchen.

The cook, Ms. Langley, confirmed that she found the letter, addressed to the Duke, mysteriously laying on the preparation table in the kitchen. She had not seen who put it there. This information did not sit well with the Duke. Sam ordered everyone in the tracking party to prepare to leave immediately.

"We do not hold any ill will toward you for being forced to track our son like this." Lady Clara cried as she spoke to Alex.

"Find Elizabeth Dawson and return her to her brother and do it quickly." Sir Phillip was almost in tears himself.

"Uncle Phillip, I do not want to do this task." Alex shook his uncle's hand before hugging his aunt goodbye.

"When you find Nicholas, please do what you can to spare my son's life." Uncle Phillip could no longer hold back his tears, as he spoke to Gavin.

"You have my word, Uncle Phillip. We will do all we can for Nick." Gavin nodded his head at his uncle and hugged his aunt goodbye.

"Do not fret, Lady Clara." Maxx held Nick's mother's hands in his. "I promise, we will return your son safely to you."

Lady Clara pulled Maxx into her arms and hugged him, just as she had hugged both of her nephews. Sir Phillip forced a smile and nodded his head at Maxx, as he put his arm around Lady Clara. Gavin, Alex, and Maxx waved to the sad couple as they left Kinsley Estate, with the Duke following closely behind them.

It was dark when the tracking party reached London. With the loss of daylight, Alex could not properly follow Nick and Elizabeth's trail. Alex dreaded telling the Duke that the trail had gone cold.

With the tracking now halted until morning, Maxx and Alex insisted on going to the Blume'N Brew for the night. The Duke and his guards would return to Greyham Court but first they escorted the others to the pub.

Miss Nancie was not pleased to see them. Still, she played the proper host and sent drinks to them at Maxx's favorite table.

"I will return in the morning and we shall resume our search straight away." Sam looked at Alex.

"I will do what I can but here, in the city, it will be harder to track them." Alex smiled at Miss Nancie as she poured him a drink. Miss Nancie did not smile back at him.

"If Alex cannot find their trail, we will have to start questioning some of the shop owners for possible sightings of Nick and Elizabeth." Gavin wanted Sam to know that they would do their best to find his sister as quickly as possible.

"London is a pretty large city, so the questioning may take a few days." Maxx opened a bottle of rum.

"I do believe that you have your own mission to see to, do you not?" Sam stared at Maxx.

"I have not forgotten your request. I will start on that within the hour." Maxx decided to not use a mug and drank straight from the bottle.

"See to it that you do." Sam stood up. "I will see the rest of you in the morning after breakfast."

Once the Duke was out of the pub, Miss Nancie locked the doors. She had Jerry to announce last call so the few pub patrons would leave soon. Dealing with the Duke tonight had greatly irritated her nerves. She also figured that Maxx, and the others, would prefer some privacy, so closing early did not bother her at all.

"What mission is he talking about." Gavin did not like the sound of this.

"I have to make a little trip for the Duke. That is all that you need to know." Maxx avoided making eye contact with everyone.

"You are sailing tonight?" Miss Nancie was alarmed. She had not expected this.

"Aye. I have already sent the crew to the ship. Paul and I will join them shortly." Maxx pushed the unfinished bottle of rum away. He should probably be sober for this trip.

"Where exactly is this 'little trip' taking you?" Alex grabbed Maxx by his arm. He did not like the hold the Duke had over his friend.

"France." Maxx looked over at Paul while the others erupted in chaos.

"You cannot go to France!" Miss Nancie was frantic.

"You have been avoiding France as much as possible because their troops have sided with the colonist in America." Alex pulled on Maxx's arm until Maxx looked at him.

"I have no choice." Maxx jerked his arm away from Alex.

"If the Duke has asked you to something shady and you get caught…" Gavin could not say the words.

"Then the king will have me rightly hanged for treason." Maxx said the words the others could not say.

"How do you get free of this deal with the Duke?" Gavin asked as he walked with Maxx to the door.

"I do not know just yet." Maxx looked over at Miss Nancie and Alex. Both were still sitting at the table, stunned from hearing what Maxx had to do tonight. "Get your brother free of the Duke and take care of my little blonde friend while I am gone. We should return within two days."

Maxx and Paul hurried to the docks. Within half an hour The Em left London Harbor bound for France. Maxx prayed that they could make this journey without being caught. High treason was a crime he did not wish to be caught at.

Chapter Twenty-Five

Nick and Elizabeth huddled close together in the small room. They could hear the shouts of men all around them. There was much more activity tonight than there had been before.

"Do you think that my brother has found us?" Elizabeth whispered. Nick position her behind him in case someone burst through the door.

"That is a strong possibility." Nick looked at her over his shoulder. "No matter what happens, never forget that I love you."

Nick leaned back and gave Elizabeth a quick kiss. As the voices grew louder, Nick put his hand on his sword and waited. To his surprise, the footsteps retreated, and the voices soon faded. Without warning, the room shook with a strong jerk and the footsteps above them started again.

"What just happened?" Elizabeth grabbed Nick's waist to support herself.

"It is alright." Nick turned around and put his arms around Elizabeth. "We just set sail."

"Captain, can I have a word?" Ollie followed Maxx and Paul below deck.

"Let me rest for a few hours and we will talk." Maxx hurried into the captain's quarters.

"It has been a long day. I am sure that the matter can wait." Paul put his hand on Ollie's shoulder. "Surely it is not that important."

"Did the Captain see Miss Nancie before boarding? If so, I am sure that she informed you both." Ollie was still nervous.

"Ollie, what is going on?" Paul had not been informed of anything by Miss Nancie.

Ollie opened the cabin door to the left of Paul's cabin. He found it empty. Immediately, Ollie was alarmed. This was where they had put Sir Nicholas. Ollie hurried to the cabin on the other side of Paul's and quickly opened the door. He was relieved to find Nick and Elizabeth inside.

"This is a problem." Paul shook his head when he saw the couple. "We best tell the Captain right away."

Paul hurried into the Captain's quarters without even knocking on the door. Maxx was sitting behind his desk, taking off his boots.

"I take it that the matter could not wait a few hours." Maxx was greatly annoyed as he looked up at Paul.

"The matter most definitely cannot not wait a few hours." Paul was frustrated.

"Well, bring Ollie in and let's hear it." Maxx propped up on his elbow on his desk.

Maxx's eyes widened with shock when Nick and Elizabeth followed Ollie into the Captain's quarters. When the shock wore off, and to everyone's surprise, Maxx almost fell out of his chair laughing.

"I do not see the humor in this." Paul was greatly concerned over the matter. "If the Duke finds out that they were on this ship, he will tighten his grip on you even more."

"What does that mean?" Nick did not understand.

Paul proceeded to tell Nick, Elizabeth, and Ollie about the deal that Maxx had to make with the Duke to help free Alex from prison. Paul had a feeling that Maxx had aligned himself with a harsh man. It was quite possible that Maxx would never be free of this evil deal.

"Captain, if we had known that you did not approve this matter, the crew would have never agreed to help Miss Nancie." Ollie was now as concerned as Paul was for Maxx.

"It appears that our little pub owner has learned some of your tricks over the years." Paul smiled at Maxx. He had to hand it to Miss Nancie for thinking well on her feet.

"Aye, that she has." Maxx chuckled. "Remind me to commend our little blonde friend when we return to London."

"If we return," Ollie mumbled.

"Where exactly are we going?" Nick was now even more nervous about being on The Em.

"We are on a mission for our dear little Duke to the jolly land of France." Maxx leaned back in his chair.

"Is that a wise idea?" Nick now wished that he had not agreed to Miss Nancie's plan.

"Wise or not, I am bound by my word to the deed." Maxx sighed as he stood up. "I need a drink."

"What are we supposed to do for the Duke in France?" Ollie asked the question the others in the room were wondering.

"We are picking up a passenger." Maxx poured drinks for himself, Ollie, Paul, and Nick. He offered a small glass to Elizabeth. "Care for some rum, Lady Elizabeth?"

"Have you gone mad?" Nick stepped in front of Elizabeth.

"Why yes, I have." Maxx quickly drank the rum he had offered to Elizabeth.

"I thought that we did not carry passengers. Has that changed?" Ollie asked.

"Tonight, we have no choice." Maxx sat back down at his desk.

"My brother truly does have a kind heart." Elizabeth walked over to Maxx's desk. "Just know, if you have bound yourself to Sam by an oath, in business, he is ruthless."

"Thank you, Lady Elizabeth. I will keep that in mind." Maxx smiled at her before turning to Nick. "It is a lovely evening. Why don't you two go up on deck and enjoy some fresh air for a while?"

Nick nodded his head at Maxx, silently thanking him for this opportunity. Taking Elizabeth by the hand, Nick led her up on deck. He was grateful to see the sky and feel the wind on his face. Being confined below deck was not something he wanted to do for much longer.

"Ollie, do not regret helping Miss Nancie." Maxx looked between Ollie and Paul. "We all know that we are to never withhold help to one of our own."

After they had devised a plan on how to keep Nick and Elizabeth away from the Duke's mysterious guest on the journey back to London, Maxx decided to make one last stroll around on deck. He pulled Nick to the side and explained their plan for the return voyage.

"You two need to decide on what your plans will be once we are back in London." Maxx leaned on the ship's railing.

"We will. I promise." Nick looked over to where Elizabeth was standing not far away, waiting for him. "I will do whatever she asks of me."

"Spoken like a true Shaw." Maxx had seen Shaw men fall in love before. It could be bloody annoying at times.

"What would you do?" Nick quickly looked over at Maxx.

"Me?" Maxx placed his hand on his chest as he spoke. He was stunned by Nick's question.

No Shaw had ever asked Maxx that question before. Once a Shaw had fallen for a woman, their minds usually turned to mush but they strongly followed what their hearts wanted. Nick Shaw was no exception to this rule. Well, except for the part about asking for advice.

"You should do exactly what your heart wants you to do." Maxx looked Nick in the eye. "If the rumors of this little adventure that you two have taken ever gets out, Elizabeth will be ruined in society. I can only think of one way of preventing that."

"Do you believe that Elizabeth will agree?" Nick looked over at the woman who held his heart.

Elizabeth was breathtaking to him as she stood there, next to the ship's railing. Her blonde hair flowed freely in the wind. The moonlight danced on her golden strands of hair. Nick's heart almost leapt out of his chest when Elizabeth smiled and closed her eyes as she turned her face so that the wind could touch her cheeks.

"Elizabeth is kind and beautiful, make no mistake, she is also smart and witty. I would think that the thought has already crossed her mind." Maxx could clearly see just how far Nick Shaw had fallen for the Duke's sister.

"Do you really believe that to be true?" Nick suddenly felt nervous.

"It is probably what she had hoped that your little adventure would turn into." Maxx patted Nick on the back. "If I were you, when we get back to London, I would head north."

Maxx excused himself and went below deck. He was tired and needed some rest. Sleep would not come but rest was a must right now. He could not believe what he had just encouraged. He had said before that his ship was not a love boat. Maxx hoped that Nicholas Shaw would have the courage to follow through with the suggestion.

Maxx would always say that his encouragement tonight was for the matter of the heart. Love should always win in the end. Hopefully, the Duke would not kill him for suggesting this.

Chapter Twenty-Six

Nick hurried over to Elizabeth with a new kind of hope in his heart. Maxwell Spencer was right about this. He should do what his heart had been wanting to do for years. After all, his father and uncle were bold and brave enough to follow where their hearts led them.

Elizabeth was glad when Nick had returned to her. The sea and sky looked much different from the deck of a ship than it did from dry land. She could now understand why some men loved the sea. On nights like this one, there was something lingering in the air that seemed to comfort her soul.

"It is absolutely wonderful out here." Elizabeth put her arms around Nick's waist, as he wrapped his arms around her.

"Oh, it is wonderful, but I do believe that I will leave the sea life to Maxx and my brothers." Nick smiled down at her.

Nick felt as if his stomach were in knots. He wondered if Maxx was right about Elizabeth. Did she genuinely want him as much as he wanted her? Would she dare to take the next step with him? What was he to do if she refused him and retreated to the safety of her higher status world? Was it right of him to ask her to walk away from the only world that she knew? Nick sighed as his mind was flooded with these questions.

"I will never forget this night." Elizabeth sweetly smiled up at Nick. The beauty of the sea created a carefree spirit in her.

"I wish for us to share every night like this." Nick leaned down and softly kissed her.

"That would be a wonderful dream." Elizabeth hugged him tighter.

"It does not have to remain a dream." Nick cautiously approached what his heart wanted.

"What are you saying?" Elizabeth took a step back as she looked up at Nick.

"Marry me." Nick took her hands in his. "I know that I have no title, but I have loved you for years."

Nick hated blurting out a proposal like this, but he feared that if he did not say the words now, that something would happen, and he would never get the chance again. This was not a romantic proposal and Elizabeth deserved a romantic one.

Nick was determined to give Elizabeth what she deserved, starting with a proper proposal. He took Elizabeth's hand in his as he knelt on one knee. He brought her hand up to his lips as his eyes searched hers for a sign of hope.

"You truly wish for us to marry?" Elizabeth could not believe what she was hearing. This was what she too had wanted for years.

"Yes, Elizabeth Dawson. I truly wish for us to marry." Nick's eyes pleaded with hers. "I cannot promise you a life of luxury as you have grown up in, but I promise that I will love you for eternity. Would you do me the honor of becoming my wife?"

Nick grew nervous as he watched the expressions on Elizabeth's face change. She was stunned, shocked, or was she surprised, which he was not sure of, perhaps she was a bit of all three. Was she happy that he had proposed? Was this what she wanted or was he wrong to have hoped it was true? All he was sure of, was that waiting for her answer felt like he was lost in time, nothing seemed to be moving in the world for him right now.

"Yes." Elizabeth smiled at Nick. "A thousand times, yes!"

Nick quickly stood up and wrapped his arms around her waist. Elizabeth threw her arms around Nick's neck as he lifted her off her feet and twirled her around. Nick was everything that she wanted. She did not care that he had no title. She knew that Nick loved her and that she loved him. Title or no title, she wished for nothing more than to be the wife of Sir Nicholas Shaw.

After a long tender kiss, Nick knew that he had to get Elizabeth back below deck. They needed to rest for a few hours before they docked in France. Preparations had to be made to keep Elizabeth and himself hidden while the Duke's mysterious guest was on board The Em.

Once they were safely back in London, he and Elizabeth would head north, toward Scotland. They would journey to the same little town, just south of the Scottish boarder, that his parents had gotten married in. He prayed that they could make it to Camden and find a minister before the Duke caught up with them.

When The Em docked in France, just hours before daybreak, the crew, along with Nick and Elizabeth, went to their assigned stations around the ship. Maxx, Paul, Harper, and Doug were the only ones that left the ship. They each carried a crate of wine to Mr. Baston's shop.

Maxx had only traded with this one merchant in France for years. Mr. Baston was shocked to see the Captain at such and odd hour of the night. Still, the little man quickly opened the door to his shop and ushered them inside.

After they settled on a price for the crates of wine, Mr. Baston led Maxx to the private entrance to the Corbel Hotel next door. Maxx and his crew had used this hidden entrance many times over the years but never at this hour.

Maxx hated waking Mr. and Mrs. Corbel at this hour. The couple was groggy but happy to see Maxx. Their daughter, Briley, hurried down the stairs. Briley was overjoyed to see Maxx. The Corbel's son, Damien, went to stand watch at the front doors, while his parents talked with Maxx.

"If it were not for this mysterious passenger for the Duke, I would carry you all home to Hartford tonight." Maxx wanted to do this, but this mysterious passenger had the entire crew on edge.

"We are safe here, for now." Mrs. Corbel assured Maxx.

"We are ready to go at a moment's notice, when necessary." Mr. Corbel walked Maxx to the door.

The Corbel family hugged Maxx and his crew goodbye. Hopefully soon, The Em could return to France and carry the family back to England. For tonight, Maxx assumed a darker mission lay ahead of him and his loyal crew.

At four in the morning, Maxx knocked on the door of the Poncelet Hotel that was down the street from the Corbel family. The little man that answered the door was short and as rounded as he was tall. He clearly did not like being summoned at this hour.

"May I help you gentlemen?" The night clerk was upset but he was still polite.

"Tell Sebastian that we are here." Maxx gave the message, just as the Duke had instructed him to do.

The night clerk nodded his head once before he hurried to the back of the hotel. Maxx pointed toward the front doors, instructing Harper and Doug to keep watch. Paul, like always, stayed by Maxx's side.

Soon the night clerk returned with a tall skinny man following him. This man was well dressed in a business suit and a matching hat that Maxx thought looked funny on top of his head.

"You sent for me?" Sebastian asked.

"The Duke requests your presence." Maxx repeated the sentence, just as Sam had instructed, as he handed Sebastian a sealed letter from the Duke.

After reading the letter, Sebastian took his satchel from the night clerk and bid the man farewell. Sebastian walked over to the fireplace and tossed the letter from the Duke into the flames. He nodded his head at Maxx and motioned with his hand toward the front doors.

The moment they boarded the ship, The Em set sail for the return voyage to London Harbor. Paul showed Mr. Sebastian to the cabin next to his. Nick had gathered his things and moved over to the Captain's quarters. When Maxx entered the room, Nick and Elizabeth were still awake, sitting at the table.

"I have never heard Sam mention anyone by the name of Sebastian before." Elizabeth was sure of this.

"The man is mysterious, but I get the feeling that I have seen him before." Maxx sat down at his desk. There was something familiar about the man, but Maxx just could not place what it was.

"At least you have safely pulled off getting in and out of France tonight." Nick was still nervous though.

"The only thing we have to worry about between here and London is the Royal Navy and The Raven." Maxx went over and laid down on a cot that he placed across the doorway.

"Pirates? We have to worry about pirates?" Elizabeth was now terrified.

The stories of Captain Sayer had made their way into Greyham Court. Even Elizabeth knew of the notorious pirate's reputation. Captain Sayer drove fear into the hearts of everyone, even that of the Duke's household.

"Let us hope not." Maxx pulled his blanket over himself. "Now rest while you can." Maxx turned on his side to face the door with his sword by his side.

Neither Maxx nor his crew would sleep this night, but they were hoping to give Sebastian the idea that they were all comfortable with him being on board. They also did not want to let the man know that Nick and Elizabeth were on the ship. Every precaution that could be thought of was being taken tonight.

Elizabeth climbed into the Captain's huge bed. Once she was settled under the covers, Nick doused the lantern and went over to his cot next to the bed. Nick doubted that any of them would rest while the mysterious man was across the way. Guards were stationed outside the door, but this was still not enough to settle the hearts of everyone on board The Em.

Nick leaned over and gave Elizabeth a tender kiss. Soon, she would be his wife and the Duke would have to come to terms with that one day. Nick took Elizabeth's hand in his, as he laid down on the cot next to her. This was going to be a long night for them all.

Chapter Twenty-Seven

The voyage back to London took longer than Maxx had hoped. The crew of The Em was on edge all day with the mysterious friend of the Duke on board. The whole day was a curious one indeed.

Sebastian remained in his cabin the entire day. The only time the Duke's friend opened the door to his cabin, was when Ollie brought a food tray to him. When Sebastian finished eating, he would put the food tray on the floor outside his door.

The sun had set, and darkness now surrounded them. Maxx thought that losing the wind for a few hours today may have been a blessing after all. Now they could dock in London Harbor under the cover of darkness. Sebastian would be able to slip away into the shadows of the night, unseen.

Maxx and Paul had been on deck for most of the day. Around the time of the sun setting, a ship was spotted in the distance. To the natural eye, it was just another ship that was possibly heading to London. Through the spy glass, it was confirmed that the ship following them was in fact The Raven.

When they were within an hour of making port, Maxx went below deck to check on things. He was ready to get all three of his passengers off The Em. The Duke's mysterious guest had only been seen at mealtimes through the door of his cabin.

Maxx and Paul had dined in the Captain's quarters. Doing so allowed food to be brought in for Nick and Elizabeth. This was another step that prevented the strange guest across the way from being alerted to Nick and Elizabeth's presence on board the ship.

Nick and Elizabeth were relieved to know that this voyage was almost over. They were grateful to have been able to pull off being hidden away from the Duke's friend. If Sebastian told Sam they were on board The Em, it would make things harder for Maxx. They both were however alarmed to hear that The Raven was behind them in the distance. Could they survive an attack from the notorious pirate ship if an attack came?

"Are we truly safe?" Elizabeth was frightened.

"The Raven is not after us." Maxx sat down at his desk.

"Are you sure of that?" Nick looked out the cabin windows, but he could not see the pirate ship.

"If the Raven wanted us, they would have caught up with us by now." Maxx poured himself a mug of rum. "The pirates have held their distance from us for several hours."

Nick sighed deeply and shook his head. He was ready for this adventure at sea to be over with. The sooner they docked and were free of the mysterious guest, the sooner he and Elizabeth could be on their way to Camden. Hopefully, in an hour or two this would be over with.

Everyone froze when an unexpected knock came upon the door. Maxx held his hands out, signally for Nick and Elizabeth to remain still. Hopefully, it was only Paul outside the door.

"Captain, Mr. Sebastian would like to have a word with you." Harper spoke loudly from the other side of the door.

Nick and Elizabeth had no idea what to do now. They did not expect Sebastian to be at the Captain's door. Thankfully, Maxx was somewhat prepared for this. Maxx got up and took Nick by his arm.

"One moment." Maxx spoke loudly, without opening the door.

There was no time to think his plan through. Maxx pulled out a cabinet, that had shelves for books and artifacts above it. The lower cabinet and the upper shelves moved as one piece, which was a hidden door. Maxx shoved Nick inside the hidden room. He put his finger to his lips, telling Nick to stay quiet.

Once Nick was hidden away, Maxx hurried over to Elizabeth. Her eyes were wide with fear. This was a moment that they all had hoped would not happen. The quiet mysterious man across the way now made his presence known to them.

"I am so sorry about this." Maxx spoke just above a whisper.

"What…" Elizabeth was confused.

Elizabeth did not have time to respond. Maxx quickly turned her around and undone the strings on the back of her dress. In one quick motion, Maxx pulled her dress down, dropping the garment at her feet. Next, Maxx unfastened her corset and tossed it on the floor.

Elizabeth's mouth flew open as she used her arms to try and cover herself. Even though she still wore her shift and undergarments, she was still embarrassed. No man had ever seen her without her being fully dressed, until now.

Maxx paid her shock and embarrassment no mind. He jerked back the covers on the huge bed and pointed for Elizabeth to get under the blankets. Elizabeth frantically shook her head. She was not sure about this idea. Maxx could not wait any longer, he grabbed her by the arm and, as gently as he could, he pushed her on the bed.

"Face the wall, and no matter what happens, do not turn over." Maxx whispered next to her ear.

Maxx took Elizabeth's hair and tussled it about. He covered her with the blankets to where only part of her blonde hair was visible. From this view, he was sure that Elizabeth Dawson would look like any other woman with blonde hair.

Maxx removed his boots and pushed them aside. He took off his pants and let them fall next to Elizabeth's dress. Maxx's shirt was long and almost fell to his knees. Maxx gave a quick glance around the cabin to make sure that it looked alright. Satisfied at the appearance of things, Maxx opened the door.

"I just wanted to thank you before we docked." Sebastian brushed past Maxx as he walked into the Captain's quarters without being invited in.

"Personally, I am glad it is almost over with." Maxx glared at Sebastian.

"Oh, my word." Sebastian noticed the woman in the Captain's bed. "Captain, please forgive me. I was unaware that you were entertaining."

"Well, France does have many beautiful aspects about her, does she not?" Maxx looked over at Elizabeth and smiled.

"I will have to agree with you on that." Sebastian awkwardly cleared his throat. "Again, you have my thanks, Captain."

"I hope that the Duke will be pleased to see you." Maxx watched Sebastian closely. The man appeared to be quite uncomfortable.

"I am sure he will." Sebastian held his hand to the side of his face, blocking his view of the woman in the Captain's bed.

"Now, Sebastian, if you will excuse me. I am rather busy." Maxx looked over to Elizabeth's back and smiled.

"You are truly a weasel." Sebastian laughed as he quickly left the Captain's quarters.

With the door now bolted, Maxx hurried over to the hidden door and let Nick out. Nick took one look at Maxx, in his long shirt, and his eyes widened. Nick's mouth almost dropped to the floor when he saw Elizabeth's dress in a heap on the floor, next to Maxx's pants and boots.

Slowly, Nick's eyes moved over to the Captain's bed. Elizabeth was sitting in the middle of the huge bed with the blankets covering her. Her knees were pulled up to her and her arms were locked around her legs. Her long blonde hair flowed over her shoulders and was tussled about loosely. Elizabeth smiled awkwardly at Nick.

After Maxx put his pants and boots back on, Nick grabbed the little Captain and lifted him off the floor. He had heard many stories of some of Maxx's hairbrained ideas but this one took the cake.

"Put me down before I let myself down." Maxx was stern. "Do not give our ruse away now or the Duke will know exactly where you are." Nick cautiously set the little Captain back on his feet.

"I should kill you for this." Nick spoke in a loud whisper as he pointed at Maxx.

"I am afraid that you will have to get in line for that." Maxx walked over and picked up Elizabeth's dress.

"Everyone is truly right." Nick glared at Maxx. "You are a weasel."

"I was not a weasel when you needed my help." Maxx tossed the dress at Nick and left the cabin.

Nick stared at the closed door of the Captain's quarters. He was not sure how his brothers and cousins managed to put up with the outlandish tricks of Maxwell Spencer.

Nick was beyond ready to get off this ship and head to Camden. Elizabeth was his only concern. If this little ruse of the good Captain ever got out and caused Elizabeth grief, he would have no choice but to demand a duel with the little Earl of Hartford.

Chapter Twenty-Eight

Nick handed Elizabeth her corset and turned away as she put it on. With his back still turned to her, he handed Elizabeth her dress and waited patiently as she redressed herself. Maxwell Spencer should have known better than to have treated a lady in such a manner.

"I am truly sorry that you had to do that." Nick was seriously upset with Maxx's little ruse.

"Please do not let the matter trouble you so." Elizabeth put her hand on Nick's arm, once she was fully dressed again.

"You cannot tell me that you enjoyed being a part of that little theatrical display?" Nick turned around to face her.

"Enjoyed is not quite the word that I would use." Elizabeth lightly laughed as she looked up at Nick. "But it did work."

"Maxx thinks of no one." Nick was highly frustrated. "He does not think about how his actions will affect others in the future. He just lives for the moment."

"I am going to have to disagree with you on that." Elizabeth put her arms around Nick's waist. "From what I have seen of Maxwell Spencer, he puts others before himself on a regular basis."

Nick wrapped his arms around Elizabeth and held her close. The last thing his family needed, was another woman devoted to Maxwell Spencer. He did not wish to discuss their little Captain right now. What Nick wanted, was to get off this ship and be on their way. He would leave the overly free-spirited Maxwell Spencer to his brothers and cousins from now on.

Within an hour, Nick had his wish. Maxx had him and Elizabeth to wait to disembark the ship for half an hour after Sebastian had left. Maxx sent Ollie and Doug to follow the Duke's mysterious friend. Nick did not wait around to know more. He and Elizabeth hurried to the Blume'N Brew to get his horse.

Miss Nancie had Nick and Elizabeth to wait in her private dining room while she prepared them a satchel of food for their journey.

Jerry hurried out to the back of the stables to saddle Nick's horse. He was sure that the young couple would need to leave as quickly as possible. Rachel rushed into the room and gave Elizabeth a hug, she was happy to see her again.

"I got the paper the past couple of days for you." Rachel joined Elizabeth at the table.

"Thank you." Elizabeth opened one of the papers and quickly flipped to the advertisement pages.

"How will you know if a post is from your brother?" Rachel opened the other paper.

"It will be short and vague." Elizabeth ran her fingers over the advertisements.

"Like this one?" Rachel pointed to a small advertisement in the middle of the back page of the paper.

"Yes, this is it." Elizabeth's excitement faded as she read her brother's message. She sat back in her chair and looked at Nick across the table.

"What does it say?" Nick asked.

Rachel pushed the paper across the table to Nick and pointed at the advertisement. She put her arm around Elizabeth's shoulders to comfort her, as Nick read the message. Nick clearly understood the vague message that read:

E, Home! Now! S.

Nick could tell by the expression on Elizabeth's face that she was disappointed with the message she found from her brother. A part of her had hoped that her brother would listen to her and see her side of the situation. Nick could not help but to wonder if she genuinely wanted to keep running or not.

"You two be careful." Miss Nancie hugged them when they walked down to the side door of the pub.

After saying their goodbyes to Miss Nancie, Rachel, and Jerry, Nick and Elizabeth were on their way out of London. A couple of hours later they arrived at the Ridgewell Inn on the northern side of London. Nick had acquired a room for the night under a fake name.

He introduced Elizabeth to the night clerk as his wife. In a few days' time that would not be a lie.

Nick turned his back and watched out the window while Elizabeth changed into her nightdress. He knew this inn well. His family had stayed here several times over the years. This was also the inn that Roger Holden had brought Abby and Dani to the night he kidnapped them over a year ago.

Once Elizabeth had changed, she sat down at the vanity, and stared at her reflection in the mirror. The woman staring back at her no longer appeared sweet and innocent. She sighed deeply as she pulled out a brush from her satchel and started brushing her long hair. Nick leaned against the window frame and watched her for a while.

Elizabeth was beautiful, anyone could clearly see this. She was also kind and innocent to many ways of the world. She was no longer innocent to the true cruelty of others for she had seen a side of evil that Nick wished upon no one. Still, Elizabeth was a true lady in every aspect, there was no denying that either. Even the way she held herself when she walked, said that she was much more than just a common woman.

Nick knew that he could never be the higher society gentleman that Elizabeth should rightly marry. He felt greatly blessed that she had chosen him. He vowed to himself that he would spend the rest of his life trying to be the man that she truly deserved.

"Are you absolutely sure that you wish to elope like this?" Nick took the brush from her hand and started brushing out the back of her hair.

"Yes, I am absolutely sure." Elizabeth smiled as she looked up at Nick in the mirror.

"You deserve a nice wedding, with your family and friends around you." Nick was sad because eloping would rob Elizabeth of the grand wedding befitting of a lady.

Elizabeth turned around in her chair. She took Nick's hand in hers and gently tugged on his arm. Nick knelt beside her. She wanted to encourage him and give him the strength to dare believe in the wonderful life ahead of them.

"I deserve you." Elizabeth placed the palm of her hand against his cheek.

"I…" Nick tried to protest but Elizabeth placed a finger to his lips and shook her head.

How could she make him see that he was all that she truly needed? Surely, he knew her heart by now. If it were not for the rules of society and birth statuses, there would be no need for this conversation. She loved him and nothing would change that.

"Do not try to talk yourself out of marrying me just because you are worried about the things you believe that I should have." Elizabeth leaned forward and boldly placed a tender kiss on his lips.

"I just do not wish for you to regret your decision years from now." Nick placed his forehead against hers.

"If we lived in a world where it was possible to marry with both of us surrounded by our families and friends, then I would love to have a simple wedding." A part of Elizabeth wished that this could be so.

"Yet, we do not live in that world." Nick knew that this was true.

Elizabeth's family wished for her to marry within her own social status. Marrying him was stepping down several of the society ranks for Elizabeth. Nick had no right to ask this of her, for she deserved a man far greater than himself.

"Material things do not matter to me, as they do for my mother and sister." Elizabeth leaned back and looked Nick in the eye. "A life without you in it, now that would be my greatest regret."

Nick stood up and pulled Elizabeth to her feet. He took her into his arms and kissed her passionately. Elizabeth put her arms around his neck, pulling Nick closer to her. She hungrily kissed him with a passion that matched his own.

Before they were completely lost in their passion, Nick ended their kiss. She was not his wife yet, and he would not let the passion between them go any further until she was completely his. Elizabeth was a true treasure, and he would honor her in every way possible.

It had been a long day and they both needed rest. Nick led her over to the bed, they both were very tired. Neither of them had gotten much rest aboard The Em last night. Elizabeth climbed under the covers and settled down for the night. Nick took the extra pillow from the bed and made a pallet on the rug, next to the bed, with the blankets he had found in the wardrobe.

"Are you applying to be my new lady's maid?" Elizabeth teased as Nick tucked her in.

"Oh, Lady Elizabeth. I am applying to be so much more than a lady's maid." Nick smiled and gave her a quick kiss goodnight.

Nick went over and made sure that the door was bolted. He placed a chair in front of the door, as a warning if anyone tried to enter their room during the night. He doused out the lantern on the small stand by the bed, before lying down on his makeshift bed for the night. He did not like sleeping on wooden floors, but he would not disgrace Elizabeth by sharing a bed with her until they were husband and wife.

In three to four days, if no other obstacles fell in their path, they would reach Camden. Nick would find a minister and he would marry Elizabeth that very day.

Chapter Twenty-Nine

The next morning, Nick and Elizabeth went downstairs and ate their breakfast in the dining area of the inn. It was nice for them to be able to sit in public together for a few minutes. Still, not wishing to be recognized, they quickly ate their meal and hurried back upstairs to get their things.

Elizabeth followed Nick back down the stairs. As Nick hurried over to turn in their room key, Elizabeth waited for him at the bottom of the stairs. She was tying her cloak around her when someone grabbed her from behind. A large hand covered her mouth, preventing her from screaming.

In one swift movement, the man flipped Elizabeth around to face him when they were near the back door of the inn. She was pinned against the wall with the man's hand still covering her mouth. Elizabeth's hazel eyes, that were filled with fear, locked with the bright green eyes of Roger Holden.

Elizabeth tried to fight Roger off, as he pulled her through the back door of the inn. After several intense moments of struggling against Roger, while he was pulling her toward the stables behind the inn, Elizabeth managed to get his hand away from her mouth.

"Nick!" Elizabeth screamed as loudly as she could. "Nick!"

"My Lord, this is a horrible idea." Oliver Phelps protested Roger's desire to kidnap Elizabeth. "Leave the girl."

"Horrible or not, she is coming with us!" Roger growled at Oliver.

"Nick!" Elizabeth continued to scream. "Nick!"

"Shut up, you worthless twit!" Roger slapped Elizabeth across her face, just as Nick came running out the back door of the inn.

Nick pulled out his sword as he raced toward them. He would make Roger Holden pay for hurting Elizabeth, here and now. Seeing Nick running toward them, Oliver Phelps ran toward the Earl of Statham's carriage and quickly got in.

Roger Holden weighed the situation before him. Did he want the Duke's sister bad enough to fight for her? He wanted no woman bad enough to duel another man for her. Besides, he did not come to Ridgewell Inn prepared for a battle. He certainly was not going to risk his life over the broken, battered, and ruined sister of the Duke.

Roger smiled slyly at Nick, as he shoved Elizabeth to the ground. Roger, like his cowardly friend, ran toward the carriage. Nick pulled out his pistol and was only able to fire a single shot before Roger disappeared into the carriage. With a shout from Roger, the driver snapped the reins and the carriage bolted toward London.

Nick ran to Elizabeth and helped her off the ground. He took her in his arms and held her while she cried. A couple of the stable hands from the inn hurried over and offered to help them. Nick assured them that they were fine, and he waved the stable hands away. Nick quickly ushered Elizabeth to the stables.

"He hit you." Nick could see the red handprint on her face.

"He is a horrible man." Elizabeth turned her face away.

"I will see to it that Roger Holden pays dearly, for everything that he has done to you. I will not stop until he is held accountable." Nick vowed to Elizabeth. It was one vow he would keep, or he would die trying.

"Roger gets away with everything." Elizabeth, like everyone else, had seen this many of times over the years.

"I promise you that Roger Holden's time will come." Nick assured her.

Nick wanted to keep comforting her, but he knew that they had to get to Camden. There was not a moment to be spared now that they had been seen together. The Duke was bound to hear of it soon. He had no doubt that Roger would make sure that Sam knew where they were.

Nick had Elizabeth to hold the reins while he saddled his horse. He had already seen how much she carried for Toby. Sometimes, talking to animals helped to comfort a person's spirit. Well, it had always helped him when he was feeling poorly. From the look of things, talking to Toby was helping Elizabeth too.

"What a pretty boy you are." Elizabeth rubbed Toby on the head as she gave him an apple.

"You are going to spoil my horse, if you keep that up." Nick smiled at her.

"Toby deserves to be spoiled." Elizabeth continued to pet the horse.

"Can you ride?" Nick hated to have to rush her, but they needed to be moving.

"Of course. I am ready to reach Camden." Elizabeth was as eager to marry Nick as he was to marry her.

Nick helped Elizabeth up onto his horse. He led Toby out of the stables before mounting. They headed north at a fast pace. He and Elizabeth needed to find a minister that would agree to marry them before the Duke could stop them.

***

Roger Holden sat in his carriage, holding his left shoulder. Nick's single gunshot had managed to graze him. He was furious and would not let this matter rest. After stopping in London at Doctor Ramsey's office to get bandaged up, Roger went to Greyham Court.

The guards at Greyham Court were under strict orders to not allow the Earl of Statham to enter the property. Instead, the guards surrounded Roger and escorted him to the Blume'N Brew, where the Duke was meeting with the tracking party.

Two of the Duke's guards escorted Roger Holden into the pub. Every man in the pub stood up and pulled out their sword, or a pistol, and pointed it at the Earl of Statham. The Duke was the only one that remained sitting. Sam folded his hands and propped his chin on them, as he waited for his guards to bring Roger over to Maxx's private table in the back corner of the pub.

"You do not seem to be well received here." Sam motioned for Roger to sit down across the table from him.

"From this lot, I am not at all surprised." Roger glanced around the pub before looking back at the Duke. "I am, however, surprised to see that you are rolling around in the dirt with these dogs."

Roger's smug grin was quickly wiped from his face when Maxwell Spencer grabbed the back of his head and tilted it backwards. Fear rose in Roger's eyes when Maxx placed a dagger at his throat.

"I know where your sister is!" Roger shouted, hoping the Duke would come to his rescue.

"Let him go, Spencer," The Duke ordered.

Maxx continued to hold Roger's head back. His eyes bore into Roger's. This was the only man that Maxx wanted to kill. Maxx pushed the tip of the dagger slightly into Roger's throat. The blade pierced Roger's skin and a droplet of blood ran down his neck.

"Easy." Gavin placed his hand over Maxx's and gradually pulled the dagger away from Roger's throat.

With the dagger now in Gavin's hand, everyone in the pub relaxed and released the breath they were holding. Alex pulled Maxx over to a chair in the back corner. It was best to put as much distance as possible between Maxx and Roger Holden. At least until they could hear the snake out. One day, Alex would make sure that Roger Holden would never get another chance to hurt the people he cared about.

"Not here. Not now." Alex whispered to Maxx.

"We will all live to regret not doing so now." Maxx was sure of it.

Alex patted Maxx on his shoulder before turning back toward Sam and Roger. Paul came and stood by Maxx's other side. There was not a man in the pub that did not hate Roger Holden. With the Duke and his guards present, no one advanced on Holden, instead everyone held their positions.

Gavin dropped a cloth, that Miss Nancie handed to him, on the table in front of Roger. Holden quickly picked the cloth up and held it to his throat. He knew that the wound was not severe, but Roger glared at Maxx anyway. Maxx took this as a challenge and tried to stand up. Alex and Paul held the little Captain in his chair.

"I do believe that you have news of my sister, do you not?" Sam tapped the table, drawing Roger's attention. "Or would you prefer that I let Spencer finish what he started? Apparently, you have already had some misfortune today."

"This is nothing." Roger favored his left shoulder. He thought it best not to discuss his injury. "I saw your sister this morning."

"Which sister did you see? We all hear that you and Anne have become extremely chummy these days." Alex folded his arms across his chest as he glared at Roger.

"Elizabeth." Roger spoke quickly to the Duke. "I saw Elizabeth with Nicholas Shaw."

Gavin sighed as he looked over at Alex. Their cousin was on the run with Elizabeth Dawson and he was taking some huge chances. The Duke seemed to have a short temper where his sister was concerned. Gavin feared that if they did not find Nick and Elizabeth soon, that they may not be able to help their cousin in the end.

"And where exactly did you see my sister and Sir Nicholas Shaw?" Sam was already growing tired of Roger and his theatrics. "Or do I need to force that information out of you?"

Gavin stepped backwards until he was standing next to Alex. Perhaps it was not such a bad idea to let the Duke handle Roger Holden on his own. The Duke would be doing the Shaw family a huge favor if he did. Sam had already proved that he had a deep dark side, last year, when he helped in rescuing Abby and Dani from Roger.

"The Ridgewell Inn." Roger was even more nervous now. "They shared a room at the Ridgewell Inn."

"Take Lord Holden to Statham Hall." Sam ordered his Captain of the Guard. "See to it that he remains there until you hear from me."

"Very well, Your Grace." Sir Oscar Donaldson took Roger by the arm and pulled him to his feet.

"I do not wish to go home." Roger protested.

"You will go home, and you will remain there." Sam stood up and looked Roger in the eye. "If I find that you have lied to me, I will drag you out of Statham Hall and I will personally deliver you to the Earl of Hartford, to do with as he sees fit."

"You cannot do this!" Roger shouted as Sir Donaldson pulled him from the pub. Roger's protests were ignored by the Duke.

"You now have a sighting." Sam looked over at Alex. "I suggest that you start tracking."

Chapter Thirty

The members of the Duke's tracking party hurried outside to prepare their horses to travel. Gavin, Alex, and Maxx said their goodbyes to Miss Nancie. She gave each of them, and Paul, a satchel with provisions for their journey. Alex was grateful that the little pub owner was being kind to him once again. He also was becoming angry with the task that was being forced upon him.

"It is not right that I have to track my own cousin." Alex mounted his horse. "And to what end?"

"The Duke has lost his mind for sure." Paul rode up beside Alex.

"That is why we will all surround Nick and protect him from the Duke." Maxx had no intention of letting Sam harm Nick.

As they were riding out of the side entrance of the Blume'N Brew, Nick's brother Jackson joined them. Gavin wondered if Jax's presence in the tracking party was a good idea. Could Jax handle tracking his own brother?

"You do not have to join us." Gavin rode alongside of Jax. "None of us want to be here and you should not have to help hunt for your own brother."

"My mother is in pieces." Jax looked straight ahead. The sight of his mother had torn his heart out. "I have to do something, for her sake, and my own." He felt helpless just sitting at home.

Lady Clara was in such a state of distress that she had taken to her private room, which she hardly ever used, and refused to see anyone. Gavin and Alex's mother had traveled to Kinsley Estate to comfort her sister-in-law. Lady Caroline was the only person that Jax's mother would allow into her room.

Caleb had remained at Ellis Manor and continued to help Nate watch over Lord Matthew. Caleb still feared that if he left Ellis Manor, the Duke would find a way to force him into helping with tracking Nick and Elizabeth. Caleb would flee from the Duke before he would ever track his own brother.

Jax was glad to hear that there had been a sighting of his brother and Lady Elizabeth. Perhaps now they could bring this devilish nightmare to an end. Jax, like everyone else, could not understand why the Duke let Roger Holden leave so easily. The evil snake should be arrested and hanged for his crimes. Jax and the others knew that Roger had always hidden behind so many other people. It would be hard to make an arrest turn into a conviction without proper proof.

When they reached the Ridgewell Inn, the Duke was well received by the owners of the inn. Everyone was amazed at how polite and kind Sam was with Mr. Ridgewell. Mr. Ridgewell offered Sam a room where he could privately question the servants about his sister.

"Why does he not speak with us like that?" Jax wondered.

"Would you like to ask him?" Alex gestured toward the Duke. Jax shook his head.

"Your Grace!" Maxx waved his hand in the air. Sam looked over at Maxx, clearly annoyed. "We were wondering, why do you not speak kindly to the rest of us, as you have with Mr. Ridgewell?"

Gavin sighed and shook his head. Why did his brother and cousin have to give his best friend ludicrous ideas? There was no way that this situation would end well. Maxx was a great friend, but he seriously knew how to get under people's skin at times. Sam, for some unknown reason, seemed to be easily annoyed by Maxx.

"Because I happen to like Mr. Ridgewell." Sam narrowed his eyes at Maxx.

"Well, there you have it." Maxx put his hand on Jax's shoulder and rolled his eyes. "We can now end hunger, wars, and all manner of diseases with that noble answer."

Maxx turned and left the inn before the Duke could shout at him again. Maxx had about enough of Samuel Dawson's presence today. How was he going to survive the next five years was beyond his thinking for now? He had no doubts that the Duke would run him ragged before his time was up.

Alex found Maxx in the stables behind the inn. He was sitting in a chair, propped up against the wall of one of the stalls. Alex waved a bottle of rum in front of Maxx's face. Usually Alex protested his drinking. Was this a trick? Maxx narrowed his eyes at Alex. He quickly grabbed the bottle and opened it before Alex could change his mind.

"I hope you brought one of your own." Maxx turned the bottle up. It had been a hard day.

"Why, Little Man, do you mean that you will not share with me?" Alex laughed as he grabbed a chair and joined Maxx.

"I never share rum on a bad day." Maxx rubbed his forehead. Listening to the demanding little Duke all day, had given him a headache.

"I'm good." Alex laughed as he held up another bottle of rum.

"Switching to rum, I see." Maxx turned his bottle up again. "You will still never be like me."

"Thank the Lord." Alex rolled his eyes upward.

Gavin and Jax soon found them in the stables. They left the Duke to handle the questioning of the servants on his own. They pulled out a couple of stools and sat down.

"I hope you brought your own bottle, for our little Earl here, refuses to share." Alex laughed as he pointed at Maxx.

"We are covered." Paul walked in with a bottle of brandy and handed Gavin and Jax a glass.

The three Shaw men talked about what they could possibly do that would help Nick when they finally found him and Elizabeth. It was a tricky situation for sure, but they all agreed that it needed to end, and soon. The Duke was not sharing what his plans were just yet for Nick and that had them all worried.

When Alex was not looking, Maxx switched out his almost empty bottle of rum for Alex's half of a bottle. Paul shook his head at Maxx. Maxx put his finger to his lips and shook his head. Paul knew it was a bad idea, but he remained quiet. Just as Maxx finished off the half bottle of rum, the Duke came rushing into the stables.

"Good, you all are here." Sam was excited.

Sam filled them all in on what he had learned from questioning the servants at the inn. One of the stable hands had seen Roger Holden pulling Elizabeth out the back door of the inn. He even saw Roger slap Elizabeth and then run away when Nick came after him. The wound to Roger's shoulder was from being shot by Nick.

"This is good news, how exactly?" Gavin asked.

"And you are happy for what reason?" Jax did not have a sister, but he would not be happy to know that a man had slapped her if he did have one.

"I now have proof that Roger Holden hit my sister. There is now a witness to Holden's actions. Which means, the Earl of Statham can now be officially charged." Sam could not believe that he had to explain this.

"That is good news." Gavin was now a bit excited himself.

"Now, we just need to find Sir Nicholas and my sister." Sam looked over at Alex. "The stable hand said that they headed north. Do you have any idea where they would go for the night?"

"There is another inn about a day's ride from here." Alex told the Duke.

"If we were to ride through the night, perhaps we can catch them by morning." Sam started to walk away, he turned back and looked at Gavin. "Get everyone ready to ride."

"Are we seriously going to ride through the night? Is that a wise idea?" Jax was not looking forward to this.

"Think of it as an adventure." Maxx held up the bottle of rum before turning it up, emptying the bottle.

"Can he ride?" Sam walked back and looked at Maxx.

"He will be fine, Your Grace." Paul took the empty bottle away from Maxx.

"If he falls off his horse and dies tonight, that is on all of you." Sam pointed between the four men before he hurried away to give the order to ride to his guards.

"I do not understand." Alex held the two empty bottles of rum in his hands. "It usually takes three bottles of rum before Maxx is loopy like this."

"Perhaps this explains it." Paul held up the empty bottle of brandy.

"You gave him the rum, so you watch him." Gavin angrily pointed his finger at Alex.

"Paul brought the brandy!" Alex shouted after Gavin, who had walked away to start saddling the horses.

"I got the Captain." Paul helped Maxx to his feet.

"I will help Gavin with the horses." Jax hurried away.

"I do not mind watching Maxx." Alex put his arm around Maxx. "You go and help them saddle our horses."

"Very well." Paul nodded and reluctantly left Maxx to Alex.

"Little Man, you have got to slow down on your drinking." Alex helped Maxx over to his horse.

"But why? It is the only thing I can trust now." Maxx almost fell as Alex helped him up onto his horse.

"It makes you stupid." Alex handed Maxx the reins. "Are you sure that you can do this?" Alex was not so sure Maxx could ride in his condition.

"I'm good." Maxx nodded his head. The movement made him nauseous and he put his hand over his mouth.

"If you lose your stomach on me, I am going to make you wash my clothes." Alex laughed as he walked over and mounted his horse.

"Please, keep your clothes on." Maxx held his hand toward Alex as he looked away.

Paul handed Maxx a cool cloth, that one of the stable hands had given to him, so that Maxx could wash his face. Hopefully, this would help for they did not have time to give the Captain some coffee. The Duke and his guards were ready to ride.

"Little Man, you stay beside me." Alex rode next to Maxx.

"Why? Do you need my protection?" Maxx looked over at Alex from the corner of his eye.

"Oh, you trying to unsheathe a sword right now, would be a hilarious event but let us not tempt fate today." Alex laughed as they headed north from Ridgewell Inn.

Chapter Thirty-One

Nick and Elizabeth had to leave Ridgewell Inn in a hurry. Nick wanted to get them as far away as he possibly could, and he had to do it quickly. They spent the day traveling at a fast pace. He admired how Elizabeth had manage to show the strength to keep going even when she felt tired.

They had now been recognized and by someone who would gladly turn them over to the Duke the first chance he got. Roger Holden had probably already been to see Sam. If that were true, then his time with Elizabeth was now short.

They had stopped only a couple of times throughout the day and just long enough to feed and water Toby. At the river, Nick took one of his shirts and ripped it to make a cloth. He dipped the cloth into the cool water of the river. Gently, he placed the cloth against Elizabeth's cheek.

The light red handprint on her face was already starting to fade. The cool cloth would help to ensure that the mark did not cause her cheek to swell. Thankfully, this mark should not leave a bruise, as the other marks Roger Holden had given to Elizabeth did.

"There is a small village ahead. We can rest for a couple of hours and get a decent meal. Toby will sure need to rest for a few hours as well." Nick looked down the road, to ensure that they were not being followed.

If Roger Holden had a man at Ridgewell Inn, that he could spare, there were no doubts that man would be after them now. Elizabeth was tired and this was clearly noticeable to Nick. She did enjoy the sound of stopping, even if it was only for a few hours.

"Then let us hurry on." Elizabeth gave the best smile that she could manage.

Nick gave her a quick kiss before helping her up onto his horse. He led Toby from the river, back up to the road. The road was a risky move, but time was too short for them to be able to hide in the forest this time. If they did not reach Camden soon, Nick feared that he would lose Elizabeth forever.

Satisfied that they were not being followed, Nick mounted his horse. With his arms securely locked around Elizabeth, Nick urged Toby on, once again at a fast pace.

It was late when Nick and Elizabeth rode into the small village of Delane. The shops were already closed and very few people were moving about on the streets. The only places still open were the pub, the inn, and the restaurant. Nick had not been here in a couple of years and the village seemed to have grown slightly.

Nick would like nothing more than to get a room at the inn for the night. However, he could not take that chance after running into Roger Holden. The inn would be the first place that the Duke would go to looking for them. He hated it, but it looked as though they would have to ride through the night.

After leaving Toby at the village stables, Nick and Elizabeth went to the town restaurant. It was near closing time, so there were not too many guests in the restaurant. It was nice to be able to sit and relax after a day of riding hard.

"Where would you like to go, once we are married?" Nick whispered across the table.

"Let me see." Elizabeth thought for a moment. "Scotland. I would love to see Scotland."

"Then Scotland it is." Nick was more than happy to make this wish come true for his bride to be.

Elizabeth smiled up at their young server as she poured them both a fresh cup of tea. Nick loved seeing Elizabeth happy. Her smile brightened his darkest days. With her by his side, he knew he would live a full and happy life.

They left the restaurant just as the owners were locking up. There was a bit of a chill in the air tonight. Nick put his arm around Elizabeth as they walked toward the stables. He worried that the night air would be too cold for them to ride through the night. The last thing they needed was for one of them to become sick. Yet, Nick had a feeling that the local inn was not a good idea for the night.

The stable boy overheard Nick and Elizabeth while they were talking about traveling further and possibly finding another inn down the road. Will Baskin's family had been friends with the Shaw's for years. Will's father and Sir Phillip had traded together quite often.

"Sir Nicholas, my parents are away in London, but we do have a spare room that you may use for the night." Will offered as he led Toby out of the stables.

"That is awfully kind of you, Will." Nick paid the lad for taking care of his horse. "We would not wish to trouble you."

"Tis no trouble at all. My father would be sore with me if he knew that I did not offer help to you." Will locked up the stables for the night. "I am heading home now. Our farm is just up the road, north of the village."

When Nick looked over at Elizabeth, he could clearly see how exhausted she was. Even Toby still looked tired. He thanked Will and only agreed if they could pay rent as they would have for an inn. Will reluctantly accepted Nick's offer and they followed the boy to his family's farm. This was a blessing to them on such a chilly night. They could rest for several hours and leave the farm before dawn.

The Baskin's farmhouse was an older, but modest size, farm that had been very well taken care of. Elizabeth was given the spare room for the night. Nick slept on his bedroll next to the fire in the family's sitting room. Will had put Toby up for the night in their stables.

Sometime before dawn, Elizabeth woke from a bad dream. She was shaken by the images in her dreams and did not wish to be alone. Silently, she tiptoed down the hallway to the sitting room where Nick was sleeping. Nick woke up the moment that Elizabeth sat down beside him.

"What troubles you, my dear?" Nick sat up and put his arm around her.

"It is silly to say." Elizabeth nestled closer to Nick's side. "Nightmares are such dreadful things."

"You are safe now." Nick held her close, hoping to calm her fears. "It was only a bad dream, nothing more."

"I fear that it was more than that." Elizabeth's fear shown in her eyes.

"Whatever do you mean?" Nick wrapped his arms around her. If he could protect her from nightmares, he would.

"I was dreaming about when I was attacked." Elizabeth released a long breath.

"You do not have to revisit that nightmare." Nick wanted to spare her the painful memories of the horrors that she had gone through.

"I wish that I did not have to, but I think that I do need to revisit it." Elizabeth leaned back and looked up at Nick. "The dream caused me to remember some things."

"If you wish to share with me what happened, you know that I will always listen to you." Nick got up and tossed a couple of logs into the fire.

"I still do not know exactly what my sister was planning for you." Elizabeth watched the flames of the fire as they grew. "When Roger and Edmond took me from the house, I was unconscious. I think that I woke up in the stables, but I am not sure of it."

"Caleb and Alex tracked the rider, that left you in the Eastern Forest, back to the servant's gate at Greyham Court." Nick sat back down beside her.

"There is an old garden shed on that side of the house. That is probably where I was and not the stables." Elizabeth could not be certain since she had a sack over her head. "I overheard Roger and Edmond talking. Anne only wanted you in her plans because she knew that I cared for you."

"You must know that I would never choose Anne." Nick pulled Elizabeth back into his arms.

"Roger said that Anne needed an escape goat for he was not going to honor her." Elizabeth did not understand what it all meant.

"Why would your sister need an escape goat?" Nick did not understand.

"I do not know, but Roger wanted to sabotage Anne's plans and destroy your family once and for all, since they had me."

"So, that was when Roger devised the plan to have my family blamed for your death, resulting in all the Shaw men possibly being charged and executed." Nick knew that Roger Holden had an evil mind, but this plan of his was far worse than evil.

"Anne and Roger are horrible people." Elizabeth shuddered, thinking of those two. "What do we do?"

"We do exactly what we are planning on doing. Tomorrow, we continue heading north and the day after that, you will become my wife." Nick smiled at Elizabeth.

Nick was not going to let Roger Holden and Anne Dawson destroy their dream to marry. Nick leaned his head down and tenderly kissed Elizabeth. She was going to be his wife and that was all that mattered to him.

Chapter Thirty-Two

The tracking party rode through the night to the small village of Delane. The Duke questioned the inn owners while the others waited outside. Sam was upset when he discovered that Nick and Elizabeth had not stopped here for the night.

"You said that they would be here!" Sam shouted at Alex.

"I *said* that there was an inn here." Alex stood firm as he spoke to Sam. He had already had enough of the Duke's orders this morning.

"Look, there is a restaurant across the street." Gavin stepped in between his brother and the Duke. "Why don't we all go over and get a meal with some coffee?"

"We can continue tracking after we rest a bit." Jax liked the sound of sitting down for a while, he was exhausted.

"Coffee?" Maxx quickly looked over at the restaurant.

Before anyone could stop him, Maxx hurried across the street, with Paul leading their horses behind him. After tying up the horses, Paul entered the restaurant with Maxx.

"I have only seen Maxwell Spencer move like that for three things." Gavin shook his head as he watched his friend enter the restaurant.

"And what would those be?" Sam hated asking the question.

"Coffee." Gavin folded his arms across his chest.

"Food." Jax added with a chuckle.

"And rum." Alex nodded his head, sealing the matter.

The three Shaw men looked at each other and burst into laughter. Sam sighed deeply. He thought, perhaps this was not the best group of men to be traveling with.

"Come on." Gavin started across the street. "I fear that Paul is going to have his hands full with Maxx today."

Alex and Jax did not wait for the Duke to agree, or disagree, with Gavin's decision. The entire tracking party was extremely tired and needed a break. Harper took their horses to the village stables down the street, so they could be taken care of.

By the end of the meal, and several pots of coffee, everyone in the tracking party was in better spirits. Sam and Gavin spent much of the meal discussing where they would travel to next.

"Do you have any idea where your cousin has taken my sister?" Sam looked across the table at Alex. "It is surely obvious that your tracking skills are failing. Nick and Elizabeth did not come to Delane."

"North." Alex refused to say more.

"That is fine, Lord Alexander. I have no problem with doubling yours and our little Captain's debts." Sam smiled as he raised his coffee cup at Alex.

Gavin shook his head at Alex and Maxx, to warn them to remain silent. It was best to not argue with the Duke, since he seemed to have a heavy leverage over them both. They seemed to have caught a break when the young girl serving them brought over a fresh pot of coffee.

"Is there anything more that I can get for you, Lord Spencer?" The girl smiled as she refilled Maxx's cup.

"No, thank you, Tara." Maxx smiled up at the young girl. Tara seemed nervous as she glanced over at Sam.

"It is alright, Miss Tara. I may be the Duke, but I do not bite." Sam noticed how Tara's hand shook as she refilled his cup.

"It is good to see you again, Your Grace." Tara gave a slight curtsy to Sam.

"We have met before?" Sam looked at the girl closely, but he did not recognize her. "Forgive me, Miss Tara, but I do not seem to remember our meeting before now."

"We did not actually meet, Your Grace. You gave a speech at a charity event in London, last year. My family had helped with that event." Tara quickly explained.

"Well, it is nice to make your acquaintance now." Sam nodded his head and smile up at Tara.

"It is my pleasure, Your Grace. I did not expect to see you and your sister here in Delane. I hope that you both will visit again soon." Tara turned to go, but Sam caught her by her wrist.

"When did you see my sister?" Sam was now stern with the girl.

"Last night, Your Grace." Tara was nervous again. "Lady Elizabeth dined here, just before closing."

"Did Lady Elizabeth happen to mention where she was heading?" Sam wanted answers.

"I overheard Lady Elizabeth, and the gentleman she was with, speak of Scotland. I did not ask more, Your Grace." Tara eyes widened with fear.

"Thank you, Tara. You have helped us tremendously." Maxx reached over and removed the Duke's hand from the young girl's wrist. "You may go." Relieved, Tara hurried away.

"I do hope that they are not naive enough to believe, that crossing the border into Scotland will stop me from coming after them." Sam sighed as he looked around the table.

"I am sure that your sister is aware of that fact." Gavin leaned back in his chair as he looked at Sam.

"So, it looks as if Nick and Elizabeth were in Delane after all." Alex tapped his fingers on the table as he stared at Sam.

"It would seem so." Sam did not like being wrong. "Now, you track them from here."

Sam got up to go settle the bill with the restaurant owner. With the Duke gone, the rest of the men at the table relaxed a little. They all were ready for this to be over with.

"Why Scotland?" Jax did not understand his brother's actions.

"Going to Scotland prevents nothing." Alex agreed with his cousin.

Maxx and Paul looked at each other. They both were unsure if Nick's next move was a wise one. Nick had not mentioned Scotland when he was on board The Em. Since Maxx had been the one to encourage Nick to follow his heart, he and Paul remained quiet. If only their shared glance had gone unnoticed.

"You know something." Gavin pointed across the table at Maxx.

"Me?" Maxx put his hand to his chest. Playing dumb was not really one Maxx's strong suits when he was hungover.

"Oh, Little Man, you look guilty as sin right now." Alex grabbed Maxx by his wrist. "Out with it."

"Do you know where my brother is going?" Jax leaned over the table.

"Just buy your cousin another day." Maxx looked Alex in the eye. "If it is not done by then, it will be his own fault."

"Where are they going?" Gavin tapped his finger on the table, drawing Maxx's attention.

"Not Scotland." Maxx drank his coffee as he tried to ignore the Shaw's.

"They are traveling north, and you want to buy them another day." Gavin looked from Maxx to Alex. "Do you have any clue as to where they could be going?"

"Nick loves Elizabeth." Alex had a sinking feeling in his heart. "My guess would be, they are going to Camden."

"Both of our parents were married in Camden." Jax reminded his cousins of this fact.

"Did you put Nick up to this?" Gavin asked Maxx.

"Me? Why am I always in the middle of things?" Maxx refused to admit his part in this.

"Because you are usually always in the middle of things." Alex said in a matter of fact tone as he turned to look at Maxx.

"I am only always in the middle of things because your family keeps putting me there." Maxx got up to leave the restaurant.

"He is right." Paul stood up to follow Maxx.

"Of course, you will defend the dear Captain." Alex eyed Paul as he walked past him. "Carry on, the ever so loyal, first mate."

Paul shook his head at Alex and followed Maxx out the door. Sometimes he wondered why Maxx did not just stay away from the Shaw's. Here lately, these men seemed to pulling Maxx into more and more troubled situations. Regardless of what Maxx decided to do to help Gavin's family members, Paul would always be by Maxx's side, helping him.

"So, what do we do?" Jax wanted to help his brother somehow.

A huge problem with the situation was, what would the Duke do once Nick was married to Elizabeth? Was it a chance that they could take? It had become obvious to the entire Shaw family that Nick and Elizabeth truly did love each other. They were unsure which action would be best for Nick. Should they let him marry Elizabeth and face the Duke for it, or was it better to stop them before they could marry?

"I will do what I can to give Nick and Elizabeth this day." Alex released a deep breath.

"Tomorrow, we will descend on Camden." Gavin agreed with Alex's decision.

"Let us hope that my brother survives this." Jax got up and followed Maxx and Paul outside.

Chapter Thirty-Three

It was just after lunch time when Nick and Elizabeth went back to the Camden Chapel. Minister Wallace had been out for the morning, so Ms. Crook had asked them to return in the afternoon.

"I cannot believe that we are really doing this." Elizabeth smiled at Nick as they walked inside the chapel.

"Do you wish to change your mind, my dear?" Nick took her coat and hung it on a hook by the door.

"I most certainly do not wish to change my mind." This was the happiest that Elizabeth had ever been in her life.

In a way, she was grateful for the delay in them getting married this morning. The extra time allowed for her to purchase a new dress from one of the local shops. It was not the white wedding gown that she had always imagined, but still the dark blue dress that she now wore was beautiful.

Ms. Crook handed Elizabeth a bouquet of flesh cut flowers when she and Nick walked into the chapel. The little woman was extremely giddy as she hurried over to the piano. Ms. Crook loved weddings. The little woman sat down and started playing a lovely tune as Nick and Elizabeth met Minister Wallace at the front of the chapel. The minister was overjoyed to be marrying another member of the Shaw family.

To Elizabeth, this simple little ceremony was splendid. She did not require a huge glamorous ceremony in London, she only wanted to be married to the man standing before her. Nicholas Shaw had won her heart many years ago. She had not been brave enough, before now, to tell anyone of her love for Nick.

As Minister Wallace started the ceremony with a prayer, Nick and Elizabeth stood smiling at each other. Soon, the butterflies in Elizabeth's stomach would be gone. In a matter of minutes now, she would be pronounced Mrs. Nicholas Shaw. This was what she had dreamed of for such a long time now.

Before the ring could be placed on her finger, and the ceremony completed with a kiss, something horrible happened. The front doors of the little chapel suddenly flew opened as the Duke came rushing in.

"That is far enough!" Sam pointed at Minister Wallace. "This ceremony ends now!"

Ms. Crook screamed and ran to the back rooms of the chapel when the Duke's guards rushed in and surrounded Nick and Elizabeth. Nick pulled Elizabeth behind him and stood firm as he faced the Duke.

"Young man, why do you descend upon the house of God in such a manner?" Minister Wallace walked over and stood next to Nick.

"You have my apologizes for that, Minister Wallace." Sam walked closer to Nick. "But my sister will not be getting married here today."

"Have we met?" Minister Wallace did not recognize Sam. Sam's head snapped toward the minister.

"Not officially, Minister." Sam swallowed hard as he motioned around the chapel with his hand. "But your services here are spoken of quite frequently in London."

"Yes, we do have many couples from London to get married here." Minister Wallace agreed on that matter.

Sam officially introduced himself as the Duke of Greyham. He explained that Elizabeth was his sister, and he came to take her home. Minister Wallace did not wish to cause problems for the Duke. He excused himself and went to sit down on the front chapel pew. Minister Wallace had learned over the years that it was best to let the families work things like this out among themselves.

Maxx and Nick's family members, along with the men from Hartford, came in and surrounded Nick and Elizabeth. They created a shield between the couple and the Duke's guards. Maxx was keeping his promise to Lady Clara, he would not let the Duke harm her son.

"I do not wish to battle with you in a chapel." Sam looked around at the men before him.

"Then, Your Grace, I suggest that you tell us what your plans are now that we have found them." Gavin stepped forward.

"I only want my sister." Sam held his hand out toward Elizabeth.

"I do not wish to return to Greyham Court. You already know this." Elizabeth stepped out from behind Nick and faced her brother.

"Why would you force her to return there after what she has gone through?" Nick was upset. He took Elizabeth's hand in his. He was afraid of losing her.

"If you return to London with me now, of your own free will, I will not harm Sir Nicholas." Sam ignored Nick as he continued to hold his hand out toward his sister.

Elizabeth looked around the chapel at all the guards from Greyham Court. She was sure that there were even more guards outside. Nick's family probably had about twenty men total. She knew that they would be heavily outnumbered in a battle. She could not stand here and watch Nick and his family die today.

It would also be wrong to start a full fled battle inside a house of God. Now, Elizabeth regretted the delay this morning. If only they had gotten to Camden earlier yesterday. Minister Wallace would have been here at the chapel. She and Nick would have been married before the day had ended. Sadly, that was not meant to be.

As much as it saddened her, Elizabeth could only think of one way to save Nick's life. She knew that her brother was stern, and he did not tolerate foolishness. If Sam made the decision to fight, he would fight hard, until he had destroyed everything in his path. Nick would hate her for doing what she was about to do, but she had no choice. She could not watch the man she loved die like this.

"Do I have your word that Nick will go free, and unharmed, if I go with you?" Elizabeth held her head high as she looked at her brother.

"You have my word, as an oath, that if you leave with me now, I will not harm one single curl on Sir Nicholas' precious head." Sam made her a true promise.

"What are you doing?" Nick turned her to face him.

"I love you, Nick. I have always loved you." Tears filled Elizabeth's eyes as she looked up at him. "Forgive me, but I just cannot watch you die."

"And I cannot lose you." Tears also filled Nick's eyes.

"You will always have my heart." Elizabeth closed her eyes. Her heart was truly breaking.

"And you will always have mine." Nick placed his forehead against hers.

Elizabeth threw her arms around Nick's neck. This was wrong and it was so unfair. She now truly hated the world in which she was forced to live. Titles and fortunes did not always guarantee happiness. As her tears freely flowed down her face, Elizabeth kissed Nick on his cheek.

A sudden coldness surrounded Elizabeth as she stepped away from Nick and took her brother's extended hand. In that one moment, Nick stumbled as his heart fell from his chest. He had lost her.

"No!" Nick stepped forward as he reached for Elizabeth.

Jax and Gavin quickly grabbed Nick and held him in his place. They all watched as Sam handed his sister to one of his guards and ordered for a carriage to be found for the trip back to London.

"Let her go." Jax whispered to Nick.

"I know it is hard, but you have no choice." Gavin's heart broke for his cousin.

Once Elizabeth was out of the chapel, Sam returned to the Shaw family that was huddled together near the front pews of the chapel. He was glad that this ordeal was now over with.

"You all have my gratitude." Sam nodded his head at them all.

"Keep it." Nick glared at Sam.

"This Saturday evening, there will be at party at Greyham Court. I do expect to see both of your families present." Sam was polite as he extended the invitation.

"I would not hold my breath if I were you." Nick snapped at Sam.

"That would be a shame and such a pity. I do hope that you all change your minds." Sam again politely nodded his head at the Shaw's before turning to Maxx. "I will see you later in London."

"I do believe that you have something to say to Alex, do you not?" Maxx reminded the Duke of his promise.

"Lord Alexander, walk with me." Sam turned to leave the chapel. Reluctantly, Alex followed him.

"I did not like being forced to track my own cousin." Alex felt horrible that he did not buy Nick enough time today.

"Still, you managed to do a tremendous job. Your tracking skills are extraordinary. You did find my sister and I am profoundly grateful for that." Sam looked Alex in the eye. "You are free of your debt to me."

"And what of Maxx? Is he free too?" Alex asked.

"I am afraid that I cannot lose my hold on the little Earl of Hartford so easily." Sam looked back over his shoulder at Maxwell Spencer. "But, if you make sure that Sir Nicholas, and the rest of your family, are at Greyham Court this Saturday evening, then I will reduce Maxx's debt by one year."

"A year?" Alex looked between the Duke and Maxx. It then hit him. "Maxx has bound himself to you for years, to grant me my freedom from prison."

"Who knew that the little Captain had such a huge heart?" Sam smiled, pleased with how things turned out, before he walked away.

Jax helped Nick over to one of the chapel pews. He motioned the others away to give his brother a moment. Nick was completely broken on the inside. He could not think, nor did he want to move.

"It will be alright, someday." Jax was at a loss for words. He had no idea how to comfort his older brother.

"I am afraid that is a day that will never come." Nick dropped his face in his hands.

Nick's world was now destroyed. There was nothing good left for him. He was even furious that Samuel Dawson thought that him and his family would wish to join him for a party after what took place here today. There was no way that he was going to that high society party and pretend that things were alright.

Chapter Thirty-Four

In less than an hour a carriage was rented, and Elizabeth was on her way back to London with her brother. She had hoped to be leaving Camden with her husband, but that dream did not happen. She was heartbroken over losing Nick and she was furious with her brother. She was so upset that she could not even look at Sam. Instead, she looked at the carriage window and ignored her brother's presence.

"I know that you are angry, but in time, you will agree that this was for the best." Sam hated the silence between them.

"Best for who? You? Mother? Anne?" Elizabeth practically spat out their sister's name.

"I am not sure what this will be for Mother and Anne." Sam leaned back against the carriage seat. "But, in the end, this will be what is best for you."

"I am afraid that you and I do not agree on what is best for me." Elizabeth looked at Sam. "You just forced me to walk away from what is best for me."

"I assure you that we will be discussing Sir Nicholas Shaw in the coming days." Sam leaned forward and took Elizabeth's hand. "But right now, I need for you to tell me again of everything that happened to you and if you remember anything more."

"I cannot." Elizabeth shook her head and looked away.

"The only way that I can do anything to help make things right, is to hear from you exactly what happened." Sam pleaded with Elizabeth.

"They left me for dead!" Elizabeth shouted. Her emotions could not be controlled any longer. Tears filled her eyes as that horrible day came rushing back to her mind. "They actually wanted me to die!"

"And they will all pay dearly for that." Sam moved to sit beside Elizabeth.

177

"It cannot be made right. It just cannot be." Elizabeth wiped the tears from her face.

"That is probably true, but we will seek justice as fully as we can." Sam vowed as he held Elizabeth as she cried.

For over an hour, Sam listened as Elizabeth told him what had happened to her. To Elizabeth's surprise, once she started talking about what had happened, she could not stop. She told Sam everything, starting with the first slap, that was given by their older sister, Anne. She included the things her dream had caused her to remember.

Elizabeth went on to tell Sam how Nick had found her in the forest. She talked about the time they had spent at the Summer Cottage and the journey to Hartford Manor. She made sure that Sam knew that running away was her idea and not Nick's. She told her brother all the ways that Nick had saved her and protected her.

The only thing that Elizabeth did not tell Sam about, was her stay at the Blume'N Brew. She also did not mention the time that she and Nick spent on board Maxwell Spencer's ship. She and Nick had given their word to Maxx, that they would never mention the help that he and Miss Nancie had given to them.

"So, now do you understand why I do not wish to return to Greyham Court?" Elizabeth hoped that Sam would now understand. "And why I never wish to see Anne again?"

"I do understand." Sam did not wish to bring more hardship upon his sister. "But I cannot do what needs to be done, unless I take you to Greyham Court."

"No!" Elizabeth shouted. "Why would you force me into going back there?" How could her brother hear everything she just told him and still force this upon her?

"When we get to London, you will understand." Sam moved back to the other side of the carriage. "Trust me, I will not leave you alone, while you are in the house."

Elizabeth was furious with her brother. After everything that she had just told him, Sam should understand her feelings and not force her back into that house. She was now glad that Rosa had taught her how to defend herself. She would be keeping the small dagger that

Rosa had given to her, hidden within her skirts. She would not be afraid to use, even if it were on her sister, Anne.

***

After the Duke and his guards rode away with Elizabeth, Alex went back inside the chapel. He did not know why but he was furious with Maxx. Alex walked straight up to Maxx and grabbed him by the arm, forcing Maxx to face him.

"Are you insane?" Alex shouted.

"I do have my moments." Maxx jerked his arm away from Alex.

"Why are you angry with Maxx?" Gavin stepped in between his brother and his best friend.

"He has bound himself to the Duke for years!" Alex shouted as he pointed at Maxx.

"What is he talking about?" Gavin turned to face Maxx. He was deeply worried about what his friend had gotten into.

"Nothing that any of you need to concern yourselves with." Maxx looked at Gavin. "Trust me, it is fine."

"It is not fine!" Alex caught Maxx by the arm again before he could walk away. "You should not have done it!"

"What did Maxx do?" Jax walked over next to Gavin, giving Nick a moment alone.

"It is really nothing to concern yourselves over." Maxx did not wish to discuss the matter.

"How many years?" Alex asked as he released Maxx's arm. He hated the fact that his freedom came at a high price for Maxx.

"Five." Maxx dropped his head and walked out of the chapel.

Gavin and Jax stood beside Alex as they watched Maxx leave. They were all stunned to learn that Maxx's deal with the Duke of Greyham had their friend bound in service for five years. After seeing the way Samuel Dawson handled his affairs over the past few days, the Shaw men were seriously worried about what would happen to Maxx over the next five years.

"He did that for you." Jax's words did not bring comfort to Alex.

"We have to do something to help Maxx." Gavin was not going to let Samuel Dawson destroy his best friend for five full years.

"That is why we all are going to the Duke's little party this Saturday evening." Alex looked between Gavin and Jax.

"I am not going to that party." Nick said flatly as he walked up beside them.

"Oh, you will go!" Alex shouted as he pointed at Nick. "If I have to drag you there myself, kicking and screaming, you *will* go!"

"I fear that you are a tad bit delusional there, cousin." Nick was ill and he had no intention of going to that party. "And thank you kindly for tracking me."

Nick started out the doors of the chapel. His brother and cousins quickly followed him. Before leaving the chapel, Gavin made their apologizes to Minister Wallace and invited his family to Ellis Manor to visit his granddaughter, Olivia.

"You should not be angry with Alex. He was forced to track you by the Duke." Jax understood why Nick was upset. His brother's anger had nothing to do with Alex.

"I am still not going to that party." Nick mounted his horse.

"Oh, you, dear cousin, will go. You can hate it, but you will go." Alex glared at Nick.

"Why do we have to go?" Jax asked.

"Because, if Nick and the rest of us, go to this little party, it will take a year off of Maxx's debt to the Duke." Alex rode on ahead to catch up with Maxx and his men. He had enough of his cousin's attitude for now.

"Looks like we all are going to a party." Jax would gladly go if it meant helping Maxx.

"I owe Maxwell Spencer nothing." Nick spat the words out.

"I am afraid that you owe Maxwell Spencer a great deal." Gavin now rode between Nick and Jax.

"He was supposed to buy us some time." Nick was still angry.

"Maxx did buy you some time." Jax told his brother, he had seen this for himself.

"I bet the Duke would add a few more years onto the little Captain's debt, if he knew how Maxx had helped hide us." Nick did not mean what he just said. He hated himself for even saying the words, but he could not take them back now.

"You would not dare do such a horrible thing." Gavin was now furious with his cousin.

"Maxx is our friend. How could you say such things?" Jax was now ill with his brother as well.

"He may be your friend, but his is not a friend of mine." It was too late for Nick to take back the words he had just spoken in anger. He needed someone to blame, and sadly he was blaming Maxx.

"I know that you are upset, but causing Maxx more grief, is not how to go about things." Jax wanted to be on his brother's side, but on this matter, he could not do so.

"If you give Maxx up, I am afraid that there will be some serious consequences." Gavin looked over at Nick, his own anger was starting to boil. "My entire family will disown you."

Gavin nudged his horse forward, leaving his cousins behind. He did not like making such a threat to his cousin. He and Nick were the same age. They had been close while growing up. Gavin knew that Nick was deeply hurt. Any man would feel Nick's pain if the woman they loved was taken away from them. He wanted what was best for his cousin. However, if Nick caused Maxx more grief with the Duke, Gavin would side with his best friend.

"I hate to say this to you." Jax looked over at Nick. "If you go through with that threat, I fear that our own Mother and Father would disown you as well."

Jax hurried ahead to ride with the others. He left Nick to wallow in his own emotions and thoughts. There were lines that honorable men did not cross. Hopefully, his older brother would regain his head and apologize for saying such horrible things. No descent man would stab a friend in the back the way Nick had just threatened to do.

Chapter Thirty-Five

It was early afternoon, two days later, when Sam and Elizabeth arrived at Greyham Court in London. Elizabeth was terrified to be returning to the place where she had been attacked. She had not spoken to her brother all day. Sam patted Elizabeth's hand and smiled, he hoped to offer her some encouragement. Sadly, his gesture of kindness offered no hope to her.

The butler, Mr. Reed, was happy to see the Duke and his sister. Mr. Reed had been very worried about Lady Elizabeth since her disappearance from the house. He had tea ordered immediately and sent to the Duke's private study. At Sam's request, the servants were sent to summon Anne and their mother to the study as well.

Elizabeth trembled as she sat down in the huge chair in the corner of the room. She did not want to be here. In a few moments, she would be forced to see her sister again. If only she could get away, she would rush to the Blume'N Brew. She knew that Rachel and Miss Nancie would gladly take her in and hide her.

"What is the meaning of this?" Anne snapped as she entered the study.

"Son, we know that you are the Duke, but you do not have to summon us like we are common servants." The Dowager Duchess stared at her son.

"Will you both please have a seat?" Sam motioned toward the two highbacked chairs in front of his desk.

"Is this elaborate show really necessary?" Their mother was not pleased with being treated this way.

"And why are we having this party on Saturday?" Anne hated parties on such short notice.

"Yes, Mother, this is necessary." Sam turned to Anne. "You need not trouble yourself about this party, for you will not be here."

"Is that so?" Anne laughed coldly. "And why will I not be here, pray tell? This is my home."

"Son, it is all fine and just dandy that you wish to show off your authority as the Duke, but I have had enough of all these theatrics." Their mother started to stand up.

"Sit down, Mother." Sam was very stern.

When the Dowager Duchess went to sit back down, she glanced over and saw Elizabeth, sitting in the corner. He eyes widened and her mouth dropped open. It was an action that was so unbecoming of the lady that she pretended to be.

Anne looked over to see what had caught her mother's attention. Panic and something vile rose inside of Anne when she saw Elizabeth sitting there.

"So, you found the little twit." Anne sneered. "Is this what has you so riled up? Seriously, brother? Can you not just send a servant to announce your *happy* news?"

"No, we cannot do things that way. I am afraid that it is necessary to things just like this. The two of you seem to not understand my simple requests so here we are, with all my Duke authority." Sam folded his arms across his chest.

"Then let us get on with this drama, shall we?" The Dowager Duchess folded her hands on her lap as she sat back and glared at her son.

"So, I assume that this little party is to celebrate that you found our wayward sister." Anne sat back in her chair.

"As I said, you will not be here for the party." Sam simply looked at Anne as she laughed at him.

"Oh, little brother, you are quite delusional." Anne waved her hand as she dismissed Sam's words.

"Mother, you said that you would not believe the accusations against Anne, until you heard them from Elizabeth's mouth and in this very house." Sam walked over and took Elizabeth by her hand.

"Sam, please do not make me tell it all again." Elizabeth's plea was a whisper.

"I hate doing this to you. I truly do, but I need you to tell them what happened to you." Sam whispered so that their mother and Anne could not hear him.

"I cannot do it." Elizabeth wanted to cry.

"You do not have to tell it all." Sam now pleaded with her. "Just tell Mother how it started. Especially Anne's part in it all. Then, only as much as you can, up until where Nicholas Shaw found you in the forest. No more needs to be said. Trust me on this."

Elizabeth took a deep breath and nodded her head. She hoped that she was able to give enough of the story so that their mother would believe her. This had to be the reason that Sam had insisted on her returning to Greyham Court. She should have realized before now that her mother had something to do with it.

Elizabeth walked over to the desk with Sam. As she stood facing her mother and her sister, a new hatred for them both grew inside of her. She was only here now, in a house where she had been assaulted, because of these two evil women sitting before her.

As Elizabeth told her story, and as little of it that was necessary, Sam had remained by her side, holding her hand. Her brother's support meant a great deal to her. At the end, Anne dropped her head and their mother stared blankly, not focusing on anything specific.

"Now, my dear sister. Do you trust Mr. Reed and Sir Donaldson?" Sam motioned toward the butler and the Captain of the Guard. "Do you know them to be honorable men?"

"I trust them both greatly." Elizabeth looked up at Sam.

"Then they will escort you to your room." Sam walked Elizabeth to the door. "Remain there until I come for you."

Elizabeth was confused and did not understand Sam's plan here. She did not wish to do this, but she could no longer look at her hateful sister. She still had the dagger hidden in her skirts. If anyone came after her again, she would use the weapon if she had to. Elizabeth nodded her head and left the study with the two men.

"I suppose now you have a new set of rules for us all to follow that accommodates our dear sister." Anne sighed as Sam closed the doors.

"There are some new rules and they start today." Sam sat down at his desk.

"We know that you want Elizabeth to be protected. We all will see to it that she is. So, now, may we go? This all have been so very tiring." The Dowager Duchess carelessly waved her hand in the air.

"No, Mother. You may not go just yet." Sam looked between his mother and sister. "There are some major changes happening right now."

"What on earth needs to change? Elizabeth is back, safe and sound. You have had your day playing the Duke. All is fine." Anne laughed as she dismissed the entire matter.

"I warned you last year, when you played a part in the kidnappings of Lady Abigail and Lady Danielle Shaw. I told you that you had just one more time to slip up." Sam's lips tightened as he stared at his oldest sister. He had not forgotten the handprint on Danielle Shaw's face that night.

"You cannot seriously believe that you can punish me." Anne threw her head back and laughed heartily.

"Son, there is no need in doing anything drastic." Their mother was now sitting on the edge of her seat.

"Oh, Mother. I am afraid that there is a great need to do things extremely drastic. You two do not understand anything otherwise." Sam turned back to Anne. "The only reason that you have remained in this house, and in this family, is because our dear mother here, strongly begged for you to stay."

"Mother, stop him." Anne knew now that Sam meant business.

"I am afraid that Mother cannot help you any longer." Sam stood up and placed his hands on the desk as he leaned forward. "As of this day, Anne Dawson, you are disowned by this family and banished from all our properties."

"No!" Anne jumped to her feet.

"Our sister almost died because of you! Have you no shame?" Sam's hate for what Anne had done clearly showed on his face.

"Son, please." Their mother stood, with tears in her eyes.

"You have three hours, not a minute more, to go upstairs and pack what you can. A carriage will take you from this house today!" Sam shouted at Anne.

"Where am I supposed to go?" Anne asked as tears ran down her face. Anne reached for her mother. "Mother, you must do something. Do not let him do this to me."

"Mother has distant relatives in Edinburgh. They have agreed to take you in. You will work for them to pay your way." Sam sat back down.

"Scotland!" Anne shouted. "You expect me to go live with those barbarians?"

"That is exactly what you are doing." Sam pointed his finger at Anne. "The carriage leaves in three hours. I suggest that you pack what you can, or you will leave this house with the clothes that you have on."

"Samuel, please. She is your sister." The Dowager Duchess pleaded with her son.

"I am sorry, Mother, but that argument does not work anymore. Anne is a heartless sister and I have had enough of her evil schemes." Sam looked up at his mother. "If you wish to do something that will help Anne now, then I suggest that you hurry along upstairs and help her to pack her things."

The Dowager Duchess hurried from the room. She was aware that her son was at the end of his rope. He would not forgive Anne this time. Sam was within his rights, as Duke and head of their family, to give this harsh punishment to his sister. With tears in her eyes, she rushed upstairs to pack all that she could for her oldest child.

"Sam, please do not do this to me." Anne pleaded when they were alone.

"The deed is done. You have no one to blame but yourself. I do hope that you learn from your experience." Sam walked over to the door.

As Sam reached for the handle, Anne covered his hand with hers. She was frantic and sobbed openly. She had to change her brother's mind somehow.

"Please, Sam. I am sorry. I cannot be out there on my own. I just cannot." Anne would do anything to be able to stay at Greyham Court.

"I am at least sending you to relatives. That is a very generous gift to you and one that you do not deserve. So, you will not be out there alone. Now, go!" Sam stood firm in his decision.

"But, brother, I am with child." Anne cried.

"Then, I guess it is best that you are leaving now, before that scandal falls upon this house." Sam opened the door and escorted Anne to the staircase.

Sam sighed deeply. This was why Anne was plotting with Evelyn Cramer for the night of Ms. Rhodes' party. She was planning on trapping Nicholas Shaw into marriage. She would find a way to have Nick in a compromising situation and then claim that her child was his. Anne marrying Nick would have ripped Elizabeth's heart out. Sam narrowed his eyes as he glared at Anne. His sister was truly evil.

"I hate you!" Anne screamed at Sam.

"I have known that for years." Sam motioned for a guard to escort Anne upstairs. With a smile and a simple nod of his head, Sam walked away.

Chapter Thirty-Six

Elizabeth watched from a window. on the second floor, as the carriage pulled away from Greyham Court with Anne inside. She was stunned when one of the maids had told her that Anne had been disowned and banished from the family. Anne was her sister, but Elizabeth felt no sorrow for her older sibling as she rode away from Greyham Court, and their lives.

Elizabeth was now concerned with why Sam had her also packing her things. Was she to be thrown out of the family as well? Perhaps Sam was not tolerant and forgiving of her running away with Nicholas Shaw. Whatever her fate was, it would be far better for her than being in this house.

Elizabeth did not have to wait for long. Within minutes of Anne's departure, guards and servants came to her room and carried her trunks outside to another carriage. Sam was waiting for Elizabeth at the bottom of the grand staircase. He did not speak to her. Sam only extended his hand out to her.

Their mother stood in the doorway of the drawing room. The Dowager Duchess turned her back and walked away, as Elizabeth and Sam walked out the front doors. The scowl on her mother's face was enough for Elizabeth to know that she was very displeased with both her and Sam.

"Am I being disowned and banished as well?" Elizabeth asked, once they were inside the carriage.

"I see that the news of our sister has already reached you." Sam figured that it would.

"Yes, and I see that Mother is very displeased." Elizabeth never understood why their mother seemed to only love Anne.

"To say that Mother is displeased is putting it mildly." Sam looked out the window and nodded his head at Sir Donaldson. He turned back to Elizabeth. "Why would you think that I was banishing you?"

"I know that you are not pleased that I ran away with Nicholas Shaw." Elizabeth bravely held her head high.

The only regret that Elizabeth had from her time with Nick, was that it ended without them being able to marry. She only hoped that someday her brother would forgive her, but she was not going to apologize for it.

"You and I definitely need to talk about Sir Nicholas Shaw, but we will do that once you are settled." Sam's lips formed a tight smile.

Sam knew that he had to think wisely on the matter of Nicholas Shaw. Elizabeth was the one sister that he did not wish to lose. For now, Elizabeth's safety was his main priority. They would talk more about Nick once things at Greyham Court were settled.

After riding around the streets of London, for what felt like hours, the carriage pulled up to an adorable cottage on the far edge of London. The house was beautiful. It was surrounded by a huge stone wall, just as Greyham Court was. Elizabeth had never seen this cottage before.

"Where are we?" Elizabeth asked as they walked up the front steps. She had no memories of this house. Perhaps this was one of their properties that she had only visited as a small child.

Sam opened the front door and led her inside. The inside was decorated even more beautifully than the outside was. Still, it seemed a much simpler home than Greyham Court and the Summer Cottage was. Elizabeth could not picture her family ever owning a house like this.

"I do hope that you will be comfortable here for a few days." Sam led her to the sitting room. Elizabeth was already pleased with this cottage and knew that she would be extremely comfortable here.

"If she complains, even one time, I will be bringing her straight back to you." Maxwell Spencer was waiting in the sitting room.

"Why is Maxx here?" Elizabeth looked at her brother, she was confused about everything.

"Lord Spencer is in charge of protecting you." Sam walked over to Maxx. "I will see you on Saturday evening. Is everything you need in place?"

"I have everything here covered." Maxx looked over at Elizabeth and smiled. "I will make sure that Elizabeth arrives safely to the party."

"What about the Shaw family?" Sam asked. Elizabeth was extremely interested in the answer to this as well.

"Would you rather that I deal with the Shaw family or protect your sister?" Maxx asked sarcastically. "I can do one request but not both."

Sam shook his head and walked away. Maxwell Spencer was a handful, even for him, when the little Earl was in a mood. He knew that Maxx was not thrilled to be working for him. Still, the next few years should prove interesting indeed.

"Would one of you like to explain to me, what is going on?" Elizabeth did not like being kept in the dark.

"You did not wish to remain at Greyham Court. So, Maxx will keep you here until the party." Sam gave Elizabeth a hug. "After the party, things should be safe for you to return home. Now, do you have that list that I asked for?"

"Why can I not just live here?" Elizabeth handed Sam the parchment from her bag. "This is a lovely house."

"Yes, this is a very lovely house, but we do not own it." Sam kissed Elizabeth on her forehead and quickly left the cottage.

"This is all so maddening!" Elizabeth exclaimed as she turned to face Maxx.

"Sam is your brother. You have known him much longer than the rest of us have. I would think that you should be used to his unorthodox ways by now." Maxx walked over to the door and asked a maid to bring them some tea.

"I do admit that Sam is a bit eccentric, but I believe that he has now reached another level with it." Elizabeth sat down on the sofa.

Nothing about this move made any sense to her. As hard as she tried, Elizabeth could not figure out her brother's reasoning in all this. However, her spirits were lifted when she saw Rosa walk into the room. A maid walked behind Rosa, carrying the tea tray. Elizabeth hurried over and gave Rosa a hug.

"It is wonderful to see you again, Lady Elizabeth." Rosa poured them all a cup of tea. Since Rosa's arm was still in a sling, Maxx handed Elizabeth the teacup.

"We do hope that you enjoy your stay at Hartford Place." Maxx patted Elizabeth on her arm. "Will you please excuse me? I need to go speak with Paul. I will leave you in Rosa's capable hands for now."

"Do you know what has happened to Nick?" Elizabeth caught Maxx by the arm. "And do you know what my brother's plans are for Nick's family?"

"Lady Elizabeth, I am afraid that I do not have the answers to your questions." Maxx shook his head. "I was ordered to stay here with you, and to deliver you to the party on Saturday. That is all I have for now."

Maxx said no more as he hurried away to find Paul. Elizabeth figured that Maxx would not give up any of her brother's secrets, if he thought that those answers would bring her grief. She did hope that Rosa would be more forth coming with answers. Elizabeth hoped that she could find a way to ask her questions without trying to trick Rosa into revealing the answers. That was more Anne's style than hers.

"I did not know that Lord Spencer owned a house in London." Elizabeth walked into the study, next to the sitting room.

"Maxx's grandparents owned this house. Maxx's family uses it from time to time." Rosa took Elizabeth by the arm. "I have a surprise for you."

Elizabeth followed Rosa down the hall to the kitchen. Elizabeth was extremely happy when she saw Rachel in the kitchen. Rachel hurried over to give her a hug.

"Do either of you know what has happened to Nick?" This was the one question that Elizabeth needed the answer to the most.

"Sir Nicholas is at Kinsley Estate with his family." Rachel took Elizabeth's hands in hers. She knew how much Elizabeth loved Nick.

"Is he alright?" Elizabeth had to know.

Rosa nodded her head at Rachel, letting her know that it was alright to say more. Neither of them liked having to keep secrets from Lady Elizabeth. Still, they would do their best to honor Maxx's and the Duke's wishes.

"Nick is devasted and deeply heartbroken, but your brother did not harm him." Rachel wished that she knew more, so that she could help ease Elizabeth's mind.

"Lord Alexander will make sure that Sir Nicholas is at the party on Saturday." Rosa wanted to offer Elizabeth some hope, and this was all she could think of for now.

"Perhaps you can have a moment with Nick at the party." Rachel's suggestion made Elizabeth smile.

"I have no idea what my brother has planned, or why this party is so important to him. Sam has been very vague with everything lately." Elizabeth looked between Rosa and Rachel.

"Come, sit down, and we will share with you what little we know." Rosa motioned toward the table.

With her now safely tucked away, in this little cottage, owned by the Earl of Hartford, Sam had returned to Greyham Court. Elizabeth learned that Sam disowning and banishing Anne was just the start of him regaining control of his household.

Her brother had released every servant at Greyham Court that was loyal to Anne. Sam did not stop there; he had even sent away the loyal servants of their mother as well. Not even the Dowager Duchess' lady's maid was spared.

The only servants that held onto their employment at Greyham Court were the ones named on the list that Elizabeth had handed to Sam, before he left Hartford Place. She had been curious as to why Sam had asked for a list of the servants that she fully trusted. She now had her answer to that.

Since a witness had seen Roger Holden slap her at Ridgewell Inn, Sam was having his lawyer to file formal papers with the magistrate, to charge the Earl of Statham with assault. This was another reason as to why Sam had hidden her away until the party. If Roger Holden came after her, he would not find her here at Hartford Place. Very few people knew that Maxx owned this cottage.

If, by chance, Roger did find out where she was, then he would have to battle Maxwell Spencer. From everything that Rosa and

Rachel had told her, Elizabeth was sure that Roger greatly feared a battle with Maxx.

Later that evening, Miss Nancie would be joining them at Hartford Place. Together, these three women would spend the next few days, taking care of her. According to Rachel, Rosa and Miss Nancie were still a bit at odds with each other, but Rachel did not explain why.

Elizabeth's comfort and safety had been taken care of. She only hoped that she would be allowed a moment with Nick at the party. Then again, Elizabeth could not help but to wonder, since she could not have a life with Nicholas Shaw, was it right to see him again? Perhaps, for Nick's sake, it would be best if she completely let him go.

Chapter Thirty-Seven

On Saturday evening, the Duke's carriage pulled up at Greyham Court. Elizabeth had mixed emotions about going to this party. No matter how much it broke her heart, she had decided to not try and see Nick tonight.

When Sam paid a visit to Hartford Place, earlier that morning, Elizabeth became a bit defiant with her brother. She had refused to attend this party tonight, unless Sam allowed the people who had taken care of her the past few days, to attend. To Elizabeth's, and everyone else's surprise, Sam agreed without any protest.

Rosa was not thrilled about going. However, she was happy that she would be next to Paul for the evening. Miss Nancie and Rachel were extremely delighted about being invited to attend such a grand party. Maxx, however, was concerned for his friends. The ladies of London's society set were a vicious and cruel lot. He would have to keep an eye on Rachel and Miss Nancie tonight, to ensure that no one insulted them.

Even though Elizabeth had decided to let Nick go, she wore the dark blue dress that she had bought in Camden. She knew that it was wrong to do so, but her heart was having problems letting Nick go. She would do her best to smile and get through this night.

After this, she would avoid any contact with the Shaw family. Perhaps Sam could secure her a marriage in another country. She hated the thought of an arranged marriage. However, this would ensure that she would never have to see Nick again.

Elizabeth and her friends entered Greyham Court through the family's private entrance, on the west wing of the house. They found Sam waiting for them in the foyer.

"You look lovely this evening, my dear sister." Sam offered Elizabeth his arm. "May I have a word with you, before we go in?"

While Sam and Elizabeth talked in a private study, the party in the grand ballroom started without them. By the time Elizabeth entered the ballroom, the music and dancing had already started. Sam left her with Maxx, as he hurried away to greet some of their guests.

"Lady Elizabeth, would you care to dance?" Maxx held his hand out to her.

Elizabeth smiled as she quickly wiped a tear from her eye before anyone noticed it. She took Maxx's hand and followed him out onto the dance floor. Paul and Rosa remained in the back of the room and kept an eye on Rachel and Miss Nancie.

Most of the Shaw family was present for the party tonight. They came to help lower Maxx's debt with the Duke. Lord Matthew was given a huge comfortable chair to sit in, since his leg had been severely injured weeks ago. The Earl of Claybourne had insisted on coming tonight. He was grateful for all that Maxx had done to help his son, Alex.

After more than an hour, Nick and Alex had not shown up for the party. Gavin left his wife, Abby, with his parents and went outside. There was still no sign of his brother and cousin. Maxx's debt to the Duke would only be reduced if Nick showed up here tonight.

Another half an hour passed. Every member of the Shaw family watched the doors. Hopefully, Alex would be able to persuade Nick into joining them tonight. They all understood how hard this would be for Nick. The family wanted to ease Nick's pain, but that was something that only time would be able to do.

"Do you believe that Nick will show?" Jax asked Maxx.

"I would not." Maxx said flatly. Jax's eyes widened. "Your brother is hurt. He should not be forced into being here, not even for my sake."

Even though Maxx had not seen the Shaw family since they all returned to London, he heard about the Duke's offer to reduce his debt from Miss Nancie. Gavin and Alex had told her about it when they stopped at the Blume'N Brew.

Maxx looked over at Miss Nancie and smiled. She was different tonight and looked extremely happy. Nancie had always wanted to come to one of the society parties. She wore a lavender colored dress that Elizabeth had loaned to her. Maxx was exceedingly grateful for his friend. Nancie had done a lot, over the years, to help him. Jax followed Maxx's gaze over to the little woman with blonde curls.

"A friend of yours?" Jax kept his eyes on the little woman.

"Yes, she is." Max looked at Jax and shook his head. Jax clearly did not recognize Miss Nancie.

Maxx chuckled as he walked over and took Miss Nancie by her hand. He smiled slyly as he led her over to Jax. He thought that this should be an interesting event.

"Miss Nancie, this is Jackson Shaw." Maxx motioned his hand between the two. "Jax, this is Miss Nancie."

"The pub owner?" Jax's mouth dropped open. Miss Nancie folded her arms.

"You cannot tell me that you have never met Miss Nancie." Gavin put his arm around his cousin's shoulder.

"I have seen her in the pub, but not like this." Stunned, Jax eyed Nancie over. He was amazed at the difference in her tonight.

Miss Nancie did not care much for Jax's attitude. She used the fan in her hand to swat Jax on the arm.

"We do not hit." Maxx took the fan away from Nancie.

"We do not gawk at people either." Miss Nancie snapped. Her eyes never left Jax's.

"Here." Maxx took Nancie's arm and pulled her closer to Jax. "Why don't you two enjoy a dance?" With a gentle shove from Maxx, Jax and Nancie were on the dance floor.

"You will pay dearly for that, my friend." Gavin watched as Jax and Miss Nancie made the best of an awkward situation.

"You are right, but not tonight." Maxx patted Gavin on the back before he led Rachel out onto the dance floor.

When the music paused between songs, Maxx and Rachel returned to where Gavin was standing. Surprisingly, Jax and Miss Nancie stayed on the dance floor. Gavin and Maxx shared a laugh as they watched the couple.

"I see that your cousin and brother have decided to not accept my invitation for tonight." Sam now joined them. "That would be a great shame."

"I am sure that Alex is doing all that he can to get Nick here." Gavin did not understand why Nick's presence was so important tonight.

"Lady Danielle looks lovely tonight." Sam had been watching Dani all evening.

"Oh, Lady Danielle looks *very* lovely indeed." Maxx smile at Sam before hurrying over to Gavin's little sister.

Dani threw her arms around Maxx when she saw him. She was always happy to see their family friend. Maxx bowed before her and offered Dani his hand. Dani eagerly accepted Maxx's invitation to dance. She happily followed Maxx onto the dance floor.

"He greatly tests me." Sam growled.

"He does have that effect on people." Gavin chuckled. Gavin was thankful that his father could not get up and protest Maxx dancing with Dani tonight.

Before the music could end, Alex practically threw Nick into the grand ballroom. Nick stumbled but managed to keep his balance. His eyes shot daggers into Alex.

When Elizabeth saw Nick, she quickly stood up from the elegant chair she was sitting in, on the far side of the dance floor. Sam held his hand up, to still his sister. Elizabeth nodded her head at her brother and took her seat.

"Glad that you could find the time to join us, Sir Nicholas." Sam greeted his angry guest.

"Save it." Nick did not want the Duke's politeness.

"Take him and get him somewhat presentable." Sam told Gavin. "And hurry."

Gavin and Alex took Nick out into the hallway. Their cousin wanted no part of this night. Nick fought against his cousin's every move.

"Leave me be!" Nick shouted. "I am here! Is that not enough?"

"I know…" Gavin tried to speak.

"You know nothing!" Nick was furious.

Gavin and Alex did what they could to straighten Nick's hair and clothes. It was not an easy task, for Nick continually swatted at them. Finally, they gave up and pushed Nick back into the ballroom.

Sam still did not approve of Nick's appearance, but there was nothing that could be done about it now. With a wave of his hand, the musicians stopped playing. Everyone on the dance floor returned to their families, as the Duke walked out to the middle of the dance floor.

"Thank you all for being here and sharing this wonderful night with me and my family." Sam walked over and took Elizabeth's hand.

Sam pulled his sister out to the middle of the dance floor. Elizabeth was sure that her face held the signs that she had been crying this evening. The sight of Nick filled her heart. She was so afraid that he would not come here tonight.

"I am nervous." Elizabeth whispered to her brother. Sam placed a kiss on her cheek.

"Sir Nicholas, will you join us please?" Sam held his hand out toward Nick.

Everyone in the ballroom turned to look at Nick. He was stunned and hated that the Duke would make such a display of things like this. Alex gave a shove to Nick's back, pushing him onto the dance floor. Reluctantly, Nick walked over and stood next to Sam.

"You are a cruel man." Nick leaned over and whispered to the Duke. Sam pretended not to hear him as he continued smiling at his guests.

"Please forgive my family for waiting until this night to share this wonderful news with you all." Sam held his head high as he looked around the room at his guest. "Since I have been away the past few months, this was the only night that we had where we could include you all."

"Go ahead and drag it out." Nick mumbled.

"I am honored to announce to you all of the engagement of my sister, Elizabeth to Sir Nicholas Shaw. I hope that you all will return in a few short weeks, on October 5th, to witness the marriage ceremony." Sam placed Elizabeth's hand in Nick's and walked away.

Elizabeth was so happy, she had tears flowing down her cheeks. Nick was stunned and did not know what to say. As the music started again, Elizabeth quickly stepped closer to Nick and urged him to dance with her. After the initial shock settled, Nick pulled her closer to him and happily twirled Elizabeth around the dance floor, as the other guests joined them.

"Did you know about this?" Nick whispered next to her ear.

"Not until I arrived here tonight." Elizabeth looked up at Nick. "I was so afraid that you would not come."

"If I had known that this was why your brother wanted me here, I would have been here yesterday." Nick closed his eyes and held Elizabeth close.

The entire Shaw family was still in shock. Sir Phillip put his arms around his wife and held her as she cried. The only person in the room that did not look happy was Elizabeth and Sam's mother. Without saying a word to anyone, she left the ballroom.

"That was very kind of you." Gavin nodded his head in approval to the Duke.

"Regardless of what you all believe, I am not a heartless man." Sam looked at Gavin from the corner of his eye.

"Did the magistrate charge Roger Holden?" Alex asked.

"Sadly, he could not." Just hearing Holden's name infuriated Sam.

"How could having a witness not be enough?" Jax was furious.

"Because, yesterday, the witness was found, hanging in the stables at Ridgewell Inn with a note on the ground." Sam looked straight ahead. He fought to hold back the darkness inside him.

"They are claiming that he took his own life." Maxx understood what Sam had not said.

"But we all know that he did not." Sam walked away. He had to find something to be joyous about before he exploded.

Sam hurried across the room. This was a bold move for him, and one he had not planned on doing this night. There was only one way that he would be able to fight back the darkness that threatened his mind tonight, and he had to take that chance.

Sam smiled sweetly at Danielle Shaw as he approached her. The sight of her soothed his soul beyond anything he had ever known. Her soft brown eyes warmed his heart and settled his raging spirit.

"Good evening, Lady Danielle." Sam bowed before Dani.

"Good evening, Your Grace." Danielle politely curtsied.

"Would you do me the honor?" Sam held his hand out as he asked her to dance with him.

"It would be my pleasure." Dani blushed as she smiled at Sam.

Sam's heart and mind found great peace when Dani gladly accepted and took his hand. Sam's smile broadened when he noticed that Dani was wearing the amethyst necklace that he had given to her at her brother's wedding over a year ago. Lord Matthew and Lady Caroline shared a smile as the young couple stepped out onto the dance floor.

Chapter Thirty-Eight

On October 5, 1781, Greyham Court was beautifully decorated for the wedding reception for Lady Elizabeth Dawson and Sir Nicholas Shaw. Even with such a short notice, most of London's society set had shown up for the joyous and much talked about event.

"Are you sure that this is truly what you want?" Sam stood outside the church doors with Elizabeth.

"I have never been surer of anything in my life." Elizabeth kissed her brother on his cheek.

"If you are happy, my dear sister, then so am I." Sam squeezed Elizabeth's hand.

The organ started playing, cueing Elizabeth and Sam that it was time. The doors opened and Elizabeth walked with her brother toward the man that she loved with all her heart.

The gown that Elizabeth wore was glamorous. It was made of satin and was trimmed with delicate white lace. The detailed stitches were golden. Miss Claudia had done a fantastic job on such a short notice. This was probably a design that the seamstress had been working on privately for months.

The bouquet in Elizabeth's hands was tied with a dark blue ribbon. The ribbon matched the dress that she had bought when she and Nick were in Camden, when she first thought that they would marry. This ribbon allowed her to feel as though she was also giving honor to that day and that beautiful dress, which was now packed away in her trunks.

Nick stood at the front of the church and watched in awe as the beautiful vision of his wife walked toward him. Of course, he knew long ago that Elizabeth Dawson was beautiful, but today, there was an extra special glow about her.

Only a few weeks ago, Nick's heart was broken, and he wanted to give up on everything because he thought that he had lost her. Today, every wrong thing he had ever experienced in his life had vanished from his mind and heart. Standing before him was all the love and peace that his heart truly needed.

After the marriage ceremony, everyone went to the grand ballroom at Greyham Court for a wonderful reception. Even though the Dowager Duchess was not pleased with her daughter's choice for a husband, she did not protest this marriage. She feared that if she did, Sam would banish her as he had Anne.

"I owe you an apology." Nick found Maxx outside on the garden terrace. "I should have never said the things that I said in Camden."

"Since you did not act on them, let us leave them in Camden." Maxx shook Nick's hand and walked away.

"Did you enjoy the ceremony?" Sam asked as Maxx walked back into the ballroom.

"I am happy for Nick and Elizabeth." Maxx started to walk away, but Sam caught him by the arm.

"Thank you for all the things you have done for Elizabeth." Sam looked Maxx in the eye. "For doing so, I reduce your debt by one year." He was a man of honor and kept his word.

Maxx nodded his head. He was grateful that now he only had to work for the Duke for four years instead of five. Sam shook Maxx's hand and hurried away. He planned to make full use of Maxwell Spencer's services over the next four years.

After the reception, Nick and Elizabeth left in the Duke's personal carriage for their honeymoon in Scotland. They both were excited to finally visit Scotland together like they had planned to do weeks ago.

The happy couple enjoyed five days in Inverness and the Scottish countryside. Elizabeth made sure that they avoided going to Edinburgh altogether. She did not wish to have a run in with her sister. She wondered, for a moment, how Anne was doing in her new life in Scotland. Elizabeth doubted that the harsh changes in Anne's life would change her hateful attitude.

"Can you believe that we are married?" Elizabeth smiled as she nestled closer to Nick's side.

"I will be honest, for a moment there, I was worried." Nick kissed her on the cheek. "I am glad that you got the glamorous ceremony that you truly deserved. It was better than eloping in a little chapel."

"I would have been just as happy to have married you in that little chapel weeks ago." Elizabeth leaned back and look up at Nick.

"I know you would have, and I love you even more for being willing to do so." Nick would love her more as each day passed.

Nick lowered his head and pressed his lips to hers. Elizabeth's arms went around his neck as she pulled him closer to her. The passion that they had for each other no longer needed to be held at bay.

With the honeymoon over, the happy couple rode to Kinsley Estate. Elizabeth's things had been moved here, from Greyham Court, while they were in Scotland. Sir Phillip and Lady Clara waited on the front steps to greet them, along with Nick's brothers and the servants.

It did not take Elizabeth long to settle into a comfortable routine at Kinsley Estate. She preferred the simpler life she had found here over the tedious one she had grown up in at Greyham Court. It did sadden her to know that her brother was left to deal with the cruelness of their mother alone. Yet, Sam had proven that he was strong enough to handle the Dowager Duchess of Greyham.

Lady Clara was overjoyed to now have a daughter in her home. Raising three sons took a lot out of a woman. A daughter was a welcomed change for Nick's mother. She spent many wonderful moments teaching Elizabeth about Kinsley Estate and the Shaw family.

Elizabeth was overjoyed to now have a loving mother in her life. Sadly, her own mother never truly showed love to her or Sam. It was sad that the woman only loved one of her three children. Elizabeth vowed to herself and her unborn children, no matter how many she and Nick would have, that she would shower each of them with the same love that Lady Clara so freely gave to Elizabeth and all three of her sons.

Caleb and Jax started to spend more and more time away from Kinsley Estate. When their mother questioned them as to why, both of her sons credited their absence to being sick of watching the loving and romantic couple that now resided in the house. Caleb and

Jax were happy for Nick, but for them, this side of their brother was hard to watch.

Fall was giving way to the winter season. Sir Phillip's family was planning on going to Ellis Manor to celebrate the Christmas and the New Year. Since Gavin's wife was due to have their child soon, and Nate's wife's due date not too far behind, the family thought it best that the two mothers'-to-be did not travel.

On the last day of November, Nick's family was paid a surprised visit from his cousin, Alex. Alex hurried to the sitting room at Kinsley Estate. He was grateful to find Uncle Phillip's entire family present.

"I have come to let you all know that Abby had just given birth to a son." Alex announced the happy news.

"We must celebrate!" Sir Phillip got up and poured drinks for everyone.

"How is Abby and the baby?" Lady Clara gave Alex a hug. She was not a woman that played favorites among children, but Alex had always had a special place in her heart.

"Abby is fine, but Gavin had some touch and go moments." Alex chuckled. "And I have to say that little Alastair Matthew Shaw has an excellent set of lungs."

"Childbirth is also hard on the father, especially the first one." Sir Phillip knew this all too well. "I was a total wreck when all three of our sons were born. It was all my brother could do to keep me calm."

"Gavin paid Nate and I no attention. Thankfully, Maxx showed up and helped keep my brother calm." Alex was profoundly grateful for Maxx's help. He would have preferred to just punch his brother out and been done with it.

When Sir Phillip offered Elizabeth a glass of wine, she graciously refused. Her action immediately brought panic to Lady Clara. Nick's mother hurried over to Elizabeth.

"Are you alright, my dear?" Lady Clara took Elizabeth's hands in hers.

"I am fine." Elizabeth smiled up at Nick.

"You are more than fine, my dear." Nick gave her a quick kiss.

The happiness on Nick and Elizabeth's faces, and Elizabeth's refusal of the wine, brought excitement instead of worry to Lady Clara. Could this be a moment that she had been praying for?

"Oh, my dear. Are you?" Lady Clara could hardly contain her excitement.

"Yes, I am." Elizabeth could not keep the secret any longer. "Nick and I are expecting our first child."

"We were going to announce it at Christmas." Nick hugged his mother.

Caleb and Jax rolled their eyes, but they were happy for Nick and Elizabeth. A baby meant a great many changes would be taking place at Kinsley Estate. They both chuckled and went over to congratulate the happy couple.

"You should find a nice girl and settle down." Lady Clara looked up at Alex.

"You should worry more about marrying those two off." Alex pointed to Caleb and Jax. "I am afraid, that will not be an easy task."

"I am sure that you are probably right about that." Lady Clara smiled as she watched her two youngest sons. "Still, my dear nephew, your lady is out there somewhere."

"Or right under my nose," Alex mumbled.

"Awe, so she does exist." Lady Clara gave Alex a little hug. "I look forward to meeting her."

"So do I." Alex whispered as his aunt walked away.

***

Christmas and the New Year were an exciting time for the Shaw families. The first grandson, who was also the future Earl of Claybourne, had arrived and two more grandchildren were on the way.

Nate and Olivia welcomed their daughter on February 2, 1782. Nick and Elizabeth went to Ellis Manor to meet their beautiful little niece, Aurora Havanne Shaw. Nate got his wish, for it was already obvious that his daughter had her mother's auburn hair. Little Lady

Rori Shaw, as Lady Caroline called her, had quickly won everyone's heart at Ellis Manor.

"Just think, in five more months we will be welcoming our first child." Elizabeth climbed into bed next to her husband.

"You are going to be a wonderful mother." Nick placed his hand on his wife's stomach. "I can hardly wait to meet this little fellow."

"Will you be disappointed if we have a daughter?" Elizabeth looked down at her growing abdomen and placed her hand over Nick's.

"I would be honored to have a daughter." Nick placed his finger under Elizabeth's chin and tilted her face up toward him. "We can just try again for a son."

Nick held his lips just above hers for a moment as he gazed into Elizabeth's eyes. The golden streaks in her hazel eyes sparkled in the glow from the candles in the room. He thoroughly enjoyed teasing his beautiful wife like this for a moment. When they both had enough of teasing, Nick pressed his lips to hers.

Chapter Thirty-Nine

Roger Holden remained behind the walls of Statham Hall for several months. He had seen his plots and plans fail too many times to risk going out in public for a while. It was best that he did not show his face in London until he knew that he could do so without being arrested.

"I cannot believe that you have failed, once again." Harriet Holden glared across the sitting room at her son.

"Do not fret, Mother." Roger glared back at his mother. "I will find a way to destroy the Shaw family."

"You are as useless as your father was at that task." Harriet Holden was severely disgusted.

"Why do you hate the Shaw family so much?" Edmond Prescott asked Roger's mother.

"I hate them because they took your father from me!" Harriet Holden shouted.

"Do not profess that you loved Father." Roger angrily pointed his finger at his mother.

Lady Holden sat back in her chair and tried to calm her temper. She struggled to control her breathing. She had spent her youth trying to be the wife her husband had wanted, but she failed at every turn. Nothing pleased Simon Holden for he was consumed with hate over the Shaw family.

"I did love Simon, at first." Harriet Holden looked at her son. "Your father was so set on revenge against the Shaw's. He could see nothing else."

"Except the Mason Jewel." Edmond reminded Roger's mother. "Whatever that is."

"Why was father so set on acquiring that jewel?" Roger asked his mother.

"Because our holdings have been dwindling for decades now." Harriet Holden was growing tired of her son's failures. "You, like your father, could not even acquire that."

"Does that mean that we are broke?" Edmond looked over at Roger.

"That does not mean anything to you." Harriet Holden snapped at Edmond.

"Enough, Mother!" Roger shouted. "Edmond is my brother."

"This?" Harriet pointed at Edmond. "This was born to a lowlife piece of trash. This only proves that your father was an unfaithful man!"

Edmond folded his arms across his chest and looked away. He did not need Roger's mother to remind him that he was the illegitimate son of the former Earl of Statham. He could not stand his ground in this house or he would lose his connection with his half-brother. He needed Roger's protection in his many unlawful dealings.

"Mother, there is no need to insult Edmond." Roger chose to not feed his mother's angry spat. He turned his attention to Edmond instead. "I am sure that there is nothing to worry about on our financial status. Mr. Phelps here should have that under control."

"Actually, Lord Holden, we do have a bit of a problem with the financials." Oliver Phelps hated to admit the failings of the estate.

"Then raise the taxes," Roger suggested.

"That is just it, Lord Holden." Oliver was nervous. "We have raised the taxes to the extent that the tenants can no longer pay them."

"Then they will no longer be tenants." Harriet Holden was growing tired of Oliver Phelps. "Do your duty and foreclose on them immediately."

"I do not have to foreclose on them." Oliver looked away and cleared his throat.

"If you cannot do your job then I suggest that you find another one." Harriet snapped at Oliver.

"Mother, Mr. Phelps has been with us since father became Earl." Roger was not about to dismiss the man because his mother was dissatisfied with him.

"Then why can he not do his job and foreclose?" Harriet asked her son. Roger looked over at Oliver.

"My Lord, the tenants that cannot pay have all accepted their failure and have handed in their contracts." Oliver informed Roger. "I received four notices this week. The tenants have already moved on."

"I guess the Mason Jewel would come in handy right now." Edmond stared at Harriet. He did not like Roger's mother.

"The Mason Jewel is lost to us now." Harriet Holden sighed deeply. "Abigail is now married to Gavin Shaw."

"What do we know about this jewel?" Edmond leaned forward in his chair. "Perhaps we can still find it."

"Miranda Mason said that her husband only talked about this jewel when he had too much to drink." Harriet now wondered if there truly was another way to acquire the jewel. "All Miranda knew was, it is an emerald and it is attached to Lord Mason's oldest child."

"That jewel is probably lost forever." Edmond looked over at Roger. "You should probably just secure a marriage with a wealthy woman from another country."

"You should have agreed to marry Anne Dawson when she suggested it." Harriet could not understand why Roger had refused.

"I do not love Anne Dawson." Roger sighed and shook his head.

"As crooked as you are, dear brother. You are not marrying for love." Edmond laughed at Roger. "You could go to Scotland and take Anne up on her offer."

"It is too late for that. Anne has been disowned and banished from her family." Harriet glared at Roger for messing up the best offer he had. "Anne has no dowery now."

Roger was irritated from being pressured by his mother and brother. He just learned that his estate holdings were falling and now he had no plan for how to fix it. Somehow, he would find a way to accomplish what his father had failed to do.

"I will find a way to save our estate and I will destroy the Shaw family in the process!" Roger stood up and shouted.

"Not without help you won't." Harriet did not trust her son to pull off any plan against the Shaw family.

"If you have some suggestions, then out with it." Roger spat the words at his mother.

"The way I see it, you have several options available." Harriet smiled slyly at her son.

"I would love to know what those options are." Roger snapped at his mother.

Roger sat back down and waited for his mother to share her ideas with them. She had never fully helped to formulate a plan before. His mother usually only dropped casual hints that had led to his failed plans. Perhaps if they worked more closely together, they could finally end the Shaw family and save their estate.

"We need to find out more about the Mason Jewel." Harriet looked over at Edmond. Hopefully, the dirty little man would amount to something.

"We will need to get someone close to Lord Mason." Edmond slyly smiled as a thought came to his mind.

"You should continue pressuring the Earl of Hartford. That little Captain is always in the way." Harriet looked over at Roger.

"Spencer is not easy to get to." Roger had tried this and failed.

"Then keep raiding his lands." Harriet walked over to the tea cart and poured herself a cup of tea.

"I did not know that you were raiding on Hartford land." Edmond was surprised. Usually Hartford lands were well guarded.

"I am not raiding Hartford lands." Roger leaned back in his chair. "My men have only been able to cause a few break ins before the guards are alerted."

"There are three unmarried Shaw men." Harriet sat back down in her chair. "You should work on separating them from their families and find ways to kill them all."

"Why just the unmarried ones?" Edmond wondered.

"Because the three that are married with children are going to be more cautious and protective." Harriet could not believe how much of an idiot her husband had sired.

"The three that are not married are free spirited and reckless." Roger could see the reasoning in his mother's plan.

"That would take care of destroying the Shaw families but how do we save the estate?" Edmond wanted to know more about the money. He had always been greedy and wanted his fair share.

"My son needs a wealthy bride until we find the Mason Jewel." Harriet smiled at Edmond and Roger.

"And where do you suggest I find her?" Roger did not like the sound of this idea.

"I would think that you have two great choices." Harriet's smile broadened. "And both would rip out the hearts of every member of the Shaw family and the Earl of Hartford."

Roger raised his eyebrow as he looked at his mother. He did not realize just how much of an evil schemer his mother was until now. He did not wish to marry but if doing so would drive stakes into the hearts of the entire Shaw family he was all for it.

"Well, Mother." Roger was growing impatient. "Who do you suggest I marry?"

"Either Danielle Shaw or Emily Spencer." Harriet Holden was pleased with her idea.

"Why would I marry either of those women?" Roger could no longer see his mother's reasoning.

"Roger is an idiot." Edmond looked stunned at Harriet's suggestion. "There is no way he will ever get either of those women to marry him."

"Neither of them will willingly marry me, Mother." Roger agreed with Edmond but for different reasons.

"Both of them would marry you if they thought that doing so would save their families." Harriet was still beaming with pride over her plan.

Roger leaned back in his chair and looked between his mother and brother. He slyly grinned as several evil plots came to mind on how he could get Danielle Shaw or Emily Spencer to marry him. Blackmail looked to be a great option on obtaining a wife for him

"So, which option do we put into play?" Edmond thought over the suggestions Roger's mother had given them.

"Each and every one of them" Roger smiled. He was well pleased with every option before him. The three now shared an evil laugh.

Chapter Forty

As the summer months came, the Shaw families graciously refused all party invitations. They remained in residence as they awaited the birth of Nick and Elizabeth's first child. Even the Duke showed up at Kinsley Estate the first week in July. Sam did not want to miss being with his sister when she had her baby.

In the early morning hours of July 12, 1782, Elizabeth gave birth to a daughter. After a night of hard labor, Elizabeth was exhausted, but she was filled with joy at the same time. Nick had been so nervous that he was out of his mind for hours. Doctor Ramsey assure Nick that Elizabeth and their daughter were fine.

Lady Clara made sure that Elizabeth had everything that she needed. The nursery was already set up so that Elizabeth could get some rest now that the baby was here. Nick sat on the side of the bed and held Elizabeth after he lovingly greeted his little girl.

To everyone's surprise, the Duke walked around Nick and Elizabeth's room, holding his niece. Sam was overcome with joy, as was the rest of the family. Sam spoke sweetly to his niece as she held tight to one of his fingers.

"She is absolutely perfect." Sam smiled at the baby in his arms.

"She is *my* daughter," Nick teased.

"Oh, but little Miss Haily Victoria Shaw is my niece." Sam could not take his eyes off her. "Yes, you are. And you have an amazing uncle that will totally spoil you."

"I have no doubts that she is going to be a very spoiled little girl." Elizabeth smiled at Sam. "But, dear brother, try not to get too carried away."

"This little lady will want for nothing. And since I am the Duke, there is nothing any of you can do to stop me." Sam playfully narrowed his eyes at Elizabeth and Nick. Sam placed a soft kiss to his niece's forehead. "Now, which name shall we call you, my sweet one?" Sam smiled and wiggled his finger, that the baby was clinging too.

"That does not have to be decided right now." Nick was amazed at the change in Sam, but he did not see the rush in choosing which name to use just yet.

"A name is important." Sam narrowed his eyes at Nick before looking back into the face of his niece. "This is important, for it will stay with her for her entire life."

"He does have a point." Elizabeth smiled as she looked up at Nick.

"I agree with your brother, but we can decide on that tomorrow." Nick kissed Elizabeth's forehead. Elizabeth was tired and needed to rest.

"We will decide now." Sam never took his eyes of the baby in his arms. "I think that we should call you Tori, my sweet one."

Elizabeth could not help but to laugh at her brother. She had never seen him like this. One day, she knew that Sam would be a wonderful father.

Hopefully, there was a young woman out there that her brother loved, as the housekeeper at the Summer Cottage had believed. She hoped that one day soon, Sam would tell her about this woman. All though, Elizabeth thought that she had caught a glimpse of her brother's love several months ago.

"I think that Tori is perfect." Elizabeth looked up at Nick. She was pleased with this idea. "Tori is what Sam and I use to call our grandmother."

"Then that definitely settles the issue of our daughter's name." Nick like the sound of the name.

"Perhaps she will be best friends with Nate and Olivia's little girl." Elizabeth truly hoped so.

When Elizabeth yawned, Lady Clara knew that it was time to clear the room. She was amazed that Elizabeth had not fallen asleep already. Elizabeth had spent most of night in hard labor. When Elizabeth seemed to be having difficulty giving birth, everyone was grateful that the Duke had brought Doctor Ramsey with him almost a week ago.

Sam handed the baby to Elizabeth so that she and Nick could have another moment with their daughter before Little Tori was carried to the nursery. When that time came, Sam went with Lady Clara and his niece down the hall.

"At first, I was worried if my sister would be truly happy with her decision to marry your son." Sam walked beside Lady Clara.

"You were worried because your sister was marrying down from her status." Lady Clara smiled over at her granddaughter, in the Duke's arms.

"I am sorry to say so, but yes." Sam was terribly sorry for doubting it.

"Well, it did work out fine for me, so I am sure that Elizabeth will find as much joy as I did." Lady Clara opened the door to the nursery.

"What do you mean?" Sam handed Baby Tori to Lady Clara.

"I too was the daughter of a Duke." Lady Clara told Sam. "And I assure you that I regret nothing about marrying Sir Phillip Shaw."

"I was not aware of that." Sam was surprised.

Sam was deeply moved as Lady Clara went on to tell him about how she and her husband had fallen in love. He could see how happy Nick's mother was with her life here at Kinsley Estate.

"Sir Phillip proposed to me at the Winter Ball. The greatest yes that I ever said was on that night." Lady Clara smiled at the sleeping little girl in her arms.

"You were proposed to at Greyham Court?" Sam asked. His family had hosted the Winter Ball every year since it first began.

"Yes, I was." Lady Clara nodded her head. "So, I hope that you can see, as I knew many years ago, a title does not ensure happiness."

Lady Clara placed her sleeping granddaughter in the crib. She and Sam slipped out of the nursery, leaving the newest addition to their family with the nanny.

Lady Clara had thoroughly enjoyed these moments with Sam. This time reminded her that Samuel Dawson was much more than a Duke who had to rule, and sometimes that meant being stern when he did not wish to.

"Will you promise me that you will always love my sister and look out for her?" Sam loved Elizabeth very much. They had been close as children. Sadly, that closeness did not happen with their sister, Anne.

"That is one promise that I will honor until the day I die." Lady Clara took Sam's extended arm as they walked downstairs together. "And I can assure you, there is not a member of this family that does not love your sister. The moment Elizabeth fell in love with my son, she became one of us."

Sam was glad that Elizabeth had Lady Clara for a mother-in-law. He could see that his sister now had the love of a mother that she had been denied growing up. In a way, he envied Elizabeth a little. His sister now had a mother that genuinely loved her. Sadly, he still had to deal with their mother back at Greyham Court.

Lady Clara Shaw had shown Sam nothing but kindness the past several months, after Nick and Elizabeth were married. Sam could clearly see, after hearing Lady Clara's story, that marrying someone for love and not a social status was not a bad thing. Seeing this firsthand, had changed his point of view for his sister's decision. He knew that his sister would be just as happy as Lady Clara was.

***

"It looks like we are going to have a hard time getting rid of your brother." Nick pulled the covers over Elizabeth.

"Let him enjoy this." Elizabeth nestled close to Nick's side. "Sam has had to be so strong and stern because of how Anne and our mother were. Maybe our daughter can soften her uncle's heart."

Nick hoped that she was right. Over the last several months, Nick had learned much about the Duke from Elizabeth. Their childhood, even though they never wanted for anything financially, was lacking in motherly love. He had no doubts that Elizabeth's and Sam's father loved them both dearly. It was quite clear that their mother only had enough love in her heart for her first-born child, Anne.

"The colt that Toby sired was born this morning as well." Nick gave Elizabeth the happy news. "The little fellow already has a lively spirit about him"

"I missed it." Elizabeth yawned again.

Elizabeth had spent the last few months of her pregnancy, going to the stables to feed Toby apples. She was extremely excited to know that the new colt had arrived. It was sweet that this little horse shared the same birthday as their daughter.

"You were busy, my love." Nick gave her a quick kiss.

"Can we call him Spirit, then?" Elizabeth asked sleepily.

"Of course, my dear." Nick too yawned. It had been a long night for them all. "Now, my love, you need to rest."

Nick knew that she was tired. He had spent the night emotionally in pieces as Elizabeth struggled to give birth to their daughter. Even though his mother and Doctor Ramsey told him that everything was fine, he found that hard to believe every time Elizabeth cried out in pain. His father, both of his brothers, and the Duke had stayed by his side though it all.

"Will you stay with me?" Elizabeth was close to falling asleep.

"I will stay as long as you want me to." Nick closed his eyes.

"Forever?" Elizabeth's voice was low.

"Forever, will be my pleasure." Nick rested his head against hers.

"I love you." Elizabeth whispered.

"And I love you." Nick held Elizabeth close as they both fell asleep.

Capturing a Knight's Heart

For the Love of a Shaw
Book Four

By:
Debbie Hyde

Sneak Peak
Enjoy!

Debbie Hyde

Chapter One

Jackson Shaw used the back of his hand to wipe the trickle of blood from his chin. The tin ale mug, that had slammed into his face, had busted his lower lip. Thankfully, he did not lose any teeth in the incident. Jax's hair and clothes were drenched from the ale that was in the mug when it hit him.

Jax shook off the ale that was now running down his arm and onto his hand. His eyes bore into the object of his fury. He now had Edmond Prescott pinned the front corner of the Blume'N Brew pub. Edmond's eyes radiated with fear as Jax took a step toward him.

"It is time for you to pay for every evil thing that you have done to my family!" Jax shouted as he took another step closer to Edmond.

"It is time for you to die, Shaw!" Edmond dropped the tin ale mug onto the floor and reached for his pistol.

Before Edmond could pull the pistol and take aim, Jax closed the distance between them. Jax slammed Edmond into the wall of the pub. The jolt caused Edmond to drop his weapon. Jax took Edmond by the back of his head and slammed him, face first, into a nearby table.

Several other fights had erupted around the two angry men. Edmond Prescott had not come to the Blume'N Brew pub alone tonight. His friends jumped up and started more fights as distractions. Soon, the entire pub was in a brawl.

Before Jax could take another swing at Edmond, he was hit across the back with a wooden chair. Jax whirled around and snatched the two remaining pieces of the chair out of Brody Williams' hands.

Jax threw the pieces of wood onto the floor. He grabbed Brody by his shirt. With all his strength, Jax lifted the man off the floor and tossed him through the front window of the pub.

Edmond used this distraction to save himself. He rushed outside, and with the help of Randal Gates, Edmond pulled Brody to his feet. The three men quickly hurried into the shadows of London.

Jax shook off the effects of the fight and braced his hands on a table. Before he could stand up straight, the table flipped, causing Jax to fall to the floor, with the table landing on top of him. Jax could not believe this just happened to him.

A single gunshot was fired into the side wall of the pub, demanding everyone's attention. Jerry Griffin, the pub bartender, walked into the middle of the pub, his rifle still in his hands. Every member of Edmond's party, that had been left behind, took one look at the fury on the bartender's face and fled from the Blume'N Brew.

Jax groaned as he pushed the wooden table to the side. He struggled but managed to get to his feet. He turned around to find himself staring into the bright green eyes of Miss Nancie. The little pub owner was furious, and her eyes bore holes into Jax.

"Why did you flip that table on me?" Jax was furious too. He had clearly seen the little pub owner's face just before she flipped the table on him.

"It was either that or shoot you!" Nancie shouted at Jax. "Look at what you have done to my pub!"

"I did not do all of this." Jax was defensive as he pointed around the room.

"You started it!" Nancie poked Jax in the chest with her finger. Jax caught her by her wrist.

"I was after Edmond Prescott." Jax leaned toward Nancie.

"Well, you failed at that." Nancie pulled her hand away from Jax. "Prescott was the first one out the door."

"What happened?" Maxwell Spencer asked as he walked through the broken pub door.

"Need I say more?" Nancie asked as she motioned toward Jax.

"You are going to fix this." Maxx pointed his finger at Jax as he walked further into the pub.

"Did anybody die?" Paul asked. He and Maxx watched all the men getting up from the floor.

The entire front room of the pub had been destroyed. The tables were overturned. Most of the chairs were broken into pieces. The front doors hung loosely, and the huge main front window was shattered.

Nancie walked over and put her hand on the piano. Sadly, even this beautiful instrument had not been spared. The entire scene before her was heartbreaking. There had not been destruction like this at the Blume'N Brew since Captain Sayer and his pirates started a brawl. At least Captain Sayer had reimbursed her for the damages his ruffians had caused. Who was going to pay for this?

"I should have shot them all," Jerry mumbled.

"Why would you do this." Maxx asked Jax.

"I did not mean for all of this to happen." Jax was finally coming to grips with just how badly the pub had been destroyed.

"It was not all Sir Jackson's fault." Will Carter set his piano stool upright.

"Of course, it was his fault!" Nancie glared at Jax.

"Hold on, lil buddy." Maxx put his arm around Nancie. "Let us hear Jax's reasoning for this before we flog him."

"He threw the first punch!" Nancie angrily pointed at Jax.

Nancie threw her hands up. She was overwhelmed with the destruction of the pub. She went over to the only section of the pub that had been spared. Thankfully, no one had went up on the raised platform section in the back corner. Every pub patron knew that this was Maxwell Spencer's private table.

"Yes, I admit it. I threw the first punch." Jax followed behind Nancie. He tried to get her to listen to him. "I am deeply sorry that your pub has been destroyed like this."

Nancie was not listening to Jax. She sat down at Maxx's favorite table and looked around the room. Jerry set a bottle of brandy on the table for her. Rachel hurried in with a large bowl of cool water and clean cloths, that she gave to the hurt men.

"I am sorry about this, Maxx." Nancie apologized.

"Do not fret, my friend." Maxx patted Nancie on her hand. "We will fix it."

Jax watched as Maxx comforted Nancie. In this moment, Jax envied the friendship between these two. He was surprised that Maxx took the time to listen to Nancie. Maxx was able to offer Nancie's mind some peace. Still, he could not figure out how these two, unlikely people, had become such good friends.

"How did the brawl start?" Paul looked over at Jax, after he had helped to set the tables upright again.

"Edmond Prescott was here." Jax sighed deeply.

"Roger Holden is getting extremely brave sending his brother in here like that." Maxx walked over to the bar and grabbed a bottle of rum.

"That was a bad lot that Prescott was with tonight." Will continued picking up the piano keys off the floor.

"Will, what do you know?" Maxx sensed that the piano player had more information about what had taken place here tonight.

"The piano is a lost cause. We are going to have to get another one." Will stood up and shook his head as he stared at his piano.

"Will." Maxx walked over to the man and motioned toward the rest of the pub. "The brawl, what do you know about it?"

"If Sir Jax had not of thrown that first punch, he probably would be dead by now." Will nodded his head at Maxx and sat down on his piano stool.

"I am glad that somebody is on my side," Jax mumbled.

"How exactly did Jax starting this brawl save his life?" Paul was confused. The little piano player made no sense.

"That bad lot was sitting here." Will pointed at the table that was the closest to his piano. "They were planning on killing Sir Jax before he could leave the pub tonight."

Will's words stunned everyone in the pub. All eyes turned to Jax. Jax sighed deeply. He closed his eyes and shook his head. It was not comforting to know that his death was being plotted tonight.

"It looks as if Holden has a new plan." Maxx put his hand on Jax's shoulder. "Sadly, you seem to be his new target. But, since you did start this, help clean it up."

"Take this." Paul handed Jax a board and a hammer. "Start boarding up the front window."

"I do not work here, and I do not take orders from you." Jax set the hammer down on a nearby table.

Nancie was angry and heartbroken over the way the pub looked. She jumped up from her chair. She grabbed Jax Shaw by his ear and dragged him over to the front window of the pub.

"Until this pub is restored, you most certainly do work here!" Nancie pointed at the window. "Now, board it up!"

Jax looked down into Nancie's bright green eyes. He knew she was angry, and he understood why. Yet, Jax saw something more. The little woman standing before him had a huge heart. She was fighting to hold onto this pub because it was, somehow, a part of her.

Something strange and unfamiliar grabbed ahold of Jax's heart in that moment. He had never felt this feeling before and he could not name what it was that he felt. Yet, it was a feeling he could not escape. Somehow, the feisty little women, with green eyes and golden ringlets of hair, standing before him had bound him to her.

"I will do whatever you ask." Jax took Nancie's hand and brought it to his lips. His deep brown eyes never left her bright green ones as everything around them faded away from existence.

Debbie Hyde

Other books by Debbie Hyde

Christian Writings:

Stamped *subtitle*: Breaking Out of the Box
Please look for the Second Edition

Her *subtitle*: Beautiful, Loved, Wanted, Matters, Priceless!

Her: Beautiful, Loved, Wanted, Matters, Priceless!
Subtitle: Devotional Guided Study Journal

Fictional Writings:
Historical Romance:
For the Love of a Shaw Series:

When a Knight Falls: Book One
Falling for the Enemy: Book Two

Coming Next:
Historical Romance:
For the Love of a Shaw Series:

Capturing a Knight's Heart: Book Four

Fiction: Preteen – Young Teen

Rovania Forest Series:
Jasper's Journey: Book One
With Nevaeh Roberson

Debbie Hyde

About the Author

Debbie Hyde has a love for writing! She enjoys reading books in many different genres such as: Christian, Romance, Young Adult and many more. You will always find wonderful clean stories in her fictional writings.

When not reading or writing, Debbie enjoys using her talents in cooking, baking and cake decorating. She loves using her skills as seamstress to make gowns, costumes, teddy bears, baby blankets and much more.

She is currently working on Capturing a Knight's Heart, Book Four in the For the Love of a Shaw series in Clean Historical Romance and Book One, Jasper's Journey in Pre-teen – Young Adult with her granddaughter, Neveah.

Debbie started Letters To You on Facebook after God put it on her heart to "Love the lost and lead them to Jesus." This wonderful community of amazing people allows her to continue her mission to Just #LoveThemAll. Please look this page up on Facebook today. Debbie would love to see you there.

Connect with Debbie at:

Email: debbiehyde5@yahoo.com

Facebook:
Letters To You – Debbie Hyde, for her Christian writings.
Debbie Hyde & Nevaeh Roberson, for her fictional writings.

Debbie would love to hear from you and see your reviews!

Debbie Hyde

Made in United States
Troutdale, OR
12/19/2024

26907125R00131